The Académie

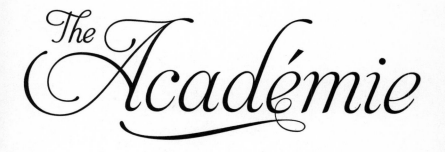

The Académie

Susanne Dunlap

BLOOMSBURY

NEW YORK BERLIN LONDON SYDNEY

First published in the United States of America in April 2012
by Bloomsbury Books for Young Readers
www.bloomsburyteens.com

For information about permission to reproduce selections from this book, write to
Permissions, Bloomsbury BFYR, 175 Fifth Avenue, New York, New York 10010

Library of Congress Cataloging-in-Publication Data
Dunlap, Susanne Emily.
The Académie / by Susanne Dunlap. — 1st U.S. ed.
        p.   cm.
Summary: Told in separate voices, teenaged Eliza Monroe, the daughter of a future
United States President, Hortense de Beauharnais and Caroline Bonaparte, relatives of
Napoléon I, and Madeleine, daughter of an actress, come together at L'Académie
Nationale à Saint-Germain in the turmoil of 1799 France.
ISBN 978-1-59990-586-0 (hardcover)
[1. Interpersonal relations—Fiction. 2. Boarding schools—Fiction. 3. Schools—Fiction.
4. Aristocracy (Social class)—Fiction. 5. Monroe, James, 1758–1831—Family—Fiction.
6. Napoléon I, Emperor of the French, 1769–1821—Family—Fiction. 7. Paris (France)—
History—1799–1815—Fiction. 8. France—History—1789–1815—Fiction.] I. Title.
PZ7.D92123Ac 2012   [Fic]—dc23   2011025662

Book design by Nicole Gastonguay
Typeset by Westchester Book Composition
Printed in the U.S.A. by Quad/Graphics, Fairfield, Pennsylvania
2 4 6 8 10 9 7 5 3 1

All papers used by Bloomsbury Publishing, Inc., are natural, recyclable products
made from wood grown in well-managed forests. The manufacturing processes
conform to the environmental regulations of the country of origin.

For Sofia, Ella, and Avery, with love

The Académie

1

Paris! I'm in Paris!

Or at least I was, for a few weeks, until Mama decided to ruin everything by sending me to school.

I wish I didn't have to go! L'Académie Nationale à Saint-Germain. Horrors. I thought this year in Paris was going to be for fun, a break from learning tedious sums and boring history. It's 1799, after all. The revolution is long over and France is becoming an extraordinary power again. Not to mention the gowns. How everyone in Virginia will be envious of me when I return with the latest fashions to show them!

"Remember, Eliza, you can hold your head up in the most exalted company in France. We're descended from the New York Aspinwalls, a very honored and wealthy family. Our money did not come from trade, and your father was first minister to France when Jefferson was president."

This is the hundredth—no, the thousandth—time my mother has told me this as we set out for Saint-Germain-en-Laye. At least she could have found a school actually *in* Paris, for pity's sake! But as usual, she had to find the best. Anything to raise us up a notch.

"Your papa—and I, truth be told—were the ones who managed to get the Marquis de Lafayette out of prison in Germany during the *Terreur*. You know I went to the jail in Paris where they were holding Madame de Lafayette, and saved her from the guillotine?" She thinks I was too young to remember, but I recall it quite well. How nervous she was, in the rented carriage with liveried servants attending, at a time when everyone who looked aristocratic risked being set upon by a mob. I can still picture the broken-down walls and rubble in the streets. They've been cleaned up nicely since then.

As for the school, I expect I'll find only the daughters of dead aristocrats, or perhaps a few grocers' daughters who have risen up in the world thanks to the new system of merit. The new manner of government gives titles and positions to those who actually deserve them. It will be easy to stand out in that sort of crowd.

Oh, why, *why* school! It truly isn't necessary. I already have enough Latin to understand erudite jokes at a dinner party. My needlework is as fine as it must be to entertain me at home on quiet evenings. I can spell tolerably well and have read most of the books in my father's library. It was supposed to be a lark to come to Paris. Mama promised we'd have a delightful home together for this year, and then go back to Virginia. Papa practices law there, and we have a lovely plantation and neighbors who come to dance and enjoy themselves with us.

"You understand, it's not for your education in the usual sense," Mama says to me. "But I hope it will be an education in other ways. It will add some polish to you and make your French not only good but flawless. Madame Campan is very respected."

"Yes, yes, I know. She was mistress of the bedchamber to Marie Antoinette. Do you suppose she went to the execution?" I wondered what it was like to see someone get her head chopped off!

"Eliza! Don't be ghoulish!" Mama swallows the last word as she is flung to the other side of the carriage. They may have rebuilt much of Paris, but the roads are still atrocious.

Once she regains her balance and straightens her headdress, Mama continues. "Ernestine has done a marvelous job on your *ensemble*." She pronounces it in an exaggerated French accent. Mama thinks her French is perfect, but I can hear the rough edges. I would never say anything to her about it, though.

"She knows everything and everyone," I say. Ernestine was a find. She used to serve in the household of a duchess and is acquainted with the finest couturiers and milliners in Paris. It is because of her that I am wearing the high-waisted gown made of silk voile with a blue satin sash and only a black silk rope with a simple gold locket around my neck.

"It is not the fashion to wear jewels in the daytime in Paris," Ernestine told me just this morning. "Ever since the *Terreur*, one's wealth is shown only in private circles where everyone is trusted."

"I should think Ernestine could teach me all I need to know about French society," I say, knowing it will vex my mother.

"Saint-Germain isn't just any suburb, you know," Mama says. Sometimes I think she can read my mind. "Many of France's wealthiest families have homes in Saint-Germain. There's a royal palace there, although no one stays in it now."

"At least you're not making me board at this school," I say.

Mama does not meet my eyes but looks out the window of the carriage. "See how pretty it is here."

"I certainly don't need to mix with bourgeois country girls who have come to Paris for some culture, afterward to return to Rouen, or Lille, or Toulouse—wherever they came from—to marry the wealthy burghers their papas have already picked out for them."

Mama says nothing, and before I can press the issue we pull up to the gates of the courtyard. The school's footman opens them for us. He's not in livery, I observe. Our Negro coachman in Virginia wears livery. Still, I expect it is another one of those practices that is frowned upon after the revolution. I can see that at one time someone's crest must have topped the gates, but it was most likely torn off by the mob. I'm pleased to see that the courtyard is well kept and quite large, and there's a fresh coat of black paint on the doors and window frames.

An elderly lady dressed entirely in black greets us at the door—well, perhaps she isn't as old as she looks; many of the people we've encountered in the salons who survived the *Terreur* have white hair, even though they are not yet forty. It was the fear, they told us. But by the lines in Madame Campan's face I can see that she would have been white haired with or without a fright.

"*Bienvenue*, Madame Monroe, and Mademoiselle Elizabeth."

"It's Eliza, *s'il vous plaît*," I say, giving her just as much of a curtsy as I think she warrants. I detest it when people call me by my mother's name.

"Madame Campan, how good of you to meet us," Mama says, flashing me a fierce look.

I suppose it was a little rude of me, and I decide I had better make up for my impertinence by being very sweet.

"But you have not brought any trunks for Mademoiselle . . . Eliza," Madame Campan says as she leads us across a large vestibule with a stairway that sweeps in a curve up to the next floor and into a spacious drawing room where tea things have been laid out.

"Oh, I'm not—" I start to speak, but my mother places her hand on my arm to stop me.

"I didn't want to delay our arrival for the sake of packing. Her maid will bring the luggage—you do have accommodations for personal maids?" Mama flashes Madame Campan her most winning smile.

My maid will bring . . . ? This was not in our plans! I am so stunned I almost forget to notice what kind of china the tea is served on, and whether the silver is plate or sterling. When did Mama decide that I would board? I don't want to be a prisoner in a girls' school! Paris is for attending parties and going out to fabulous banquets and the theater and the opera. I try to catch Mama's eye, but she steadfastly avoids me. No doubt having Ernestine there is intended to soften the blow to me.

But it won't work. She tricked me. My own mother! I feel a sensation like fire bubbling up inside me. I want to throw something, or spit. But I can't argue. Not in front of others. Instead I have to sit here like a lady.

"Ah, and here is another one of my pupils," Madame Campan says, gesturing toward the salon door. "Allow me to present Hortense de Beauharnais."

De Beauharnais . . . That is a noble name. And familiar somehow. And this girl who enters the room is utterly beautiful. Blue eyes, delicate features, and golden blond hair. She is dressed in the very latest fashion, and how she moves— she floats, hardly disturbing the air around her.

To my surprise, Mama, who considers herself superior to everyone, stands and curtsies to greet this apparition, who I can see is only a few years older than I. "An honor to meet you, mademoiselle," Mama says. "May I present my daughter, Eliza Monroe? Eliza, this is the daughter of Joséphine Bonaparte."

My teacup is about to touch my lips and I must use every ounce of concentration not to jerk suddenly and slosh the tea out and over my gown. Daughter of Joséphine! I just saw the famous lady the other night, in a box at the theater, wearing exquisite jewels and looking absolutely beautiful. Some people say she ensnared the general and he had to marry her. Others are even less kind and say her powerful former lover, the Marquis de Barras, passed her on to his young protégé.

"And I," says another voice before I can even address Hortense, "am sister to the great general himself."

We all four turn at once to see another girl enter through the same door. She is not quite as beautiful as Hortense, but very striking. Her eyes flash dark and lively. Her skin is smooth as porcelain, and her gown is of the finest silk and decorated with jewels at the neckline.

"Yes, this is Caroline Bonaparte, who has been at my school almost since her arrival in Paris. You are all close enough in age to be friends, I hope," Madame Campan says, smiling toward my mother, who looks as though every dream she's ever had for me is about to come true.

Could this be why such a plan was hatched? Because Mama wanted to throw me together with these girls—the most famous in all Paris, perhaps even the world? I suppose if

I have to be away from home boarding in a girls' school, it will at least be a compensation to keep company among the most celebrated young ladies alive.

Now when I look at my mother, she stares right back at me. She positively glows with triumph. I raise one eyebrow just a little, our private signal that I am pleased. And I follow it by looking down, to show her that I'm not entirely happy, either. The end may not always justify the means, and I expect her to make it up to me somehow.

We all sit down again. Caroline takes the place of honor next to Madame Campan. Hortense sits in the least comfortable chair, farthest away, as if she wants nothing more than to blend into the background. But that would be impossible for such a beauty.

"We have four levels here, which correspond to those at the Collège Irlandais, our neighbor, where young men study. The youngest are the Green class, which you can see from their caps and ribbons. Above them are the Pinks, then the Blues, and finally the Pearls—my crowning achievement."

"Which class will Eliza join?" Mama asks. I see that both Hortense and Caroline are wearing white caps and ribbons, and so must be among the Pearls. *Please!* I think. I want to be with them.

"We shall see," Madame Campan says. "It depends upon her abilities. We do not base our classes solely upon age. There are ten-year-olds who wear the blue ribbons, and twelve-year-olds who are still in pink."

I am fourteen, fifteen next year. I wonder how old Hortense is.

"Eliza has had an excellent education in Virginia. She is well versed in history and mathematics, as well as Latin."

"Perhaps she may assist me with the English classes," Madame says. "Then she may be in one level for some subjects, in another for others."

"Which subjects do you place the most importance upon?" I wish Mama would stop speaking and leave!

"Conversation. Most others require only the faculty of memory. Conversation requires wit."

How grand! I may yet avoid boring arithmetic and composition, and perhaps learn things much more to my liking.

2

Hortense

The men are coming for us. I cling to Maman's hand. Eugène stands behind her, trying to be protective. I am crying.

"Hush, ma petite!" Maman murmurs. "They will find us!"

I know there is danger, but I cannot stop the tears. I hear the heavy footsteps and the clanking of swords against leather. They have entered Maman's bedroom. We press ourselves into the back of the secret cupboard behind the wardrobe. I start to shake. My teeth knock against each other so that I think anyone will be able to hear them. I try to control the trembling of my jaw, but it only becomes worse. I hear the men outside in the room yanking out drawers and emptying their contents. Some jewelry clatters to the floor.

They aren't finding anything. Perhaps they will leave.

"Eh, Marcel! Ici une jolie petite fille!"

They must have found the miniature of me that Maman keeps on her dressing table. The next thing I hear is the sound of smashing and raucous laughter. I gasp.

"Sshht!" One of the men stops the others from talking.

The footsteps approach fast. The wardrobe door opens. It is only a moment before they find the latch that reveals our hiding place. A man with almost no teeth and a wicked scowl raises his knife high above his head. Maman faints. Someone stays the man's hand.

All at once dirty arms reach in to grab for us. I feel the imprint of their rough fingers—

"Mademoiselle Hortense! Mademoiselle!"

It takes me several moments to realize I have been dreaming—again. The shaking is only Geneviève, the maid who looks after me and the other girls in the school who have not brought their own servants with them. She is gentle and kind. Hers are not ruffians' hands, but slender fingers, roughened with hard work. And those other hands, and the capture, never happened in quite that way. It is my own imagination that toys with me.

"You have had another *cauchemar,*" she says, sitting on the edge of my bed and stroking the hair out of my face. I look down and see that my covers are completely disheveled.

"I'm so sorry. Is it late?"

"No, but you asked me to wake you early so you could join the American girl."

The American girl? All at once I remember. I leap out

of bed, barely letting Geneviève help me into my dress. At least it's easier now that we don't wear corsets and panniers! I choose something simple from the wardrobe. Though my family name means nothing now, I don't want Eliza to be in awe of me. I'm no one, really. I was even apprenticed to a seamstress when I was only nine years old.

My father left us before I was born. I never even knew him, though I wrote to him in prison at Maman's instruction. I felt sorry for him. Maman told me he had worked so hard for the revolution and then was called a traitor. I remember the day he mounted the guillotine. Our governess, who took care of us when Maman went to prison soon after Papa, would not let us go and watch. I don't think I would have wanted to, although I saw others beheaded. The vision of those brutal executions haunts me. So many familiar faces. They are not the same, though, when they are dead. They are like specters, or wax figures made horrible to frighten children.

I shake off the memories and in a matter of minutes I am downstairs. But as I approach the breakfast room I hear voices—Caroline's voice.

I am too late to warn Eliza not to believe everything she says.

"You mustn't be fooled by her manner. She can be very—"

I know what Caroline will say next, so I quickly open the door to prevent her and walk in. Only the two of them are there. I hear footsteps above and know that soon the others will join us at breakfast—silly girls in the younger classes, some from noble families, others whose fathers are in the Directoire and who have ambitions to marry well.

"Hortense, *ma chérie!*" Caroline rises from her place and kisses the air next to my cheek one after the other. I make no pretense of doing the same. I see she has placed herself at the head of the table. Madame Campan does not breakfast with us, instead having her tea and brioche in her room and joining us in time to conduct the first lesson of the day.

"Good morning, Mademoiselle Eliza," I say, taking my place next to her. The maid pours out tea for me. Caroline sits down again and bumps the table so that my tea sloshes into the saucer. No matter. She has quite taken my appetite away.

"I was just giving Eliza some hints about how to manage here," Caroline says.

"You mean, about the cold bathing every day, and the lessons where we must carry our books upon our heads?" I smile. She has been talking about nothing of the kind. I wonder if she knows that I am aware of what she has been trying to do to me ever since my mother married her brother.

She must be. Caroline is not so clever as to hide her distaste for me.

"Ah yes," says Caroline. "Madame Campan has some rather antiquated ideas about education, I'm afraid, but she is intelligent, and there is a good library here. All the political writings of the ancients, and Shakespeare—translated, of course."

I want to laugh aloud to hear Caroline speak of the library, which she has entered but once. "I hear she has a well-thumbed copy of Machiavelli," I say, knowing that Caroline can have no idea what I speak of. She could barely read when she arrived two years ago. I'm astonished at how glibly she pretends to be educated.

Whether she understands my jab or not I do not know, because she deftly changes the subject and studies Eliza, looking her up and down as if she were a new toy. "Dear Eliza, I see we shall have to do something about your hair."

"What's wrong with it?" Eliza asks. She looks cross. Perhaps Caroline has not yet influenced her enough to make her hang on Caroline's every word and believe all she says.

"It is so beautiful! I did not mean to criticize. Only with such hair, I know my own maid could work magic with it. But perhaps she should not. You would quite take away all my beaux."

Now Eliza's cheeks glow pink. She *is* young. Perhaps too young to be thinking of men and love just yet, and perhaps Caroline has embarrassed her. I know Caroline is disingenuous. She has only one interest. It is General Murat, whom she longs to marry, but whom her brother will not permit to see her.

"I would be honored if she would try," Eliza says.

Oh, dear. The process has begun. No one is immune. Caroline even worked her cunning upon Madame Campan in some way, although I feel that at heart Madame does not like her. She accepts her because we must all be Republicans now. But she would prefer to have her fashionable school filled with girls like me, who have titles and lineage, even if it extends to Martinique on my mother's side. That is why she gives such preference to the Auguier sisters, Marthe and Jeanne.

I am thankful that our little dance is interrupted by the younger classes in their green, pink, and blue caps. I don't know them all, but the Blues—Marie, Constance, Émilie, Marguerite, and Catherine—are promising girls who will take their places in society and be a credit to the school.

"Bonjour! Bonjour!" they call out, full of the energy of children, although they are between eleven and fourteen years old already and could marry in another few years. Caroline reaches into her reticule and pulls out sweets for them— absolutely forbidden before evening tea. Yet if I told Madame Campan, I would only become the enemy. I smile at Eliza, but her eyes are drawn hungrily to the sweets. I shake my head just a little. She turns her attention to the brioche on her plate.

Chatter fills the air and I sit quietly, sipping my tea. Before long the school bell tinkles in the distance.

"There is our signal," Caroline says, standing and crooking her arm with the clear expectation that Eliza will take it, and so she does.

"That's the school bell?" Eliza asks. "Where I went to school in Virginia the schoolmistress rang a great loud bell that could be heard clear across my father's fields."

"Did you go to school with Negro children?" asks Constance, always the one to say something awkward.

Eliza draws herself up. "Certainly not! Our Negroes are slaves and do not go to school."

I shudder, recalling the slaves I saw in Martinique when Maman and I went there long ago. I must find a way to tell Eliza that slavery is not spoken of in Europe now.

"I'm fascinated by the Africans. My brother has been in Egypt," Caroline says.

My brother has, too. He was badly wounded, at Napoléon's side. Caroline knows it was a wicked thing to remind me of. But I do not even look at her, just lead the way to the schoolroom for our lessons.

3

Madeleine

There is no heat in my attic room, and the blanket that covers me is threadbare. I hear a mouse scratching in the corner, but even he does not stay, finding a hole that might lead him below, where the rooms are warmer. Although I am in the heart of Paris, one would never know it. The lights have almost all been extinguished and the sounds of revelry have died away. I could be anywhere in the world, it is so quiet and dark. It must be very early in the morning.

Somewhere in Paris, girls like me are in school. Or perhaps they are not exactly like me. Those whose fathers were aristocrats and who have any money or friends after the *Terreur* might perhaps be in convents. Perhaps others, the daughters of members of the Directoire or merchants who have become wealthy through other people's misfortune, are at private schools run by elderly ladies who are trying to put bread upon their tables.

I am in a school of my own, where I have been learning the skills I need to make my way in the world. I've been here almost as long as I can remember. It's the school of life, interpreted for the entertainment of those who can spare the price of a ticket. Others know it as the Comédie Française.

We came here—my mother and I—after my papa threw us out of his house. I was very small, but aware enough to understand his stinging words. I slept in a small attic room, hardly bigger than a closet. The door was not stout and I could hear everything that went on below. I knew those times when my papa came to her and they laughed and drank wine and tumbled into bed.

I also knew when other men were there. Maman was very beautiful, and still is. But her beauty has made her cruel.

And so on that night when Papa found her with the director of the theater in her bed, I was not surprised by what he did.

"You and your half-breed spawn can go to the devil!" my papa said, his voice trembling with rage.

A moment later he yanked open the door to my sleeping cubby and dragged me to my feet. I saw his face go from blind fury to a kind of dawning awareness as I peered up into his eyes. While my mother and her maid threw all her gowns and jewels into baskets and trunks behind him, he knelt down in front of me and took hold of my shoulders.

"If only you did not have so much of your mother in you, I would keep you, raise you as a lady, so you could make a good match." I could see behind his eyes to the molten emotions that coursed through him, although I didn't understand what they were.

"I have not been naughty, Papa," I whispered.

He enfolded me in a fierce embrace, broken when my mother took hold of his collar from behind and made him stand. She slapped him, hard. "You are lucky that I choose not to run you through with a dagger!" she hissed, as if he were the one who had been unfaithful.

Since then I have learned a great deal about jealousy.

The theater director could do no less than take us in after that time, but he would not avow us openly. Instead, he made Maman his new *étoile*, the exotic star to attract crowds who wanted to ogle and gloat over her misfortune. And it turned out that Maman has talent. She enters into the characters she plays. Sometimes, when she adopts the personality of a noble heroine, she even makes me like her.

But as soon as she steps off the stage and the applause has died away, she becomes the bitter monster I know only too well.

Tonight I have retired to my attic room to sleep while

my mother attends a ball. I am not sad or sorry to be alone. I have a letter from my beloved. He has returned!

I shall come for you soon, ma chérie. *I must attend upon the general tonight. We are to go to a ball, a celebration of the recent victories. But it is just the beginning. Something big will happen soon, something that will change the way France is governed. The Directoire must look to its back, or it will soon find itself out on the street. But I should not tell you this, except that I know I can trust you. Oh, how I wish I could present you to my mother and my sister as my wife! That, too, will come. Adieu.*

I pray that he will not encounter my mother, for I know they must be at the very same ball. Maman would not go anywhere that was not at the precise center of everything, where she couldn't show herself to the greatest advantage.

I cannot blame her. She has suffered much as well. The only way she knows to survive is to be the most beautiful, most desired woman in her world.

Despite her wishes to the contrary, I have found it impossible to remain a small child, hidden in the background. I have grown, and now I am beautiful. I am still petite and dark skinned, but my big eyes and youthful curves are a threat to her. She sees the way her gentlemen friends cast their hungry gazes over me when I help her maid put away her costumes or bring her cape before she goes out to supper.

Now she sends me away when they come, and dresses me in the meanest rags she can find.

But still, if what my secret friend says is true, I am loved. At first I didn't believe it. But it has been some months since the first time he sent a note to me after a performance. He does not know the full extent of my life here, how desperate I am. I am afraid to let on, afraid that it will drive him away.

He says he will marry me, when he comes of age. We are both young, although many girls my age are already promised. I'm certain Maman has forgotten how old I am, and conveniently ignores the fact that she should be looking to my future. I have no intention of making that future in this theater, in a world where nothing is real, where every night people pretend to be in love or to hate and then hang up their characters with their costumes.

I close my eyes and imagine myself in some other place, not in my cold attic room alone, but cradled in my sweet one's arms, wearing a beautiful gown, whirling to music in the warm candlelight of a glittering ball, and I fall asleep at last, contented.

4

Eliza

I spent my entire first day at school observing Hortense and Caroline. I hardly had to observe! The bad blood between them is so obvious it could be embarrassing in any other setting. Here there is no one to pretend for. Even the young ones watch and wait for an opportunity to play one girl against the other. I thought the young students were all Caroline's creatures in the morning. But by the end of the day, I wasn't certain. Hortense has a quiet command that draws some of them to her with their needlework, as if copying her motions will make them more like her. And it is clear that Madame believes Hortense to be the ideal student. There is something about Hortense. Not just her beauty. She is fragile, as if some secret weighs on her, or some sorrow is always in her mind. I find myself wanting to protect her, despite the fact that she is older than me.

As to where I am to be in this intriguing game—I have not yet decided. I promised my mother I would write to her each day, and so now I must try to remember every detail, every nuance of expression and meaning so that I can get my mother's advice on how to play along without exposing my own hand. What is that hand exactly? What do I want to accomplish for myself in this place?

I can see that the school itself is a grand enough setting now that I have resigned myself to being here. In addition to the large, airy parlor, there is a dining hall big enough for all forty students to sit down to dinner. And this leads to a ballroom. It must have been a lovely place once, although the chandeliers are swathed in netting and the gilding on the trim is worn off in most places. Still, I could imagine dancing here, my gown trailing behind me and my jewels glittering in the candlelight. . . .

That is not likely to occur here, however. A school is hardly the setting for an elegant ball. So what, then? What do I want?

And suddenly, I know. I want to fall in love. Paris is so full of dashing young officers, and between Caroline and Hortense, I must be able to meet some of them. Oh, I know I shall likely return to Virginia and marry someone from a good family. But there is always the possibility of a lieutenant or a colonel, or perhaps even a marquis. . . .

And there is a school full of boys just across the street. One of the younger girls told me they sometimes watch them from the windows on the second floor as the boys take their exercise in the garden of the old convent building that houses them. I imagine they must be much more interesting than the rough lads in Virginia, who are good only at plowing the fields or killing birds with their guns. I have heard that there will be a tea party here in a day or two, and that some of the students from the boys' school will come. Madame Campan thinks it's important for us to learn how to behave among young men so that we are not flustered when we first go out in society.

It will be difficult to accomplish even a flirtation, though, that is not fully in view of everyone. I promised my mother that I would behave and follow all the rules. One false step, she said, and she would send me back to Virginia while she remains in Paris to enjoy the society. She is thinking of the time at school last year, I know, when I found out that our teacher had a lover and threatened to expose her for it if she did not make me first in the class. I did not know the man was my teacher's fiancé. She went to my mother. I had to be very obedient after that, and was never first, no matter how hard I tried. My spirits were so low. That is when Mama decided to bring me back to Paris.

It is very quiet in the school. I expect everyone is asleep except for me. As my pen scratches on the page, I imagine it being as loud as a banging gong. This is the hour when Mama and I normally go over the day, whether we are in Virginia or in Paris. She sends the servants away, brushes my hair herself, and we talk. Whenever I feel uncertain about something that has happened, she helps me sort out the meanings and threads. So what if the daughter of a minor Virginia landowner pulled my hair and called me a snob? She is not worth bothering about, my mother would say. Her family rose to prominence only because her grandfather was a thief and swindled his partner out of his half of the business. And if the teacher pays more attention to a boy who wants to go to Harvard, I must simply accept that I am only a girl and there are other ways to make a name for myself.

A small blob of ink drops onto the page. I have been sitting with my hand poised above the paper. Yet I still hear scratching. At first it is quiet, but it becomes louder.

"Eliza!" The whisper is just audible. I lay down my pen and go to the door of my room. Those of us with maids have private rooms. The other girls sleep in dormitories on the top floor, one for each class. Except for Hortense, who as one who has been at the school for a long time—Caroline told me it has been four years—has her own room down the corridor.

I open my door and am surprised to see Caroline standing there, not in her nightdress but in an evening gown and a velvet cloak.

"Come! We have no time to lose."

She brushes past me into my room and heads straight for my wardrobe, opening the doors and rifling quickly through my gowns. She pulls out my best evening dress and tosses it on the bed.

"Quickly!"

Not a word of explanation. She simply expects me to dress and go with her! Where? I can't help wondering. But if I am to dress for evening, it must be a party! Perhaps I will meet someone handsome and dance.

"I'll tell you all about it on the way. There's nothing to worry about. I simply need your help. Do you have any jewels?"

While I slip out of my nightdress and into the silk gown with lace at the neck, she plunges her hands into my jewel case, tossing aside a few pieces until she reaches my pearl ear bobs and sapphire necklace.

"These will have to do. Now get your cloak. It's cold."

As we run quietly as ghosts through the dark corridors of the school, I realize that Caroline never gave me the opportunity to deny her, that she simply assumed she could command and I would obey. From all I've heard of her famous brother, this presumptuousness is a family trait.

An unmarked but very comfortable coach awaits us outside the gates of the school. As soon as we close the door behind us, the driver cracks his whip and we lurch forward over the cobbles.

"I only hope we are not too late!" Caroline says with a cross glance at me, as though the lightning speed with which I prepared myself had somehow delayed us.

I reach up my hand to pat my hair. I hadn't yet taken it down for the day, but if I'd known I was going anywhere, I would have repinned it to catch up the strands that had fallen loose.

"You're fine; don't worry. No one will look at you." Caroline chews the side of her thumb and stares absently out the window. Her words hurt, just a little.

"Where are we going?" I ask since she hasn't volunteered any information.

"To Paris. To a party at a lady's *hôtel particulier.*"

I want to ask which lady, thinking it possible my mother will be there, but the abrupt way Caroline answers discourages me from saying anything more.

And besides, isn't this what I want? To go out to parties? I just didn't expect to be doing so in secret in the middle of the night, without my mother's knowledge or approval. Why does Caroline need me by her side? What purpose will I serve?

The carriage is racing through the streets toward the gates of Paris. How will we get through at that hour? Must we pay a toll? I didn't bring any money with me.

Caroline remains silent most of the way. I think about trying to make small talk, but it feels out of place in these circumstances.

After what seems too short a time, I hear the coachman telling the horses to pull up. I see a gate and a watchman ahead and the lights of Paris beyond. Caroline sits forward in her seat, fumbling for something tucked into her cloak. To my surprise, she draws out two silk masks.

"Here! Put this on!"

I quickly tie mine over my eyes, positioning the slits so that I can see out. Caroline has fastened hers remarkably quickly. Though she thinks I don't notice, I see her take a small note from the folds of her cloak. The watchman comes to the window. She smiles and leans on the top of the door.

"*Merci, monsieur,*" she says, putting out her gloved hand with the folded note tucked into her palm. I catch the fellow's eyes. They are that lively dark brown I have noticed in the faces of some attractive Parisian gentlemen. He casts them rapidly over the note, and almost before I can register his reaction, he yells "*Allez!*" up to the coachman and we are off again.

"Are you planning to tell me why we're going out at this hour?" I ask, by now so mystified and curious I can stand it no longer.

Caroline turns to me, now smiling and calm, the way she was at school earlier. "We are going to meet a particular friend of mine, at a masked ball."

"Why have you brought me with you?"

"Because, my dear Eliza, I wish to make you my particular friend as well. And in order to do that, we must have a secret together, *non?*"

We arrive at the gates of a very grand house. I see many coaches ahead of us, letting out their passengers at the door.

All the ladies are masked, but not costumed. They are the kind of masks that make the wearers feel protected but do not fool anyone acquainted with them. If my mother is here, she will surely recognize me. I pray she has either not been invited or is at home with one of her headaches—ungracious as that sounds.

After we descend from the coach Caroline takes my arm as if we are sisters, or at least the closest of friends. She is rather short, and so anyone might think we were quite close in age, not separated by four years.

We enter the ballroom after letting a maid take our cloaks. I have never seen anything so dazzling. It's as if all the jewels women hid away during the revolution and the *Terreur* are on display at the same time, glittering in the flicker of thousands of candle flames.

"Don't gawk!" Caroline hisses in my ear, squeezing my arm a little too hard. Her eyes scan the guests. She is affecting ennui, but I can tell she is searching for someone. I don't have to be a genius to guess it is a gentleman.

"*Merde!*" she whispers. An elderly lady standing nearby turns quickly and glares at her, but Caroline doesn't notice.

"What?" I ask.

"See, over there?"

She lifts her chin toward a corner of the room, where a knot of men in uniforms with sashes is standing, their backs to the dancing couples in the center. They are clearly in deep conversation with each other. I shrug. "What is it?"

"My brother is with them. I did not think he would be here."

I still don't know who Caroline is looking for, but if Bonaparte is here then surely Joséphine cannot be far. As I look around, I see the most extraordinary lady, her skin so dark I could almost imagine she is one of the slaves who work our land, but she is dressed in a column of silver silk, with jewels draped over her. Perhaps she has darkened her skin because of the party? "Who is that?" I ask Caroline, turning her so she can see.

She tosses her head. "An actress. She is all the rage at the Comédie Française, I'm told. She is supposed to be the estranged wife of a *vicomte*, but that is only by her word."

I continue to stare at the woman, fascinated. She has sharp, high cheekbones and large eyes. Her lips are full, but that is the only feature aside from her dark skin that makes her appear to be a Negro.

"Don't act like a child!" Caroline says, forcing my attention away from her. "Look! There he is!" She points toward the group of men again, but not in the direction of the one I recognize as Bonaparte. "He's looking this way!"

Before I can get a good look at whom she means, she yanks me around so that I almost lose my slipper and drags me after her as she walks rapidly away. I am practically limping, until I manage to slip my foot more securely into my shoe. Caroline pulls me into an anteroom that is empty except for a maid who stands ready to fetch something for whoever asks her.

"You see, that is my secret. It is Murat. I am in love with him." She whispers fast and low, her eyes glittering.

"Why is it a secret?" I ask.

"Because my brother will not consider it. And right now, I don't know if Murat even notices me. He is so handsome. All the ladies love him. I must see him, alone. And I will need the help of my friends."

Now I'm beginning to understand. She wants me to do something for her, perhaps carry messages. I hear my mother's warning voice in my mind. *One false step, and it's back to Virginia.* "Oh, Caroline! I can't help you. I'm only young, after all."

She takes hold of my upper arm and squeezes so her fingers are digging into me and I have to grit my teeth not to cry out. "Oh, but you must—you *will*! Because now I have your secret, too."

My secret? So that's why she woke me and brought me here. She can hold this over me forever. My first instinct is to be angry. But then, I have to admire her. It was cunningly done.

"Well, then, Caroline, what next?" I say.

She smiles.

5

I don't know what's woken me, but I am completely alert. I light my bedside candle and glance at the clock. Three in the morning. Thank heavens the Republic decided to leave the clocks alone when they changed everything else into units of ten.

It wasn't a dream. I heard a sound, quiet and close. I listen, holding my breath.

There it is again. A stone, against my window. A small one, not loud enough to awaken anyone but me.

It must be Eugène.

I leap from my bed and run to the window without even putting on my slippers. I unlatch the window and throw it open. My heart is pounding with joy. My brother must be well enough to steal away and visit me as he once did, when we were both schoolchildren and he would walk from the Collège Irlandais across the street in the old convent buildings.

I look around, eager to see Eugène. But no one is standing below my window. I hear only the wind gently rustling the few remaining leaves in the trees.

Just as I am about to close the window and return to my bed, I hear something else. I swear it is the sound of someone stifling a laugh. I look toward the shrubbery below and see it move, and then I catch sight of the scrap of a lady's cloak as a figure runs around the corner of the building and out of sight.

It could only be Caroline. Once, when she first came to the school and I thought we would be friends, I told her about Eugène's signal to me when we were young; in return she told me that she was in love with someone of whom her brother disapproved. She would not tell me his name, but I felt so sorry for her I vowed I would help her.

Now she has changed. She uses her knowledge about me to torment me. How can she be so cruel? And what was she doing outside at this hour? Whatever she is up to, there is no need for her to involve me. I don't understand her vindictive behavior. She and the rest of her family have been so horrid, are trying to destroy my mother because they think Bonaparte could have married a wealthier woman, and that my mother is too old for him.

But now I am awake and there is little chance of falling asleep again.

I decide to write a letter to my brother. I won't send it, of course. It will sit with the others in my drawer, and I will give them to him when I see him again, which my mother promises will be soon.

I sit by the window and lay my head on my arms. I close my eyes, hoping for rest.

The sun on the island is hot and voluptuous, like a huge, ripe fruit in the sky. Clouds skirt it, casting shadows only on the inland mountains, not relieving any of the heat that makes the puddles from last night's rain evaporate before noon. I see a slave woman, carrying a newborn infant in a sling made of calico. It is a pretty picture, laid out in front of me as I sit on the veranda.

All is quiet until the stillness is broken by an angry voice, the Creole patois, loud and harsh. It is the voice of the slave master. The woman I watch making her leisurely way stops smiling at the sun and looks fearfully over her shoulder. She quickens her steps, heading to the house where the laundry is done, an even hotter place than the outdoors. Her bare black feet kick up the dirt beneath them, pounding. My heart keeps pace with her feet. But the slave master is faster, because he is not carrying a baby, only a whip, which he holds over his head.

I want to leap out of my chair and run, put myself between the slave master and the young woman with her child, but I am made of lead and cannot move. I want to cry out for Maman, but my throat is dry and my scream is only hot breath with no sound.

So I can only watch, helpless, as he reaches her and brings the whip down on her back, flaying the light fabric that covers it and the skin beneath. The woman looks up, and her face is my mother's, only dark as night. The infant starts to cry. She curves herself around it like a snail shell. My own back feels the sting of the whip, the heat.

Tears cool my face.

I jolt myself out of my terrible dream. I must have been more tired than I thought. The sun wakes me, warm on the back of my neck. The pain I felt in my dream is the stiffness of the awkward position I have been sleeping in. My mouth is open, but no sound comes out of it. I haven't had that dream for a long time. I never actually witnessed such a beating. I heard my mother speak of them, begging her mother to stop the abuse. But no one ever did anything. And the slaves, inflamed by the ideas of the Republic across the Atlantic Ocean, rebelled. We left Martinique in secret, just before the terrible bloodshed began.

I look around and see that my bed has been made. Why didn't Geneviève wake me when she came in?

I dress quickly and descend to breakfast. I am late. The others are nearly finished, and I can hear excited chatter and laughter. All eyes turn to me when I enter, and the conversation stops suddenly. I don't know why, but I look at Eliza, not Caroline. She is young enough that perhaps her face will tell me more than that of my stepsister/aunt-in-law/whatever she is.

I'm not disappointed. Eliza's eyes are cast down, studying her empty plate. She has learned fast, I see. Her hands remain in view of all, forearms resting delicately on the edge of the table, fingers curled. Just yesterday she would have had them folded in her lap like a peasant. The slight pink glow brushing her cheekbones tells me she is hiding something.

"Apparently someone stole out of the school last night and did not return until the early hours of the morning," Caroline says, lifting her teacup to her lips. She has a way of flaring her nostrils slightly when she sips her tea that makes it appear that she dislikes the taste.

By the way no one will look at me I realize that I am the suspect. They suspect me because I am the one who is late to breakfast. This really is low. And it confirms what I thought last night, that it must have been Caroline who tricked me with the stone at my window. Was Eliza with her? That would be too bad. Why must she also spread rumors that implicate me? I decide I must find out more.

Because Madame does not come down to breakfast, I am spared knowing immediately how far this lie concerning my nocturnal activities has spread. This morning I have my music lesson, the most wonderful hour of my week. No matter what treachery Caroline is hatching, she cannot take my music away from me.

"Ah, Mademoiselle Hortense, *vous êtes ravissante!*"

Monsieur Perroquet greets me with his usual extravagant compliment. He bows and I curtsy. He takes his place at the spinet, where he has already spread the music out on the desk. Monsieur Perroquet is gray haired but youthful. He must once have been very handsome, and his manners are impeccable. The other girls make fun of him because he always arrives in a cloud of cologne and wearing a carnation pinned to his lapel. His clothes are old-fashioned: he wears a ruffled shirt beneath a cutaway, and breeches with hose and shoes with buckles. I find it oddly *charmant*.

I expect to begin with the usual *vocalises*, a comforting routine that takes me away from the pains and sorrows of the present, but Monsieur Perroquet touches my shoulder lightly. "Excuse me, mademoiselle. I should like to introduce you to my son, Michel—my apprentice, as it were—who will soon be teaching students of his own. Madame Campan kindly permitted me to bring him here to observe my methods."

I turn, and a young man comes forward. He is the image of his father as I imagine he must once have been, only dressed in the fashion of today. I hold out my hand to him. He takes it and bows over it, brushing it with his lips. "*Enchanté*, Mademoiselle Hortense." His hand trembles just a little, giving his stiff greeting a certain poignancy.

Before he takes his seat on the other side of the music room, our eyes meet. His are a crystalline gray, the color of an old diamond my mother possesses and dark enough to be interesting, but remain transparent and honest. A slight smile spreads across his face, as though he is trying to prevent his lips from betraying the pleasure he feels. Something awakens in me, and my fingers tremble as I touch the sheet music on the stand. I start to warm up my voice as Monsieur Perroquet plays the gradually ascending chords. I make mistakes and must start over. I feel myself blushing.

"Mademoiselle Hortense, an audience is something you must become accustomed to," Monsieur says. "You will be called upon to entertain your guests, and you must be able to do it without showing any nervousness or fright."

"Yes, monsieur," I say, relieved that he mistakes my tremblings for nerves rather than complete confusion at the sight of the first young man I've ever met who awakens something deep inside me. Only one other person has ever come close to making me feel this way, and he is as forbidden to me as my own brother would be. Michel has music at his core, and I feel that he might understand my own deep connection with music. He looks at me and sees more than simply the famous Joséphine's daughter. Sympathy hangs in the air between us. That knowledge calms me, and I am able to continue the lesson unperturbed, but suddenly alive to possibilities I have never before imagined.

6

Eliza

I have found it difficult to concentrate all day. I am tired, of course, from our adventure last night. Caroline and I stayed, and we both danced. I danced! I have never before been treated like an adult, not just dancing among children and with my girlfriends, but with dashing young men. I was very glad I had been taught so well by my tutor in Virginia. The intricate steps were wasted on those galumphing farm boys, but here . . .

Three different officers took me out on the floor. I danced a quadrille and a polonaise. A contredanse, then a mazurka. Then another quadrille.

I think I would have danced more if Caroline hadn't kept pulling me aside and trying to get us to stand nearer to the generals, who weren't at all interested in dancing.

But even more remarkable than the dancing was a scene I witnessed between two extraordinary people.

Caroline left me at one point near the punch bowl, warning me not to slake my thirst with it if I was unaccustomed to strong drink. When she'd disappeared from view, I took a cup anyway, thinking it would be odd to stand near the table and have no intention of partaking of refreshment. At first I drank deeply, for the dancing had made me quite thirsty. But my head began to buzz strangely. This was more powerful than the wine we sipped at dinner, and so I merely pretended to drink after that.

I backed away so that others could come, and found myself in the entrance to an anteroom, similar to one Caroline had drawn me into several times to whisper confidences. At first I thought it was empty, and was about to turn my attention back to the couples who were dancing, when a young officer strode into the room from another entrance, stopped in the middle, and put his hand to his head as if it ached.

I turned away, but not before I noticed how handsome he was. Far more so than Caroline's General Murat, who seemed rather coarse and broad lipped for my taste. This officer was also younger, and slender, but not weak looking. He had a delicate nose and fine eyes rimmed with dark, curling lashes. He stood straight, but not stiffly, as though he must be a wonderful dancer. I imagined myself twining through his arms on the dance floor, certain he would be able to guide me through the most complicated steps with ease.

He stood there only a moment alone, though. Just as he prepared to leave the way he had come, he stopped. Someone appeared in the doorway.

At first I could not see her, but as she advanced slowly, smoothly, I saw it was the dark lady who had so fascinated me when we first arrived. Her skin shone, as if she'd put on some oil to catch the sparkle of candlelight. She approached him unhurriedly, and he made no attempt to avoid her.

"So, monsieur," she said once she was about an arm's length away from him. "You make a habit of visiting the Comédie Française, and yet you do not venture backstage to greet me." She circled him, still slowly, as though a vast audience were watching her. Only then did I realize that, by now, they must both be aware of me. I turned a little, pretending to find something fascinating just outside the door of the chamber, but making sure I could still see them out of the corner of my eye.

"I mean no disrespect to the greatest actress of the present day," the young man replied to her.

"No disrespect is a world away from respect—and admiration." Her voice was dark and smoky, just like her appearance.

I caught sight of the young officer turning his face away as she reached her hand out to him. Spurned, she backed away. "The stage has its generals and kings, you know," the actress said. "To get what you want in it, you must rise through the ranks."

She turned, and as she left gave a throaty laugh, like a blue jay about to raid a nest.

I got out of the way just before the officer came striding through the doorway where I stood, went to the punch bowl, and quickly drank two glasses down.

"Eliza! There you are!"

Caroline had found me. She dragged me off to fetch our cloaks.

"Who was that young man?" I asked her, assuming she would know.

"Which young man? I didn't notice him. No one of consequence, I'm sure."

When we returned, Caroline insisted on playing a trick on Hortense, and I felt a little bad about it. But I didn't know how to deny her, and I was too tired to try.

I shall find a way to make it up to Hortense.

7

Hortense

It is the hour after supper, when we sit in the parlor with Madame and read or do our needlework. She sometimes talks to us about the events of the day, pointing out an article in the *Gazette* that she thinks is important, indicating particular *bons mots* that have been uttered by famous hostesses. While she also prepares us for the rigors of running a household, Madame is well aware that many of us will be under great scrutiny as hostesses. That is the subject of her words to us this evening.

"As ladies, you can exert much more influence than you might imagine. I believe, for example, that your mother, Mademoiselle Eliza, was able to visit Madame de Lafayette and work alongside her to secure her husband's release from prison."

I glance at Eliza, who has positioned herself on a low stool at Caroline's side, a book that she pretends to read open in her hands. She is clearly pleased by the reference to her family.

"But in order to work on behalf of one's husband, a lady must maintain the utmost discretion and never call censure upon herself, or give others cause to doubt her sincerity or cast a shadow upon her character."

I feel Madame looking in my direction and lift my eyes from the needlework on its frame in front of me. Her face is all questions, but only I can see it. Madame Campan possesses a rare skill of being able to convey without words exactly what she means, all the while keeping her thoughts hidden from anyone else in the room. I see now that she has heard the rumor that I left the school last night. No doubt my fatigue from a disturbed night's sleep shows, and her concerns are reinforced.

How shall I contradict such a rumor without implicating anyone else? I dearly wish to know how it was discovered that someone had departed after the school gates were closed—and who discovered it. I know well enough who has started the rumor that I was the miscreant. I decide that the only reasonable course is to talk to Madame Campan as soon as I possibly can.

The mantel clock's delicate chime strikes eleven. The youngest ones have already gone to the dormitory, leaving only Caroline, Eliza, Catherine, and me. Caroline stands and reaches her hand out for Eliza. I expect Eliza to take it, but before she can, Catherine, who is a year or two younger than Eliza, jumps up and takes Caroline's hand.

"Thank you, Caroline, for being so good as to see that Catherine goes to bed immediately. No reading by candlelight, mademoiselle," Madame Campan says with an indulgent smile. Catherine is an intelligent girl, not as attractive as some of the others and tending to plumpness. She awakens my sympathy every time I see her round brown eyes looking up into Caroline's face.

I stand and start to walk toward Madame, but to my surprise Eliza appears before me, smiling, and threads her arm through mine. "I'll walk with you, if I may," she says.

I cannot interpret the look Caroline gives her. I would expect it to be cross, but there is a kind of triumph in it.

Eliza's actions prevent me from my planned conference with Madame, unfortunately. But perhaps it will be good to have an opportunity to speak with this young American girl alone. As we walk up the stairs, I say, "Would you like to join me in my room for a cup of tea? Geneviève will bring it for us."

I know that Eliza has her own maid, a saucy creature named Ernestine. She spends her days hiding away in Eliza's room, pretending to be caring for her gowns and jewels, staying aloof from the other servants. Even Caroline's maid, Hélène, does not refuse to help the others during the busy hours.

We enter my chamber, which is the smallest of the private rooms, but quite adequate for my needs.

"How cozy," Eliza says, looking around for a place to sit.

There is only one chair, at my writing table, and I motion her to it. I sit on the deep window seat and ring for Geneviève. She comes with two cups of chamomile tea, having already anticipated the need. "Good night, Geneviève. The cups can remain here until morning," I say. Eliza opens her eyes a little wider as if I have just committed some terrible faux pas, but wisely says nothing. Perhaps she is learning a few important lessons from Caroline after all.

"So, Eliza, how are you enjoying your first days at our wonderful school?"

She sips her tea before answering. I think she is perhaps trying to put off saying something to me, but I simply wait in silence.

Before she has a chance to answer, she notices the miniature of my brother, Eugène, which I keep on my dressing table. She seems startled by it. "Who is that?" she asks, her voice carrying a hint of surprise.

"That is Eugène. My brother."

She walks over and picks it up, holding it near the lamp. "He's very handsome, isn't he? What uniform is he wearing?"

I don't really want to talk about Eugène right now. I am still bitter and disappointed after thinking he had surprised me last night and then discovering it was a trick. "I'm told he's very popular with the ladies who follow General Bonaparte's troops."

"Then he is back in Paris?"

"Yes. But I haven't yet seen him." Eliza knows something, or has heard something, I realize, for she is too young to be entirely successful at hiding her emotions. By the look on her face I see that she has let something slip.

"I . . . I have just heard . . . the generals have returned."

"They have been here a month already. But I still have not had the good fortune to spend time with Eugène," I say, letting my breath out in an involuntary sigh. "He was injured badly. It was his head and we don't know for certain that he is entirely cured."

After gazing at it for a moment or two longer, Eliza puts the miniature back and comes to me. She kneels down and takes my hand, laying her cheek against it. Her warmth and sincerity surprise me. "I'm so sorry. I didn't know. I wish . . ."

She stops. She wants to say something to me. "What is it? You must trust me. I do not play the games that others around me play."

"It's Caroline," Eliza says, standing and returning to her chair, as if the name alone is enough to distance her from me.

"Ah, Caroline," I repeat.

"We did—that is, she made me—but not really . . ."

Poor Eliza. She is no match for Caroline's scheming. "What has happened?" I press gently.

"We went out. It was us, last night. Now she has a secret that could get me sent back to Virginia."

"But you, too, have a secret." I point this out, knowing that no doubt Caroline has managed things so that she is in control. "Why did you go out? Where did you go?" *Was it just to torment me?* I want to ask. But I don't.

"There is someone Caroline is in love with, whom she means to marry," Eliza says.

"Ah. So she is still in love with Murat."

"You know? I thought it was a secret!"

I could laugh at the look of shock on Eliza's face, but I'm not inclined to be so cruel.

"It is no secret that Caroline loves him. Only whether he returns her affections. Murat is a man of the world. And my stepfather does not encourage Caroline in her infatuation."

"But he is a great general!" Eliza insists. "Second in command to Bonaparte himself, so Caroline says."

"Caroline is young, and Napoléon is rising to ever greater prominence. I believe her brother wants her to marry better in the end." As I picture Napoléon, I have to suppress a sigh. I know how ambitious he is. When he wants something, he gets it. That thought frightens me, especially for my mother. And a little for myself. Maman is not ambitious for power, only for love. How I wish she had fallen in love with someone less important! Someone with less strength, fewer charms, and someone much less complicated.

"I see," Eliza says, her brow furrowed as if she doesn't

really. "Caroline wants me to take messages for her. Or, at least, to help her find ways to convey them. I am afraid I will be found out, but I don't know how to deny her." Eliza stares into her teacup as if the answers she seeks might be hidden there.

"Why are you telling me this, Eliza?" I ask.

"Because I think you should know something else..."

What can she tell me that I don't already know? Caroline and her mother and brothers and sister hate me and my mother and will do anything to destroy us.

"You should know, Hortense, that Caroline will stop at nothing to separate your mother from her brother. And I truly mean nothing." She puts her teacup down on the desk. "I've stayed too long already."

Eliza stands and curtsies to me, formal once again. I have discovered nothing I did not already know, including the extent to which Caroline has the young American in thrall.

But there is something about Eliza's visit that unsettles me and causes me to dream of terrible things.

8

Madeleine

Maman woke me when she returned from the ball that night.

"I need your help while I undress. I sent Marianne to bed. She has a cold."

This was a lie; I knew it. Maman has no patience for the illnesses or indispositions of those who serve her. I imagine it is because she was born a slave herself, and fears somehow losing her position. But she is royalty in the theater. She need not worry.

I got out of bed as she commanded me and went with her to her room. Before I could even unfasten her necklace, she ripped the silver gown off her shoulders and let it slither to the floor. She stood before me in all her naked beauty.

"What are you staring at?" she asked, a hard smile on her face. "Do you see what it is that drives men wild with desire? Even your father—your oh-so-virtuous father—could not take this from me, and nor will you."

I said nothing, having learned that to respond was to risk a thrashing. I reached down to the floor to pick up the gown I would have to mend in the morning.

I heard my mother step to the screen that hid her untidy pile of clothes, and by the time I looked up again she had donned a silk dressing gown. "I met a very interesting young man this evening," she said, taking her seat at the dressing table and gesturing to me to remove her necklace and earrings.

Again, I said nothing.

"He was a handsome young soldier. I have seen him here, in the theater. I thought he looked too young and insignificant to bother with, but he was among the generals this evening. He is aide-de-camp to Napoléon himself, apparently."

I could not prevent my sharp intake of breath. I prayed Maman did not notice it. But when I looked up, our eyes met in her mirror.

"I thought I would invite him to supper the next time he comes to see a performance. Would you write a note for me, that I might have it ready?"

I've become accustomed to writing and reading all Maman's love letters, all the lewd declarations from both merchants and aristocrats. She can neither read nor write. But this time . . . I knew who she was talking about. I would be inviting my true love to an assignation with my mother. The thought brought bile into my throat.

Maman yawned and then climbed into bed, blowing out the candle that had illuminated the room, leaving me standing in the dark.

I knew the way through her chaotic mess of upholstered stools, discarded shoes, and upended empty wine bottles, and so I crept from her room noiselessly.

Today, I sit with the quill in my hand, holding it above a blank sheet of paper. I wait so long that the ink dries upon the quill, and I must clean and trim it and dip again. I could write anything I want to: Maman would not be able to decipher the letters, having disdained the exercise when Papa tried to teach her before we left Martinique.

But he who will receive it—will his response not betray my own treachery? And what if Maman shows the letter to someone else? I have no doubt that she knows exactly what she is doing. She has seen me with him. She can tell that I am in love. She knows that in forcing me to do this for her, she is breaking my heart.

I wonder if every woman behaves this way. When only her beauty can give her the means to live, is it not understandable that she would do everything in her power to ensure her survival—even if it means destroying her own children?

Yet it seems wrong. There is Marianne—my one friend—to

prove it. She cares for me as I imagine a sister would, even though she is poor and lowly, with no prospect of rising above her position as a dresser in the theater. Only Marianne dares insert herself between me and my mother at times, and yet she manages to retain the trust of my mother.

If Marianne reads the letter, she will lie for me. I know it.

And so at last I start to write. I tell him all, including that he must pretend to make an assignation with my mother. I explain it by saying that she is concerned for my well-being and does not want me to enter into an alliance where I will be cast off because I am unworthy.

Once the letter is written, I scatter sand across it, then lift the edges and make a funnel to return the sand to the little jar. I fold it carefully, then drip the wax that will seal it so that it falls exactly across the paper's edge. I take up the seal with my mother's initial, but I pause before pressing it into the still-liquid red wax, the color of blood. I blow on it softly, then press my lips against the wax, feeling the heat.

I follow this with the seal. Maman would notice if it was missing. But I know my kiss was there first.

9

Eliza

Time has simply flown here at Madame Campan's school. I didn't expect it to be so wonderful, I confess. Our lessons are far more interesting than school in Virginia, and I have learned a great deal about society and how to comport myself in company.

Today is the day of the cotillion. It is a tea dance, and we are to assemble in the parlor, where the furniture has been rearranged so that a few couples can dance at a time. There is really only room for one square, but it will be enough to teach the younger ones, I suppose.

"There isn't much space," I whisper to Caroline, who looks bored already.

"The point isn't to dance, but to converse. You wait and see."

None of the visitors has arrived yet, but the servants

have brought in the spinet from the music room and set it up in the corner.

"Hortense has taken a great deal of trouble over her appearance," Caroline says, nudging me in the ribs.

Hortense stands over to the side, surrounded by some of the Blues, who are wearing their best gowns. She looks much as she always does, except that she has a string of small pearls around her neck and a little lace tucked into her bodice. It occurs to me that Caroline is being facetious. Yet unlike Caroline, Hortense's expression isn't bored. I think she's looking forward to the day.

"Does Hortense have a friend at the Collège Irlandais?" I ask.

Caroline laughs. "I'm afraid there are few young men there! Once they're over fourteen, they either join the army or go into their fathers' businesses."

Now I understand why Caroline is so cross about the cotillion. There will be no one here for her, or even Hortense. As for me . . .

My thoughts are interrupted by the sound of the bell tinkling. By the way the young students are acting, it's clear the boys have arrived. Although I'm interested, I decide I ought to pretend not to care, since that is what Hortense and Caroline must surely do.

The younger classes all turn at once to watch the entry of the guests. I admit, they are mostly a pathetic lot! The majority of them are shorter than I am. Perhaps only three or four are my age or a little older, and one of those has a face so cratered with blemishes that I feel sorry for him. I confess I am disappointed. I had imagined the boys in Paris would be handsomer than those in Virginia.

They march in and spread out among us, each going up to a different girl and bowing. It's quite comical. It seems they have been given some very specific directions about what to say and do, so that it appears that each one is acting out the same little play. There are fewer of them than there are of us, so I am mercifully spared this ritual.

I turn back to say something to Caroline, but she has wandered off. I decide to go to the tea table. There are some very pretty pastries arranged on trays, and I find I am thirsty.

As I reach for the cup a maid has poured for me, I hear someone close behind me clear his throat. I brace myself for disappointment as I turn around.

"I beg your pardon, but would you do me the honor of allowing me to make your acquaintance?"

To my complete surprise, standing before me is a young man. Not a little boy. I didn't notice him among those who entered at first. He is an inch or two taller than I am, and he has hair of a nondescript sandy color and blue eyes. Although I prefer the looks of men who are darker, he is not unpleasant, and certainly better than I might have hoped for. I curtsy.

"Armand de Valmont, at your service," he says, making a pretty bow that would not have been out of place in the court of Versailles. Only then do I realize that he's speaking to me in English. For a moment, I am nonplussed. I have said nothing yet, so how does he know I am not French?

I put my teacup down on the table and hold out my hand to him, rapidly trying to think of what to say. "Eliza Monroe" is all that comes out of my mouth. Questions at this early stage of our acquaintance would be impolite.

"*Messieurs, dames!*" It is Madame Campan. She walks among us, pulling couples out of the assembled group and drawing them toward the small dance floor. Armand and I are among them. I look around, trying to see where Caroline and Hortense have gotten to.

Caroline is pretending to help the youngest ones with their ribbons. She is hiding, I see, from the boys. Hortense, on the other hand, stands like a statue near the spinet, where a young man sits, awaiting the command to play whatever is requested of him. She does not look at him, but I can feel her attention focused on him rather than on the rest of the company, and it makes me curious.

But I have no time to puzzle it out. Madame places four couples facing each other on the small dance floor.

"You have all been taught the steps of the quadrille." She holds up a well-thumbed little book, a manual of dance, which I have never seen before. Fortunately, I know how to perform the steps. "Your mother tells me you are an accomplished dancer, Mademoiselle Monroe, and so you and the Vicomte de Valmont shall lead the dance."

Although I am pleased by the notice, I blush. The spinet

strikes up a lively introduction, but I have hardly heard it, a little shocked to discover that my unassuming partner, who I was quite prepared to walk away from as soon as it could be deemed polite, is a marquis! He clears his throat, and I begin to dance just in time to avoid looking like a simpleton in front of the entire school and our guests.

I begin with confidence, knowing that first we must cross over and change partners, then return—the *chaine anglaise*. After that, we execute a few *balancés*, before beginning the *chaine des dames*. Madame Campan is nearby to nudge the younger girls when it is their turn. "Ladies, it is up to you to introduce a topic of conversation during the dance," Madame says, as she taps the youngest couple to start their figure in imitation of the one my partner and I and the opposite partners have just completed.

"Where did you learn English?" I ask the marquis, in French.

"We are taught it at school," he answers, in English. "Which is where I assume you learned to speak French?"

I can't help feeling a bit foolish about my question. "But you speak it so well," I say, hoping that flattery will save the day.

He nods and smiles. "We French have learned a great deal from you Americans. Including how to rise up against a monarchy."

The figure we are dancing makes me turn away, so I can't see whether his expression conveys sincerity or not.

"Ah," I say, once we are facing each other again. "But the guillotine was a purely French invention."

I hear a sharp intake of breath and catch the eye of Hortense, who has moved away from her position near the spinet and is close enough to overhear me. I feel ashamed that I could make such a comment in her hearing, remembering that her own father was a victim. And my partner is a marquis. Perhaps he lost members of his family in the *Terreur.* But that wasn't my fault!

Madame claps, ending the dance in what would normally be the middle of the patterns. She motions us all to leave the floor so that others might have a turn.

"I didn't mean . . . ," I say to my partner as he bows to me politely.

"The pleasure is all mine," he says, ignoring my confusion and reciting the formula they have all been taught. He walks away and approaches Hortense, who appears to be acquainted with him. I watch their easy conversation from across the room, and my stomach sinks. What a miserable failure I have made of my first cotillion, even though it was only an artificial one. *I don't care about him anyway,* I think, consoling myself with the fact that I don't really find him attractive, even if he is graceful and noble in appearance. What's a marquis in this day and age? I see that the cuffs of his dress shirt are worn, and when he turns away, I spy a small patch near the hem of his coat.

The cotillion drags on for an hour before the visiting

students assemble to return to their school across the street. We all line up by classes and curtsy to them. I try to avoid looking at the marquis, but I can't help it. As he rises from his deep bow, I find he's staring straight at me and not smiling.

After dinner, while we are in the parlor once again, now returned to its normal appearance, I seek out Hortense.

"You're acquainted with Armand de Valmont?" I ask, handing her a small pair of scissors so she can snip her embroidery silk.

"We have known each other since we were children. He is a fine young man."

"Why is he not in the army? Surely he is old enough?"

She lifts her eyes and peers at me. "You wish all young men to go away and fight, perhaps to be killed?"

I cannot help blushing. Why must I always be so stupid in conversation? It isn't at all what I mean! "No, only Caroline implied—"

"It is true that many young men choose the army as the fastest way to achieve glory and wealth. But there are those who have different aspirations." She focuses on the tiny stitches and I can't see her expression. But I notice a delicate flush has spread up from her neck into her face. It cannot be the fire; we are turned away from it. Can she be in love with Armand de Valmont?

I do not know her well enough yet to pursue the

question. But if she is—perhaps there is more to him than I thought.

I think about the day and its odd events, and despite my initial impression and unfavorable encounter with the Marquis de Valmont, I find myself wondering, as I drift off to sleep, whether he or Hortense's brother, Eugène, is handsomer.

10

Hortense

The cotillion was nothing but torture for me. I found myself forced to pretend I did not notice Michel, that I was unaware that every note he played on the spinet held a message for me. He was very polite, and very correct, and hardly looked toward me most of the time. But whenever our eyes chanced to meet, I could tell that he was trying to say something to me alone. It was the continuation of the conversation we had begun in the music room the other day, when I first met him. Something about him touches my soul. It is a safe feeling, unlike that other, which frightens me so that I can hardly breathe sometimes.

His choice of music—it cannot have been pure chance that led him to the very melodies I most adore. Yet how could he have guessed? Surely he would not have known something I have never told anyone, choosing only from his own heart songs that speak of love and desire, that imply the meeting of minds and hearts.

But I am being foolish! How can someone I have so recently met know anything at all about my heart? How can I, having thought I would never be able to imagine love, be certain that I have at last found a worthy, attainable object of my affections?

The cotillion was mostly uneventful otherwise. The only other occurrence of note for me was my conversation with Valmont. I remember him from when we were young. Maman had taken my brother and me to his family's elegant mansion to play. I found out only later that her motive was to borrow money from them, since my father's family had all but disowned us.

Those times were difficult, but harder ones followed. Like so many others, Valmont lost both his parents—and all his family's wealth—in the *Terreur*. The relatives who care for him now are distant, on his mother's side. They were far enough away from the aristocracy to avoid danger during Robespierre's reign. Their pity rescued him from complete want, but now he has become a burden. They object to supporting him at school, and are pressing him to accept a commission in the army. For most young men, that would be a perfectly satisfactory fate. How surprising that Eliza mentioned it! But Armand is an artist. To become a soldier is unthinkable to him. "I want to create, not to kill," he said to me. How I sympathized with his torment! And indeed, he has talent. His paintings are exquisite. If they would but allow him to earn his living that way, I think he could make a good name for himself. There is wealth enough in the new France to pay for skillful portraits. He says he is nearly finished with the one I sat for over the summer, but he will not show it to me until it is perfect.

His only other choice, I fear, will be to make an advantageous alliance. Valmont is handsome enough, and as he grows into a man, he is becoming even more so. He and Eliza made a pretty picture together. If she were just a little older, perhaps a match with her would be the answer. Her family is wealthy, or they would not be able to send her to school here, and as she's American, the question of her background hardly arises. Unfortunately he disdains the Americans, blaming them for igniting the revolution here by their example. I fear he was not very polite to Eliza.

The hour is late, yet my mind will not cease its ramblings. I take out a quire of paper and line it with the special implement my stepfather gave me for my birthday last April, after I had written a song for him when he returned from the campaign in Italy. Its five nibs allow me to quickly ink in perfectly spaced lines for the staves where I can place the notes that comprise my music—an operation that used to take a great deal more time. Soon I have lined half a dozen sheets.

I pause and hold this valuable instrument, examining

it, turning it over in my hand. It was so like my stepfather to think of giving it to me. He appears to be focused on only one thing: glory for France. And yet, he has been a true father to me ever since he married Maman. That is what I, in turn, must focus on. Everything he does for me is as a father, who cares for me and Eugène as if we are truly his.

And yet, Napoléon is younger than Maman by six years. And she was just twenty when I was born. Only fourteen years separate me from my stepfather. Many girls marry men who are much older than they. How can I blame myself for idolizing Napoléon, who rescued us from poverty and ignominy?

Now, I hope that thoughts of Michel will drive away the hopeless infatuation I have allowed myself to indulge in for a man who is doubly forbidden to me: as the preeminent general of France and as my mother's husband. Now, I shall let the musical link between Michel and me have expression in a new composition.

I ink in the notes on the staff I have created, letting them flow out of me. As the notes form, so do words. I close my eyes and hear the tune. But no matter how hard I try, what finds its way onto the page is not a love song. It is a patriotic anthem. I force myself again and again to think of Michel and the sweet, thrilling feelings he inspires in me, yet my hand betrays me. Before long, I have fashioned a new, stirring piece, an anthem that lauds France's new glory.

What is love? I love France. I love my Maman and my brother so fiercely that I would do almost anything to protect them. I love Napoléon because he has been so kind to us after the fearful days of the *Terreur*. I have witnessed my mother fall in love in a way I could never imagine for myself, where she will set her children aside in an instant for a man who promises her protection and who adores her.

My love for my family has left little room for any other feeling, except for one. It is that quiet, personal love I bear for music. It feeds me, takes me away from the agonies of the present, letting me wander off into other worlds where all is beautiful and kind and people aren't cruel to one another—and they don't die. Music is the only love I have that gives itself to me without expecting or needing anything in return.

And now, Michel. He is music. And yet, he is a man. That's what I saw when our eyes met. The possibility, just the possibility, that my spiritual love could have a physical embodiment.

What am I to do? He is only the son of the music master. He could have a noble background—there is nothing to say he does not, except that I imagine if he did his father would claim it loudly to enhance his reputation among the bourgeois families whose daughters are his students.

How strange it is that only five years ago no one would admit to having noble blood, because it could lead to torture and death. Now, as the specter of those days begins to fade, the old lines are redrawn. Madame Campan treats her aristocratic pupils differently from the others. The nuance is subtle, but unmistakable. Those lines, I fear, will make it more and more impossible for someone like me—the daughter of a *vicomte*—to marry someone like Michel—the son of a music teacher.

Somehow, in this quiet hour before sleep, I have managed to complete my anthem. The melody is there, and the words, and I have noted the harmonies. It's a sketch only, but anyone who knows how to read such things would see on these sheets the heart and soul that created something from the mere suggestion of an idea. I cannot say where the impulse comes from; I can but attest that it takes me over with a power few would understand.

It is for this reason that I have come to an important decision. I have decided that I shall open my heart to Michel—if he wishes to receive it. It may be a foolhardy thing to do, but the time has come, I feel, to seize my life. Until now, I have looked to Maman for guidance in everything, never giving her a moment's resistance or questioning her at all when she has said, *You shall go to school here; you shall wear these dresses; you shall befriend these young ladies; you shall make yourself look beautiful for this party.* . . . Now I shall have my own reasons for what I do. I will not do as I have done in the past: willfully ignore the stirrings of my heart and discourage the person who is the cause of them. Instead I will embrace the troubled feelings I have, and press upon them, even loving the pain they cause if that is the result.

How else will I ever know if I can take the next step, from girlhood to womanhood?

11

Today I have my first comportment lesson with Madame Campan.

"I advise you to study the movements and actions of Hortense, Eliza," she says at the beginning, before we have started. Everyone is there except for Caroline, who is often late.

"Let us begin with the correct manner of greeting a bishop, or other high-ranking cleric," Madame Campan says, drawing herself up as though she is preparing to enter the audience chamber of a queen. I cast my eye around the parlor, with its old-fashioned, slightly worn furnishings. The paneling on the walls is delicately carved, but the paint on it peels here and there. Three paintings—all portraits from before the revolution, with the ladies' hair powdered and piled up high—gaze down upon us disapprovingly. I see the faintest outline on one wall of a space where another picture hung once. Perhaps it was sold in a time of need.

I listen to the young students saying, turn by turn, "I am honored, Your Grace" or "Charmed, Your Eminence," and realize that in Virginia there is little need for such knowledge. People are either "mister" or "doctor" or "mistress" or "miss."

"Mademoiselle Eliza, perhaps you could tell me how to greet one of the members of our own Directoire, our equivalent to your Congress. What would you say after being introduced?"

Before I can answer that I would say, "Good afternoon, Congressman" or "Enchanted to meet you, sir," we are interrupted by Caroline, who sweeps in, a hat upon her head and gloves in her hand as though she is preparing to go outside.

"I beg your pardon, madame," Caroline says with a pretty curtsy, making up a little for her rude interruption before, "but I have just received a message from my mother, who insists that I go to Paris to be with my family."

"Oh?" Madame Campan says, clearly put out that the message went directly to Caroline instead of passing through the proper channels. "What can be so urgent that you must depart like this, in the middle of an important lesson?"

"She did not say, but I believe it may have something to do with the ball she is arranging in my honor."

A ball? Caroline has said nothing of such a possibility, and I cannot imagine she would not be crowing about it if she could. I certainly would in her place. And of course, after our late-night excursion, I know how devious Caroline can be.

Madame Campan smiles, although I have observed that she is capable of adjusting her expression to suit the moment, without letting any hint of her real feelings seep through. "Of course, Caroline," she says. "Your future will be decided soon and you will be making such arrangements yourself. When will you return?"

"I am afraid that is not certain as yet. I shall send word."

I don't know why, but the idea of Caroline leaving just now, just as I am beginning to understand how things work in this school, fills me with dismay. "Must you truly leave, Caroline?" I ask.

"Yes, but I shall return soon. I will write to you every day while I am gone. Do not be downhearted," Caroline says.

I see that she has no feeling of obligation or friendship for me, and is just as quick to drop me as she took me up. I cannot help the sigh that escapes me, and I look toward Hortense. She gazes back at me with a sympathetic expression. Could she really be so good as to understand my fascination with Caroline, even though Caroline has been revealed to me as her enemy?

"I suppose you will attend parties while you're there," I say, looking back at Caroline with a slight smile. I remember what Hortense said. I have a secret to keep for her.

One of Caroline's eyebrows twitches almost

imperceptibly. I see her shoot a quick glance at Hortense, then approach me.

"If she does, I hope she will practice some of her skills of discretion and conversation," Madame Campan says, reminding me that we are not alone, but are putting on some kind of delicate ballet of hints and suggestions for the benefit of the entire school.

"What shall I do, then?" I ask.

Caroline's face brightens. "Would you like to visit my mother with me—with Madame's permission, of course?"

"Oh! May I? Must I ask Mama first?" I turn to Madame Campan, as though it is really her decision about whether or not I go with Caroline.

"Your *maman* gave me permission to allow you whatever diversions I thought would be advantageous to your education," Madame says. I can hear the "but" in her voice, though. "*Tout de même*," she says, "I hesitate to interrupt your studies, so recently begun."

"I shall ensure that she keeps up with her lessons," Caroline says.

"Please, madame?" I clasp my hands together like a child. Perhaps that is overplaying my game, but I can see from Madame Campan's softening expression that it has worked.

"*Eh bien*. But you must return in three days, regardless of how long Caroline is to remain." Three days! Much can happen in three days, I have already discovered. I smile.

"The drawing master will be here soon," Madame says.

"I must prepare to leave," Caroline says.

"So must I," I echo. Besides, drawing is my least favorite lesson. I am hopeless at it, and only frustrate my teachers. And I have seen Hortense's work. It is very skilled. I smile at Hortense, who has the good grace to smile back.

Within an hour we are settled in a fiacre with our valises tied to the back. "Will I meet Madame Bonaparte?" I ask Caroline.

"My mother? Of course," she says.

I realize my mistake. I should hold my tongue, but I cannot help wanting to know. "I meant, actually . . ."

"You mean Joséphine. Hortense's mother." Caroline looks cross. "Very likely. But there are some things you ought to know about her first."

"I know that she is a Creole, from the island of Martinique. My mother told me. And that her first husband was executed in the *Terreur.*"

Caroline takes hold of my arm and turns me toward her, almost angrily. "Joséphine's first husband was estranged from her almost from the hour of their marriage," she says. "Hortense never knew him. He abandoned the family before she was born."

I cannot help feeling a trifle shocked. She continues. "But that is not the worst of it. Joséphine became so accustomed to admiration that she had many lovers, and has continued this habit even while married to my brother."

"How can that be? When Hortense is so—"

"So virtuous? I wouldn't assume her appearance and her character to be one and the same."

This is as close to a direct insult to Hortense as Caroline has come with me.

It seems impossible that it was only a week ago that my mother and I made the trip from Paris to Saint-Germain. My life has changed so dramatically since then. I'm not certain that what I have learned is everything my mama hoped I would learn, but the lives the young women lead in France are certainly much more interesting than in Virginia.

Caroline is quiet on our way, and so I have a little time to reflect. I asked Hortense last night about the Marquis de Valmont, thinking she might confide in me that—although he is younger than she is by a year—she is in love with him. But instead, she thought I was the one who is fascinated with Valmont. "Oh, no!" I protested. "I just saw you speaking with him, and he appears so sad in a way."

Hortense sighed. "He has reason for sadness. He has a great talent that his family will not permit him to exercise, and so he must do it in secret, during stolen hours of the night, with only a few candles to illuminate his work."

She told me that he is an artist. I immediately thought of the empty space on the wall of the school's drawing room. "Perhaps we can persuade Madame Campan to commission a painting," I suggested.

Hortense's laugh surprised me. "Even if he does not go

into the army, Madame Campan would hardly encourage him to take up a trade."

"So how is he to support himself then?" I asked. In Virginia, young men become apprentices, or study the law or doctoring. Everyone has to earn a living, even if they come from a wealthy family.

"Perhaps you can save him," Hortense said, a strange look in her eye.

I smiled and our conversation ended, but I have been intrigued since then to discover what she means by me saving someone like the Marquis de Valmont.

After an hour or so we pull up at a fine house in the Rue du Rocher, a short way down from the church of the same name. There are three carriages outside, none bearing crests but all looking as though they are preparing to depart. We enter only to be stopped at the door.

A plump older woman dressed in black scurries up to Caroline and greets her with a kiss. Caroline turns to me and says, "I'd like to introduce my American friend, Mademoiselle Eliza Monroe. Eliza, this is my mother, Madame Bonaparte."

I curtsy, but Caroline's mother hardly pauses to glance in my direction. Instead, she takes hold of Caroline's shoulders, pulling her down to her level and talking directly into her face.

"We must go to Malmaison at once. At once!"

Caroline stands upright and shakes her shoulders, as if shooing away a bothersome fly. "Why?" she asks, not making any effort at politeness or affection.

"Because your brother is there, and so are . . . others."

"Which others?"

"Barras. Captain Charles . . . the rest." Madame Bonaparte makes a face as though she has tasted something sour. The names mean nothing to me, but judging from Caroline's expression, they are not popular with her family.

"I see. Then we must go at once." Caroline turns to me. "Eliza, the servants will take care of your bag. Don't remove your cloak. We depart immediately."

Instead of climbing back into the fiacre, we make the two-hour trip out to Malmaison in a much more comfortable private carriage. Caroline and I sit next to each other, with her mother across from us. Caroline's brother Joseph and another young man climbed into one of the other carriages and left before we were quite ready to go.

Almost as soon as the motion of the vehicle is steady, Madame Bonaparte closes her eyes and leans into the corner of her seat. Within minutes, she is snoring softly.

"I detest Malmaison," Caroline says. "It's in a terrible state of repair. Or it was. The workmen were still there the last time I was forced to visit, in the summer, just after my brothers returned from Egypt. Napoléon was furious."

Caroline looks out the window with a cold smile upon

her face. "Joséphine had spent an enormous sum on the place and at the time was planning to spend even more to make it truly habitable. And the gardens! They're like a forest run wild. You'll soon see for yourself."

I want to ask her more. Who are the people her mother referred to? By the time we have traveled the twelve kilometers to Joséphine's country retreat in virtual silence, the questions have only multiplied in my mind.

As we pass through the ornate gates, I gaze out the window of the carriage. "How lovely!"

This is not the chaotic wilderness Caroline described. It is as beautiful a park as any I have seen. Caroline sits forward on her seat and stares out the other side. She slides the window down with a bang that makes her mother start but does not wake her, and leans her head out as if she cannot believe what she sees.

On my side, I drink in the serene sight of manicured gardens and trees that have been trimmed, statuary, and peacocks strolling the grounds.

"She must have spent a great deal more of my brother's fortune," Caroline murmurs.

Soon we draw up to the main door of the château, whose proportions I note are very pleasing. Two footmen trot out in perfect unison and open the doors of the carriage. Caroline's mother awakens and takes the hand of one, who helps her descend.

"It's magical!" I whisper. I feel as if I have been

transported to a fairy-tale castle, where everything is goodness and light.

Caroline says nothing, nor does her mother. We walk up to the double doors, which open as soon as we reach them.

A maid appears to take our cloaks. We hear men's voices coming from behind the closed doors that lead off the vestibule to the right, opposite another pair on the other side. In front of us is a curved marble staircase, and everything gleams with fresh paint.

"You are the only one who can do it! You are the hero of the hour!"

"You do me too much honor," comes a response, in a clipped, accented voice.

"It is my brother!" Caroline whispers. Her face glows with genuine delight. All signs of petulance are gone.

"The question is how to manage it," the first voice says. "You need stalwarts by your side, because there may be trouble."

"You know I can be counted upon. I have shown myself willing to die for you," says a third voice. And I recognize it. It is the young man I overheard at the ball, and whose picture sits in a frame upon Hortense's desk. It is Eugène de Beauharnais, Hortense's brother.

I look at Caroline, who, with her mother, has drifted closer to the door. I think they would press their ears against it if they could, but my presence must inhibit them a little.

"I know the men are behind you." At the sound of a fourth voice, Caroline gasps.

"What is it?" I whisper, going to join her by the door.

"It's Murat. He is here."

Before we can listen to anything more, a footman appears from behind the stairs, strides over to the doors, and knocks. All conversation within stops. He enters, closing the doors behind him.

In a moment they fly open again, and this time a short man strides through, his jacket unbuttoned, a huge smile lighting up his face.

"Maman! Caroline! What brings you here? I thought you were in school having your rough edges knocked off." He chucks Caroline under the chin before throwing his arms around Madame Bonaparte. Caroline is still smiling, but she rubs her chin. I see that his gesture has annoyed her.

Caroline turns her attention through the open door to the others in the room. All three of the men in military garb make deep, graceful bows in our direction, and we curtsy in return. I cannot help staring at Eugène, wondering if he recognizes me from the ball. He is not looking in my direction, though, but at Bonaparte.

"But, Caroline," Bonaparte says, "where is Hortense?" He glances at me, obviously disappointed.

"She had to remain at school to help Madame Campan," Caroline says, a note of vexation in her voice. She recovers quickly, though, and introduces me. I curtsy to him, awed at being introduced to the most famous man in Europe. For someone with such a gigantic reputation he is very short.

"Monroe? Monroe?" he repeats, leaning toward me and examining me with his intense, dark eyes. "*Enchanté, mademoiselle.* I believe your father has been to Paris."

My cheeks flame red at the honor of knowing the great Bonaparte is aware of my father. I wish I could think of something to say, but words simply will not come.

Bonaparte turns away abruptly and addresses his mother. "We are nearly finished here. If you would wait in the music room?" He steers her in the direction of the doors on the other side of the opulent vestibule.

The footman opens the doors and we step through.

"Caroline! Madame!"

Seated at a harp as though she were posing for a picture is a beautiful woman I immediately recognize as Joséphine. Close by her side, perched on a footstool, sits a gentleman, also in uniform. He picks up some sheet music that has fallen to the floor.

"Ah," says Madame Bonaparte. "I see we're interrupting you."

"Not in the least," Joséphine replies, smiling graciously. "Captain Charles was about to join the others."

He looks up at us. Caroline turns her face away as if the sight of him repulses her.

I am intrigued, enchanted, charmed, and curious. I only

wish Hortense were here to talk to later, to explain everything to me. Somehow I think Caroline sees the situation
very differently, and may be less than fair to Joséphine. I
want to like this beautiful lady despite the gossip that swirls
around her like tendrils of mist.

I see them even now, reflected in Caroline's eyes.

12

Madeleine

Maman is to go out again this evening. I am so very relieved! The performance went well. She had to appear for ten bows; the audience was ecstatic. When she is happy and feels adored, I am able to relax a little.

"So, you did not steal my scenes from me this evening," she says, even as I take the brush from her maid and force it through her coarse, curling hair. I am the only one who can style it when she goes out in society. The French maids don't know how to manage it, trying to force it into the smooth, Grecian coiffures that Joséphine has made famous and that most ladies now wear. I let my fingers make the tight, skull-clinging braids that achieve the same effect but keep her hair from springing wildly from its ribbons.

"No, Maman," I say. "I couldn't possibly do that. You are the greatest actress who ever lived."

The line has lost its meaning for me, I have uttered it so often. It is a game we play, now that I am a woman. It started the time the theater director noticed this and decided to give me a more prominent role onstage.

"I shall wear my emeralds tonight," Maman says. That is another fiction we maintain. Her "emeralds" are ropes of green glass beads, artfully cut to catch the light. "The Duc d'Alger will soon be here. We attend *un bal masqué* this evening."

It always seems to be a masked ball with her. I suspect her gentlemen do not feel quite comfortable taking her to places where she would be recognized for who she is and yet not be somehow part of a display, an atmosphere of carnival. I fetch her mask with its exotic feathers and see that she is well wrapped up in her furs. The cough she developed when we first came from the islands has never left her, although she pretends she is only clearing her throat. One of her lovers was a doctor and brought her opium for it. She continues to take the opium, but her cough does not abate.

"The duke has arrived," the maid says as soon as my mother is ready. That is my signal to disappear. I do not mind that my mother does not wish her admirers to catch a glimpse of me because they might desire me. Nor do I mind that she does not want them to realize she is old enough to have a daughter who is sixteen, and a woman. I have no wish to please her elderly paramours, with their scented handkerchiefs and gifts of gold jewelry. My beloved is worth fifty of them. And I have been successful—at least in these last few days—in thwarting her attempts to lure him. He sent me back a brief note when he received mine, saying that the next time he came to the theater he would ask for me, and me alone.

As I tidy away the pots of makeup and wipe the spills from the dressing table—a task that should fall to the maid, but Maman has always made me do it—I remember the day I met him. It was after my first real performance, in which the director had cast me not as an urchin on the street or a child in the background, but as the daughter of a nobleman. My mother had protested, but he managed to smooth her ruffled feathers by making her a handsome present of a painted fan.

I had few lines to say, but one of my scenes required me to sing a simple song in the drawing room, an interlude between the dramatic romance of which my mother was the heroine.

When my song was over, the audience erupted in rapturous applause. I looked toward the wings, where the theater director stood. He motioned me to stand and bow, so I did.

That night I received the worst beating of my life. Maman's blows cracked two of my ribs, and my face swelled so that my eyes were mere slits.

She told the director that I had caught a bad cold because the costume I wore did not cover me enough, and that she had her own island medicine to tend to me. I remember hearing her tell him, through the door behind which I lay on the floor without even a blanket to cover me, "She is all I have. Please do not expose her to such danger again. If she is to go upon the stage, she must be wrapped in shawls. And singing—it is out of the question."

But she was too late. He—my love—had seen me, had heard me, by chance on that night. It was Marianne who came that evening to tell me that a young man had asked for me. My mother made her send him away, but kept the flowers he brought. White roses.

The young man returned, night after night, asking why I no longer appeared onstage. Marianne greeted him, managing to keep him away from my mother after that, realizing that it would be better for me if she did. I so wanted to go and talk to him, and would have managed it with Marianne's help. But my bruises prevented me. I did not want him to see me in such a state.

Finally, three weeks later, I again had a role to play upon the stage. But my mother had her way, and I was the poor foundling once more. The audience hardly noticed me. I was just as glad. I had no wish to suffer a beating again.

"Mam'selle Madeleine. *Psst!*" Marianne whispered to me as I made my way up to the dressing rooms to shed my costume and do my chores.

"What is it?" I asked.

"He's here!"

She didn't have to say his name. I knew who it was. Quickly, I let my ragged shawls drop to the floor. Marianne scooped them up and pointed down the stairs. "I told him to wait there."

I blew her a kiss as I went to him.

At first we stood in awkward silence. I could not stop staring at his face. He was so handsome! And such kindness in his eyes.

"Would you . . . permit me . . ." He could hardly stammer out the words.

I stepped forward and placed my fingers upon his lips. They were soft and delicate. He kissed my fingertips so lightly I hardly felt it. Then he took my hands in his, and we simply gazed into each other's eyes for what seemed a long time. I saw sadness in his, and longing. I don't know what he saw in mine, but he drew closer to me, and I knew he wanted to kiss me.

I looked away and took a step backward. Oh, how I wanted to kiss him! But I did not want to be like my mother. When I looked back up at him, he appeared so disappointed that I nearly lost my resolve. But I smiled at him and said, "You are most welcome to return, kind sir, although I am watched constantly."

It wasn't much, but it was enough to make him understand. He took my hand and bowed over it formally.

Since then, there have been many kisses, each one sweeter than the last. I have fallen so deeply in love with him that I am no longer myself, but part of this wondrous creature who saw me when I should have been invisible.

"I shall take you from here, as soon as I am of age," he said. It was a promise. It *is* a promise.

But he has been of age some months. He was in Egypt, fighting, like all the officers in France. Still, he has not come for me. I keep a small package of possessions ready for when he arrives to fulfill his promise. A handkerchief. A scarf my *maman* no longer wears. A Bible and a book of poetry. Warm stockings. A comb. The necklace my grandmother gave me in Martinique. It's all I have.

He will take care of me. I know it.

13

Hortense

I feel that I can breathe more easily when Caroline is not at school, as if no one is judging me. Out in the playing field, I run about like the young ones, feeling like a child again. It is good for me. I had so few opportunities to participate in childish games when I was younger, always having to stay with my mother and soothe her troubled spirit.

I think of Maman now, happy, I hope. Bonaparte is good for her, if she can be satisfied by one man only. The prospect of her happiness makes whatever I must endure from Caroline worth tolerating, and makes my own sadness seem less important. And I don't believe Caroline is evil. She has simply not been brought up to care, neglected as the youngest in a family where her mother thought little of the education of her daughters.

"Come, Hortense! Chase us! You're the fox!"

The young ones' voices recall me from my daydreams, and I run, chasing but trying not to catch them, just to have them run around, laughing and screeching with delight, their cheeks glowing pink from the wind and the exercise.

I stop to catch my breath and cast my eyes around the fenced-in lawn. On the far edge I see a young man on a horse looking over the fence at us. I don't know why this stranger makes me feel self-conscious, but I smooth my hair back into place and call out to the girls, "Let us play a quieter game." They cluster around me, and before I make them sit in a circle I glance back at the horseman.

Then I realize that he is no stranger. It is Michel, the person who has been occupying my dreams from the moment I first saw him. He stares at me. I can feel the imprint of his gaze as if he had his finger on my cheek. Just before I look away, he puts his hand to the brim of his hat and makes a slight bow. I am thankful that he is too far off to see the blush that suffuses my neck and face, and that running in the fresh air is enough of an excuse if any of the young girls notice. We sit to play our clapping game, and when next I raise my eyes to the fence, he is gone.

Supper is quiet. The exercise has made some of the youngest ones so tired I can see their eyes drooping at the table. Madame signals to the matron of the Pinks and the Greens to take them up to bed.

I spend as little time as I can sewing and listening to

Catherine read from a book of memoirs before retiring to my room. My candle lights the way up the broad staircase, since the sconces have been doused earlier.

At the top I spy the shadow of a person by my door. For an instant, my heart races with fear.

"Mademoiselle Hortense!"

It is Geneviève. I breathe again, although my hand trembles. I don't understand why she is whispering. "Yes?"

"This is for you." She looks up and down the corridor to ensure that no one is watching her and gives me a small, folded paper.

I take it from her. "What is it?"

"He asked me to deliver it personally." She does not answer, but scampers past me to the door that leads to the servants' stairs at the other end of the hallway. I enter my room, glad to close the door on another day and be alone with my turbulent thoughts.

I sit at my desk and open the paper, which is not sealed. I wonder, briefly, if Geneviève has read it.

Dear Mademoiselle Hortense,

Forgive the presumption of writing to you, only I do not know when we will next have an opportunity to speak. My father has assigned me some of his pupils to teach, and you are not among them. I fear his reasons are only too wise, since I have been able to think of nothing but you since we met.

I am only a humble music teacher, and if you say the

word I will never address you again. But I cannot help feeling that your heart reached out to mine in those brief times we have been in each other's company.

If I can hope at all, please come to the gates after eleven this evening, so that I may assure you of my eternal regard.

Yours with respect and admiration,
Michel Perroquet

Although I am alone, I blush, but not with shame. I have been hoping for this! Some acknowledgment that he feels as I do, that there is a possibility of something fine and noble between us. I thought perhaps he simply chanced to be in the vicinity earlier, when I saw him beyond the fence. But he must have come to deliver the letter.

His words are passionate. But is he sincere? Does he assume that I have had lovers already, and therefore dares to make my acquaintance in such a bold manner? For it is bold indeed. He must know that he could compromise me by sending a letter, that the very fact I have read it puts me in a difficult position. Surely he would not take such a step if he were not truly in love with me.

I hear the clock in the vestibule chiming eleven. I reread the last portion of his letter. Should I meet him? That is even more dangerous a request. Apart from any damage to my prospects, his father could be dismissed—losing a valuable source of support—if Madame ever found out.

Then something else occurs to me. I try to beat back the little demon of suspicion that nips at my imagination. What if this is an elaborate trick planned by Caroline to further blacken me in Madame Campan's eyes? To make me leave the school in the dead of night for what I think is an assignation, and then have me apprehended. She has done many things as bad, if not worse, and I am afraid that I must face the possibility.

Yet I know facts about Caroline that could similarly ruin her. I could, for instance, tell Madame Campan that she and Eliza stole out the other night, and that she sends letters regularly to General Murat—despite her brother's prohibition.

No. Caroline has too much to lose. And the handwriting is not hers. Besides, when I read the lines again, I see such sincerity in the words, as if the writer could not bear to wait any longer to profess his love.

I fetch my cloak from the wardrobe and, quiet as can be, I tiptoe down the stairs and out through the front door.

As I approach the gate, locked at this hour, of course, I see no one standing there. I slow as I reach it, counting myself foolish for being duped. I should have trusted my instincts, the ones that told me he could not love me after so short an acquaintance. Someone, somewhere, is laughing at my expense, even if it is only the spirits of spurned lovers.

With a deep sigh, I take hold of the iron bars and rest my head against them. Their coldness soothes my hot brow.

"Hortense?"

It is a man's whisper. I gasp. A figure emerges from the shadows and walks toward me. Michel! Soon he steps into a pool of moonlight, and I see his eyes shining.

"It is you! I didn't dare hope." His voice, though quiet, trembles with emotion.

"*Shhh!*" I say. "I cannot stay long."

He moves very close, so close that I can feel the warmth of his body, catch the impulse of his breath on my cheek. "A moment is enough. Ah, Hortense!" He takes my hand and pulls it through the bars of the gate, planting the most delicate of kisses on my fingers. I draw my hand back. "Your hand is so cold!" he says. "You came without your gloves."

I realize at once the implication of what he says. I am not acquainted with the ploys of love. My mother, I realize, would have burned the letter and ignored him until at least two more made their way into her hands. "I only received your note a few moments ago, and didn't want to miss you."

"The sound of your voice has been in my ear ever since I heard you sing. I thought I would perish having to be so near to you the other day without being able even to speak to you. I can no longer hear any other voices, including those of the young pupils I teach, and have made a terrible job of it lately."

I don't know whether to believe him, but cannot take my eyes off his full lips, his deep eyes. "We should not meet like this. We are permitted to receive guests at tea on Sunday. Perhaps you would honor me..."

"I would lie here and let horses trample me if it meant I could see you again!" he says, too loudly.

"Hush!" I put my finger to his lips. He closes his eyes and kisses my hand again. The blood races to my face and weakens my knees.

I am about to tell him that I must go when I hear something. Horses' hooves, and the squeaking of carriage springs. Most unusual on this quiet road at this hour. "Go—now!" I say, turning and running back into the school. I look over my shoulder once. He is still there. I will him to disappear into the darkness as I enter the vestibule and run silently up the stairs.

I reach my room, panting with exertion and excitement. I dip my fingers in the basin of cool water on the stand and splash it against my face, dousing the fire in my cheeks.

The carriage I heard does not pass by, but draws up at the school gates. I hear the coachman calling out to be admitted. Who could it be at this hour?

The footman makes his way slowly to the gates. I look out my window, watching as he carries a lantern across the courtyard, his ring of heavy keys dangling from his hand.

The carriage pulls in and I recognize the crest. It is Bonaparte's. Could Caroline have returned so soon?

But no one descends. The coachman speaks to the footman, who returns inside. I hear some commotion. Madame Campan is awakened.

"Who dares disturb us at this hour, after all the pupils are abed?" she says in her crispest, most authoritative voice.

"Madame Bonaparte sends her carriage for her daughter, Hortense, who is required to attend her on most urgent business," the footman replies.

I sit at my desk, pretending to be writing a letter when Madame Campan's soft knock follows. "Come!" I say.

"Ah, you have not yet readied yourself for bed, I see. Just as well. Get your things. Your mother needs you," she says with a smile that is not unkind, although I know she is vexed to have been disturbed.

What could have happened? I wonder. Maman has never before sent for me so urgently. Perhaps she is ill. Or something has happened to Eugène.

It is no use fretting. I will find out soon enough. I close my eyes and lean my head against the side of the carriage, distracted by the memory of Michel's gentle kiss on my fingertips.

14

Chère Maman,

 You will be amazed—and pleased, I think—to hear that I am staying at Malmaison for three days. Caroline Bonaparte invited me. Hortense is not here, but I have met General Bonaparte, the Vicomte de Barras, Joséphine Bonaparte, and Madame Bonaparte, Caroline's mother.

 Also staying here are General Murat, Captain Charles (the less said about him the better . . .), Joseph Bonaparte, and Eugène de Beauharnais.

Eugène! I could not believe it when I saw the miniature on Hortense's table, but it was indeed he whose unfortunate scene I witnessed at the ball. But here, even after we were properly introduced, he did not seem to recognize me, so he must not have noticed me at the ball. I am relieved. I would not want him to think I knew something shameful about him. He is much too noble to carry shame.

Eugène is older than Hortense, but only by a little. The difference in our ages is not very great, not if there is love.

What am I saying? He barely looked at me today. We sat opposite each other at the dinner table, but he spoke only to General Murat, who was on his right. Poor Caroline—her brother Napoléon made her sit as far away as possible from Murat. She was next to old Barras, who leaned into her and stared down the front of her dress the entire evening. I suppose he was handsome when he was younger, but I don't like that thick-lipped French look. And he took the measure of every woman in the room except me—but then, I suppose in his eyes I am not yet a woman.

And I also suppose I should be grateful that I am not the center of attention here. It gives me the opportunity to observe closely without the others taking much notice. Since I took little part in the conversation at the dinner table, I could listen and try to remember all that was said.

There was a great deal of talk about the Directoire. No one seems to think the directors are doing their jobs. Even Barras, who is chief among them, believes there should be change.

"But we cannot return to the old system! Monarchy would set us back a hundred years," said Murat.

I looked at Caroline to see her reaction. Barras was doing his best to block her view, but I could see she was torn between trying to guess what her brother thought and watching Murat. He is indeed handsome, I must admit—especially compared to the Bonaparte brothers and Barras. But I still prefer the looks of Eugène.

Mama, Eugène is magnifique! How can I begin to describe him? His brows are delicately arched over eyes that are both dark and clear at the same time. He has a noble nose with flared nostrils, and lips that are fine and beg to be kissed. . . .

I suppose I had better not write that to my mother. I have plenty of paper, so I crumple up the second street and start anew. She will be more interested in the conversation, which touched on matters that will affect all of France and perhaps the world.

Oh! I almost forgot to tell you. There was another man present. He was very quiet, but when he spoke, everyone paid attention to him. His name is Sieyès. He was the one who first started the talk about the failures of the Directoire.

"They have bankrupted the country through their bad management," said Sieyès.

Murat spoke up next. "They have not eliminated the monarchy, but have become a pentarchy! Five people with only one head among them!"

This made everyone laugh, except Barras, who is the leader of the Directoire right now. After that, he had to speak.

"I know the weaknesses of our present system. The needs of the country have outgrown it. We need a stronger central government, one that can manage the workings of our new nation in all its complexity."

His comment reminded me of the many similar conversations I have heard at our own dinner table in Virginia.

Everyone agreed with that, and then Joséphine stood, so we ladies had to leave the men to talk. I wish I could have stayed behind.

But I did see something interesting afterward, when the men all entered the grand salon. Joséphine had been playing her harp and singing to us. She has a lovely voice, and I just couldn't help looking at her the whole time. It's not that she's extremely graceful or even as beautiful as Hortense, but there is something in her expression I find completely irresistible. I did think it rather unkind of Caroline to whisper throughout her performance.

The men greeted Joséphine first. I watched them, trying to guess which of them might be in love with her. Barras, for all his ogling, didn't seem to be. Napoléon's face lit up with pride when he saw her. Captain Charles is smitten, obviously so, if for no other reason than that he tried very hard to act uninterested.

It was the quiet Sieyès who surprised me, though. He

held her hand a little longer than the others did, and I saw that she put a small note into his palm.

I wonder if Caroline noticed it? She doesn't like Joséphine at all and makes no pretense about it.

My hand aches from writing so much. I hope my mother appreciates the way I keep her informed of everything. I shall have to finish my letter tomorrow, though—

Heavens! What's that? A carriage has just come into the courtyard. It is well past midnight and everyone has gone to bed. Who would arrive at this hour?

A glance out the window reveals only a cloaked figure stepping down from a carriage. I glimpse a lady's dainty shoe, and the door below opens right away.

There is little noise in the house. Whoever just arrived does not want to disturb anyone, so cannot be carrying vital news. I slip my arms into my dressing gown and crack open the door to my bedroom, listening for some telltale sound.

I see a flickering glow advancing up the stairs. I retreat a little, leaving my door open just enough so that I can see but not be seen, and I wait.

A lady's gloved hand, then her entire figure still enveloped in a traveling cloak rounds the corner from the stairwell. A moment later the candle illuminates her face.

It is Hortense! I don't want to startle her, so I wait a little longer, hoping she will pass my door and I can whisper to her and draw her in. I cannot imagine what has made her arrive so mysteriously in the middle of the night.

I watch her approach, preparing to beckon her when she is near enough. But she pauses at a door on the other side of the corridor. I see her lift her hand to knock, then lower it, as if she cannot decide what to do. She takes a step to continue, then turns abruptly back and knocks softly.

A moment later, the door opens, and Bonaparte himself steps out, wearing a black brocade dressing gown. "Hortense!" he whispers.

"Maman sent for me," she says, and looks down at her feet.

"And you came to me first?" he asks.

In the dim light, it is hard to see, but I detect a faint blush in her cheeks. "I trust you to tell me what is happening, whether there is some real emergency or something Maman has imagined."

He shakes his head. "It is unfair of her to involve you. These are matters between us, alone. I advise you to go to bed and think no more of it."

"Think no more!" Her voice rises, and Napoléon touches his finger to her lips. It seems as though she leans into that touch, very slightly.

What is happening? Can Hortense have feelings for her stepfather? Or is it the other way around? My heart pounds with confusion and shock. I must do something to prevent an indiscretion.

I open my door wide, yawning as if I have just heard something that awakened me, hoping Hortense does not realize I have seen her. "Ah! It is you, Hortense! I heard something and thought I would see."

"We will speak in the morning," Napoléon says, with a slight inclination of his head. Before I can greet him he has vanished behind the closed door of his bedchamber again.

"It's been a lovely day, Hortense. Come and sit with me a while and I'll tell you about it. Perhaps someone will bring us tea or warm milk."

I can see Hortense is embarrassed. I reach my hand out to her. She takes it without a backward glance and steps with me into my room.

15

Hortense

How much did Eliza see? I am so ashamed. No one knows that this is the reason I have chosen to spend so much of my time at school, when I really don't need to continue my lessons.

"Sit a moment," Eliza says. I see the questions in her eyes, and a little shock. Who would not be shocked? Although Bonaparte is only my stepfather, I should not be so drawn to him.

"Thank you," I say. "But don't let me keep you from your bed. You have had a tiring day, too." Best to pretend nothing happened.

She smiles and goes to the bellpull by the fireplace. I hear the tinkling far away in the kitchen. No doubt someone will come soon. I've already awoken them with my arrival.

"I was up, writing to my mother," Eliza says. "Why have you come in the middle of the night?"

Well might she ask. "My mother sent word asking me to hasten here immediately." Her note had implied that something important was going to happen, and that she wanted me by her during that time.

"I think you are right," Eliza says, slowly pacing around her room and rubbing her hands together against the cold. "I'm not certain, but there was talk at dinner among the gentlemen—"

"Who else is here?" I shouldn't interrupt, but I must know.

"Murat, Sieyès, Captain Charles, Joseph Bonaparte, and your brother."

I notice that Eliza casts her eyes down when she mentions Eugène. Has something happened? "Is my brother well? Tell me, please!"

"Oh! Yes, exceedingly, I believe."

Now she is blushing. Ah, I see it. Poor Eliza! She is smitten with him. Who wouldn't be? I think Eugène the handsomest young man in France. But Eliza is very young, and I believe he is in love with someone else. His last letter— before he was injured—hinted as much. Should I tell her? Perhaps not, since she has not yet confided in me. "What were the gentlemen saying?"

"That the Directoire is ineffective and has nearly bankrupted the country."

"That is hardly news. But the Directoire is our foundation,

our government that is not a monarchy and that so many were sacrificed for." Including my own father, and many of our friends.

"I don't know, but I had the feeling that Sieyès wanted your stepfather to do something."

"He didn't say anything more?" I wonder if Eliza is canny enough to hide such knowledge, if she happened to over-hear something she shouldn't.

"No, nothing. But . . ."

"But what?"

We are interrupted by a soft knock on the door. It is Marie, answering Eliza's call.

"Bring us tea," Eliza says. She's not very kind to servants, I've noticed.

Once Marie has gone, I say, "You implied that there was something more."

"Only what I saw . . . ," Eliza begins.

My God! She did see it? "Don't speak of it. It's not nec-essary."

Eliza cocks her head to the side. "But I thought such things were commonplace in Paris, among the privileged."

How can such a thing be commonplace? My heart starts to beat faster and I feel the color drain from my face. "I assure you they are not. I'm afraid my journey has tired me. I must be ready to see my mother first thing in the morning. I'm sorry to have put Marie to unnecessary trouble."

"I did not mean to . . ." Eliza's voice trails off.

"Please don't worry. I'm just tired," I say, turning and putting my hand on the doorknob.

"Good night, Eliza."

She curtsies to me, her face a picture of bewildered sadness. I let go of the doorknob, take her by the shoulders, and kiss each of her cheeks. "Take care that you do not spoil your American innocence here, my dear Eliza. You have much yet to learn."

A soft knock announces Marie's return with the tea tray.

"We don't want it now," Eliza says, and waves her away. I slip a coin into Marie's pocket for her trouble. She smiles as Eliza closes her door.

Sleep claims me almost as soon as I lay my head on my pillow but not for very long. I awaken at the first gray light of dawn.

I dress quickly and pull on my warmest shawl. The sun is trying to dispel the mist, but at this time of year—appropriately named *Brumaire,* or "season of mist," by the Directoire—its attempts are feeble at best.

I pass Marie, whose night must have been as short as mine, carrying wood into the salon so that the fire is blazing when the others rise. She curtsies to me, but I see by her look that she is annoyed, despite the little gift I gave her last night. I shall have to make her another present.

I run out of the front door into the wooded part of the

garden, wanting to get as far away from the house as possible so that I can think.

It is not five minutes before I see the figure of a man ahead of me and start to alter my course. But then he turns around and looks straight at me, and instead of walking away I run toward him, faster and faster, until I can throw my arms around his familiar neck.

"Eugène!" I cover his face with kisses. "I am so happy to see you well."

He picks me up off my feet and twirls me around. "I am delighted—and surprised—to see you, my dear sister! I thought you were still at school."

"I was, but Maman sent for me. I arrived late last night."

He holds me away from him and looks me up and down. "You're very thin, and you have shadows under your eyes."

I pretend to pout. "Is that anything to say to a lady?"

"You don't need me to tell you how beautiful you are! But I do worry. Has something happened?"

"No, nothing at all is wrong, except the usual trivial matters."

"The Bonaparte clan is still tormenting Maman, I see. Caroline hardly said a word to me yesterday," Eugène says.

We begin to stroll along, arm in arm. I am so happy to be with Eugène that I almost forget to notice how beautiful the grounds are, and how Maman has done so much to improve them in so short a time.

"Caroline and I have a new source of competition. You met her yesterday."

Eugène looks puzzled. Then he remembers. "You mean the little American girl?"

"Yes. Her papa is quite important, so Maman says. He got the Marquis de Lafayette released from prison during the *Terreur*."

"And I hear that he is likely to be voted into the American government soon. There is talk of the Senate, or a governorship."

Eugène's knowledge surprises me. "I have not heard so much, and she is with me every day!"

"Perhaps she doesn't yet know. Bonaparte has a way of keeping very well informed. I swear the man never sleeps."

I can't help shivering, wondering how much Eliza guessed at last night.

"It is chilly," Eugène says, looking up at the sky, which has not fulfilled its promise of sun. "Let's go have breakfast."

We turn and walk back to the house.

"There is something I particularly wanted to talk to you about." Eugène squeezes my arm in his elbow. "I didn't know I'd have an opportunity so soon."

I have a suspicion about what, but I'll let him think he surprises me. "Have you at last been promoted because of your stellar service to our stepfather as aide-de-camp?"

"No, alas. Sometimes I wonder if he even notices I'm at

his side. . . . It's more personal than that." He stops and faces me. "I am in love."

I can't help feeling a little jealous. "Is she a beautiful heiress? A princess? A general's daughter?" I ask, teasing him as is my right.

"No." He smiles. "That is just the problem. I need you to help me."

"How can I help? You know Maman would do anything for you. She will be delighted."

"Perhaps not about this. Madeleine and I are so in love, but I fear . . ."

Madeleine? It is quite a common, unpretentious name. I am a little afraid of knowing more. "Why would Maman not help you if you are truly in love?"

"She is having difficulties of her own right now, and will hardly welcome the fact that her son wants to marry an actress in the Comédie Française."

16

Eliza

Although I am tired from all the excitement of yesterday, I cannot help rising early. To be a guest in Joséphine's house—it is simply too extraordinary an occurrence to waste by sleeping.

I summon the maid to help me dress, but no one else seems to be awake yet. I decide that I may as well take a turn in the garden, and give myself some time to absorb my surroundings at the heart of everything that is happening in France. My papa described it to me as a very volatile time, and I'm beginning to understand what he meant.

At first I think only about Joséphine. How gracious, how graceful she is! Last night at supper she had a way of making everyone at her table feel as if the entire meal, the entire evening revolved around them. Except for me, of course. Although she did make an effort to draw me into the conversation, asking questions about Virginia as though she was really interested.

But much more fascinating conversations claimed her attention, and I do not hold it against her that she paid me so little attention. No wonder Captain Charles is in love with her.

I could not help noticing the way Bonaparte, if the conversation drifted at all from matters that concerned him, gazed at Captain Charles, and then at Joséphine. He did not look happy. In those moments I also saw Caroline glance over, her attention for just a moment drawn away from Murat. Could it be that there is some strife between Napoléon and Joséphine?

I am so wrapped up in my thoughts about last evening that I almost forget to notice the garden, beautiful even at this barren time of year. And I almost fail to notice altogether that I am not alone. Ahead of me on the path is Caroline. I am about to call out to her when I see her back away as if she is trying to remain hidden. What has she seen?

I stay where I am for a moment, then see another path that leads away from the main avenue but closer to where Caroline stands. I follow it. Before long, I am aware of what has stopped her. Hortense and Eugène are also in the garden, and she is listening to their conversation.

"Oh, Eugène! You know Maman will be heartbroken."

"We're speaking of my heart here, not hers. And I shall no doubt rise far in our stepfather's retinue nonetheless. She need not use me as a pawn, to dispose of in marriage as she pleases. I can thrive without that. Perhaps Bonaparte will give me charge of a battalion soon. Surely she can have no greater hopes than that!"

Eugène! He is in love with someone, someone he thinks his mother will not approve of. My heart beats a little faster. Surely not . . . But what if it is I? What if—like me—he was instantly smitten upon seeing me? I have heard that it can happen this way, love. Yet we have hardly exchanged glances, let alone any words of consequence.

And Caroline is smiling. Why would Eugène's romances please her?

"Will you help me tell her?" Eugène pleads with Hortense. Her eyes are cast down. She doesn't look pleased. Perhaps I am mistaken. . . .

"I will try. But you know I cannot guarantee that Maman will accept a common actress for a daughter-in-law!"

A common actress? Of course he does not speak of me. How could he? But there is some comfort for me in the fact that Joséphine cannot be happy about his choice, if he has indeed truly chosen. And perhaps he will need comforting, a shoulder to weep upon, when his hopes for romance are dashed.

I am so absorbed in my own thoughts that I don't notice that Caroline is now striding toward me. I have to decide quickly what to do. I choose to act naive, pretend I am just returning from a stroll and wish to walk with her back to the house.

"Caroline!" I call out.

She rushes forward, her finger at her lips. "Hush!" she says, grasping my arm and hurrying both of us back to the house.

"What is it?" I ask, knowing full well that she does not want to reveal her presence to Hortense and Eugène.

"Oh! Only that everyone is still sleeping, and we must not disturb their rest at this time." She is whispering. "Joséphine does not stir until the afternoon on most days, and becomes very cross if anyone wakes her before then."

I doubt that Caroline actually knows this to be the case, but decide to let it drop.

By now we have entered the vestibule, and a maid appears from nowhere to take our wraps. We wander into a salon, a small one, very elegantly furnished and welcoming. The pianoforte and music stand suggest this is the music room. "It's so beautiful here I never want to leave," I say, brushing my hand lightly over the long silk drapes at the windows. "What color is this? Does it even have a name?"

"It looks the color of a rainy day to me," Caroline says. Indeed, I have to admit that the mist outside the window matches the fabric inside, as if there are no boundaries between one place and the other.

"Do you know that the entire army could have been supplied with new boots for the cost of decorating this room alone?" Caroline's voice is knife-edged with bitterness.

"But Madame Bonaparte surely used her own money for this," I say.

"Certainly not! She has none of her own. Her children—were it not for the generosity of my brother—would be penniless." I cannot help feeling shocked, not so much by the fact that Hortense's family is not wealthy, but by the fact that Caroline would say such things to me.

I don't quite know how to respond, and am relieved to hear Hortense and Eugène entering the house just then.

"There is Hortense!" I cry and run to the music room door.

"Eliza! Good morning. You're up early as well, I see." Hortense enters, followed by Eugène. Her hair is disheveled, the bow tied around her midriff is coming loose, and there are streaks of wet on her dress. "It started to rain, so we ran all the way from the folly by the lake." She is breathing fast and her cheeks are pink. Eugène's too. His boots are muddy and he has left a trail of dirt on the pale carpet.

"Hortense, ring for the maid to come and clean the dirt before it damages my brother's carpets," Caroline says.

I exchange a look with Hortense. If I were in her place, I would say something to Caroline, who really has gone beyond rude. Whatever Caroline thinks of Joséphine, Hortense should not be treated so badly.

"There is no need. I'll go down myself and apologize," Eugène says, more to his sister than to Caroline.

"Oh, no!" I say, seeing a chance to do something kind

for Eugène. "Please, let me." I run to the door, but somehow trip and, to my horror, I nearly bump straight into Eugène. He must think me such a fool! Now everyone will know what I feel, that I cannot be easy in Eugène's presence.

Before I can make my apologetic way out the door, Joséphine's maid enters and curtsies.

"Mademoiselle, monsieur, your mother wishes to see you immediately!"

Eugène and Hortense exchange glances before rushing away to attend the summons.

I am about to say something to Caroline, but before I can open my mouth, Madame Bonaparte enters. She looks pleased as a fat cat.

"My dear," she says to Caroline, "have you breakfasted? Do join me. I have some interesting news."

Caroline's mother has a strange accent, which I can only imagine is Corsican. Madame Bonaparte looks at me as if to say, *Can she be trusted?* I cast a quizzical glance at Caroline.

"Come, Eliza," she says after a brief pause. "Best friends have no secrets from one another." She takes my arm and together we cross the vestibule and enter the breakfast room.

17

Eliza

As we enter the room that has been equipped for break-fast, with dishes full of eggs and cold meats laid out on a sideboard, I am not thinking of Caroline and her mother, but of Hortense and Eugène. Why did Joséphine summon them?

My stomach gives a fierce growl. The smell of food has awakened it. I start to help myself immediately, but I stop when I see that neither Caroline nor her mother is eating anything. They take their seats and sit in silence for a moment. I bring my half-full plate to the table, wondering if it's all right if I take some nourishment.

"You know that your brother has finally seen that the whore has been unfaithful to him." Madame Bonaparte glows with pride. I am shocked. Joséphine? Unfaithful? Surely the admiration of Captain Charles is simply that. And yet, I remember the way Bonaparte looked at her last night.

"And how exactly did this come about?" Caroline asks, also restraining her glee, I see.

"It seems some *billets doux* were discovered by one of Napoléon's servants, just last night. He felt he must give them to his master, of course."

The two of them laugh like schoolgirls, although Madame Bonaparte is older than my own mother. I wonder if the letters are real, and if so, what they could say. Although behavior like Joséphine's would be cause for gossip in Virginia, I have always thought such things were quite accepted here. At least, that is what Mama has told me.

Even if she does flirt with Captain Charles, Joséphine is noble, charming, and beautiful, and both of her children have kindness and spirit. What could Caroline and her mother find to object to in that? Of course, they must be envious. Caroline is beautiful, too, but her mother, Madame Bonaparte, has a sharp edge to her. It's in the way she speaks and moves. She seems more Spanish than French in her looks, and her French is not very good. I think mine is better.

A terrible commotion coming from upstairs interrupts Caroline and Madame Bonaparte's conversation.

"Bonaparte! Bonaparte!"

I hear the screams of a woman. It does not sound like Joséphine, but I cannot imagine who else it might be. The three of us sitting at the table look at each other and we all jump up at once. I cast one longing glance at my plate of breakfast, but it's not enough to keep me there when clearly something important is happening up above us.

Madame Bonaparte goes first, followed by Caroline. I keep a slight distance behind them.

We sweep up the curved staircase and follow the corridor to its end, where Napoléon has his suite of rooms, just opposite my guest chamber. I can't believe what I see before me. Joséphine is on her knees, a handkerchief clutched in one fist and a crumpled letter in the other. On either side of her stand Hortense and Eugène, looking down at their mother, who is now rocking on her heels like a lunatic.

"Mother, please come away!" Hortense speaks soothingly to her. So far they haven't looked up at us. How embarrassing it must be! I could never imagine my mother displaying such volatile emotions.

"Bonaparte! There is only you! *Chéri!* Think of my children," Joséphine continues, heedless of anyone around her.

Eugène sees us first and his face hardens. I shrink back. I don't want him to think I'm enjoying this spectacle.

"This is a family matter," he says to Madame Bonaparte.

"Yes, I believe it is," she replies, standing her ground.

"Maman, come with me." Hortense is trying to pull her mother to her feet, but Joséphine will not rise.

"You speak to him, Hortense, *ma petite!* He will listen to you. He loves you like his own daughter."

Her words are so choked with sobs it's hard to understand what she is saying. I cannot help but look at Hortense, who sees me. Her eyes are sad—resigned almost. I remember what I saw last night, and I don't know what to think.

"Maman, if I talk to my step-papa, will you go to your room and wait for me?"

Joséphine looks up into Hortense's eyes. I see her tears dry up like a puddle in the summer sun. She takes a deep breath. "Oh, my darling, *ma petite Eugénia*! Would you?"

I am surprised by the nickname. So Hortense is the female version of Eugène, to her mother.

Eugène takes Joséphine's hand and finally gets her to rise up off her knees.

The three of us—Madame Bonaparte, Caroline, and I—are stuck to our places watching this family drama. Once Eugène has taken Joséphine away, Hortense turns, her back to Napoléon's door, and stares at us. I have never seen her look so angry. I didn't think she was capable of it, and I realize it must look to her as if I am on the side of Caroline and Madame Bonaparte.

"Please go somewhere else to gloat. Or better still, don't gloat at all. You cannot imagine the life we have led, but at least we have each other."

At that, she turns away and raps softly on the general's door. "Papa! *Cher* Papa, it is I, Hortense. I want to speak with you."

I look down, not wanting to witness Hortense's humiliation. "Come, Caroline," I whisper. "Let's play cards."

I am surprised when she comes with me, as does Madame Bonaparte. The three of us go into the game room, which it appears is always ready with cards and dice, and sit down to play an indolent game of bezique.

18

Hortense

When I enter the room, at first I cannot see where Napoléon is. He is not sitting on the divan or at the desk. His bed—a narrow cot with a hard mattress—is perfectly made. At this hour, I can only assume he has not slept in it.

"So, Hortense, she has sent you."

I whirl around at the sound of his voice. He is next to the door. His eyes are red. Not from drinking, which is what most men in his situation might be tempted to have done. Napoléon hardly drinks at all. His mind is always at work, calculating. And yet, he has much passion for my mother. I see that clearly. Whatever it is—pride, love, desire—he has been crying. I almost cannot bear to look at him.

"Sir, please have pity on my mother, your Joséphine. She is weak, but she loves you in the only way she knows how to love."

His face does not change expression. I send my deepest gaze into his eyes. He must see that my mother needs him—that *we* need him.

"I ask little of her. I do not question her expenses, although my mother thinks I am foolish. I ask only for her loyalty, and this she cannot give." His voice is rough and icy at the same time.

"What evidence, pray, do you have that she is disloyal? Has she not worked with every bit of guile and wit she possesses to help you rise in the government?" I try logic. I try reason. But I know even as I utter the words that reason is not what is required.

I have hardly noticed Napoléon's gradual approach to me until he is standing only an arm's length away. "She was once like you, I imagine." His voice barely rises above a whisper. "So pure, so beautiful."

My mother and I are alike, more than I sometimes care to admit. We both sing. We both love nature and the outdoors. We both like to be surrounded with beauty and kindness. And, as I have come to understand recently, we both feel the keenest pleasure at the admiration of a man, and an answering pull that comes not just from the heart, but from somewhere deeper. Hidden. Forbidden.

And it is worse now—now that I have glimpsed the possibility of something finer, now that I have felt that pull, have been drawn to the pure desire of Michel. His gaze, his soft tenderness—surely these are the things I should value above the commanding presence of my stepfather.

I have never been so completely alone with Bonaparte before. He is vulnerable, I see. Saddened by the betrayal he feels from my mother.

"She adores you, you know," I say, reaching out to touch his shoulder.

He frowns. It is a stern look I have only seen him wear when I observe him among his generals, plotting and planning. Does he think of Maman as an enemy? Perhaps an enemy to his peace.

"Why must she send you? You are innocent. This is no affair of yours." He turns his head away so that I cannot look into his eyes.

"But it is, Papa," I say, forcing myself to own the closeness of our connection. "If you leave us, Maman will be beside herself with grief. As will I." The words catch in my throat, and I struggle to hold back tears.

"You don't need a papa. You need a husband." He turns to look at me again.

What is he saying? I feel the room spin around me and notice that I have not been breathing. I stagger. I feel his steely strong hand grasping my arm. I lift my face to his. Can he guess at the confusion in my heart?

"If I remain with your mother, will you do something for me?" he asks quietly, close to my ear.

My heart slows and the room comes into focus again. He did not mean what I thought he might. I am disappointed and relieved. "Anything. I will do anything for the sake of my mother's happiness."

"And for mine?" he asks. "Little Hortense, I wish you and your brother were my children in fact. Everything would be simpler." He pats me and lets me go once he sees I am again steady on my feet.

"What shall I tell Maman?" I ask.

"Tell her she may come to me."

19

Eliza

"What is the matter?" I decide that if I don't ask a direct question I may never find out the truth, and even then I'm beginning to understand that Caroline and her mother see things very differently from Hortense and her mother.

Caroline and Madame Bonaparte look at me at the same time, with the same expressions of glittering triumph in their eyes. It makes me wish I had my mother here too. "I expect my brother to take possession of Malmaison and turn Joséphine and her family out on the streets at any moment," Caroline says.

"Do you really wish for such a thing?" I ask.

"She won't be on the street," Caroline says. "No doubt the wily Barras will take her in, and she has relatives."

"Barras!" says Madame Bonaparte. "Not if Madame

Tallien has anything to say about it. He has never been in Joséphine's power."

Madame Tallien is almost as famous as Joséphine. I saw her at the opera when I was with my mother, who would not allow me to be introduced to her by a mutual friend. Madame Tallien is still married, and openly the mistress of the Vicomte de Barras, whereas Joséphine was a widow when she was said to be entangled with the *vicomte*.

I gather up the cards after losing the game and shuffle them together. I don't know what to say or do, and am about to pretend that I need to excuse myself for personal reasons, when who should walk in but Eugène. I begin to deal the cards for a new game.

"My mother is most gracious to give you permission to visit us here," he says, encompassing all three of us in one sweeping gaze. "And I would therefore ask that you respect her in her own home."

His words sting like a whip. I wish he wouldn't include me in his hard stare. I don't know where I stand in this tortuous confusion of plots and lies.

Without giving anyone a chance to reply, he continues. "I bring you the welcome news that Maman has recovered from her indisposition, and wishes to speak with you, Caroline."

Caroline looks up from the cards she has fanned out in her hand, genuinely surprised. It is the first time I have seen her taken aback by anything.

"She can have nothing to say to my daughter that I too may not hear," Madame Bonaparte says, leaning heavily on the table and rising from her seat.

"Be that as it may," says Eugène, "she requested only Caroline." He strides to the door and stands there, his arm inviting Caroline to pass through. She looks back and forth between her mother and Eugène, rises in a decisive move, and glides past us all and through the door.

"I shall return to my chamber." Madame Bonaparte walks slowly out. She is quite stout, and Eugène must move a little to let her go by without brushing against him.

Now only Eugène and I are left. He cannot go without committing a breach of etiquette, to leave me alone in a room in a house where I am a guest.

"Do you play cards?" I ask. Stupid question! Of course he plays. All soldiers gamble, I've been told.

"I do." He doesn't move and I'm not certain what to do, but I know I want him to linger.

On impulse, I look out the window. "The rain has stopped, and I haven't yet seen the garden properly." I'm a little amazed at my boldness. He looks around, as if hoping someone will call him away on some urgent business.

I should let him go, but I'm not sure how, when suddenly he looks at me with a smile that releases all the tension in his face. "Please. It would be my pleasure to stroll with you, although my mother has changed things so much since I was last here that I cannot be certain we will not get lost." He crooks his arm in my direction. I rise and take his elbow, enjoying the feeling of his stiff uniform and the strong forearm underneath it.

As if by magic, before we go out the beautiful door to the garden, a maid appears with a heavy shawl. Eugène drapes it over my shoulders. I am in heaven.

"So," he says, after we have walked far enough away from the house that no one inside will hear us, "can you tell me why my sister is so unhappy?"

I keep walking for a bit, wondering what exactly to say. I can hardly tell him what I saw the other night! "I don't know what you mean. She seems very happy to me."

"I gather you don't know her very well then. Perhaps you are a *Caroliniste,* rather than a *Hortensiste.*" He smiles, but it's not a cheery one. "My stepfather's family does not approve of my mother."

I wish I could contradict him, but after all that I've witnessed in the past weeks—at school and now here—I know he'd see through it immediately. "I am neither of one party nor the other," I say, measuring my words as if they have the power to either kill or cure a sick patient. "Both Hortense and Caroline have shown me kindness, and I am grateful to your mother for allowing me to be a guest in her house."

"Very nicely said," Eugène says, bending to pick up a stone and throwing it in one strong, graceful movement into a dense copse of evergreen trees. "I understand your father is poised to assume a place in the government of the United States."

His words surprise me. "My father is a lawyer in Virginia. I know of no such possibility."

He stops and turns to me. "Forgive me. I hear much in my position as Bonaparte's aide-de-camp. I assumed you would know. Your mother's departure for New York was reported in the *Gazette* this morning."

I feel as if he has struck me a swift blow to the stomach. My mother? Gone from Paris? Why did she not tell me? I pretend to have a slight cough, trying to cover up my confusion. "Oh, of course. I knew it was a possibility, but not that it would happen so soon. My mother... my mother..." I cannot make myself continue the lie. My throat tightens into a knot that hurts all the way down to my heart, and I feel the sting of tears starting into my eyes.

"Are you unwell?" Eugène asks, placing his hand gently on my shoulder.

His touch unlocks the tears I'm fighting to keep hidden, and to my embarrassment I give a choked sob and they begin to stream down my face.

If Eugène had been a typical American brother, he would have told me not to be so silly and that I should act like an adult, that doubtless my mama would explain everything as soon as she could. But he isn't American, nor my brother, and certainly not typical. Instead he puts his arms around me and holds me close to him, stroking my hair. "Please don't upset yourself, Mademoiselle Eliza. If I had known you were unaware of events, I would never have said anything. Please forgive me. Here." He holds me away from him and removes his handkerchief from his pocket, using it to dab at my face. "There is simply too much crying this morning. Or perhaps it is afternoon, and we must return for the *déjeuner*."

I take a deep breath, noticing that my tears have wet a patch on the front of Eugène's uniform, and I recall the warm feel of his embrace, the smell of wool and a man's body, reminding me a little of my father. Somehow, it comforts me. "I am better now. I don't know why I reacted so stupidly," I say.

"It's quite all right. You are young. And perhaps you have not seen as much of life as my sister and I have."

I want to tell him I am not that young, that I am old enough to fall in love, but I cannot. I see by his expression and his glances back toward the house that he is eager to return. And I also see that whatever I may hope, he considers me only the impressionable young friend of his sister. I feel hope drain away from me.

"Yes, I believe it is time to rejoin the others," I say, pulling myself up and trying to act as calm and grown-up as possible.

He reaches for my hand and places it on his arm. We walk together back to the house.

Just as we come into view of the main front door, I see a woman striding toward us in a black hooded cloak. She is moving very quickly, as if she has an urgent errand. We stop. She approaches, flinging back her hood at the last second so that we can see who she is.

"Maman!" Eugène exclaims.

Before I can curtsy my greeting, she peels off her glove and slaps Eugène hard on the face.

20

Madeleine

The air crackles in the theater tonight. The last time I remember this feeling was after Bonaparte's victories in Italy. I was just a child then, yet despite the air of celebration, something dark and sinister seemed to lie beneath everyone's faces. We are a people grown used to bloodshed and horrors, thanks to Robespierre. Although the murders have stopped, their specter can still be felt in the streets, around each corner, in the shadowy spaces between costumes on the racks in the theater.

Maman is to play one of her favorite roles. Fanchette, in *Le mariage inattendu de Chérubin*. This play was written by a woman, Olympe de Gouges, before the revolution. Maman loves the irony of playing a lowborn daughter who is engaged to a peasant but desired by a wealthy citizen. Fanchette is supposed to be a young girl, though, and my mother requires more and more thick makeup to carry her through the deception.

I am on my way to help the seamstresses with the mending when the sound of voices coming from within Maman's dressing room stops me.

"This role is beneath you, Vicomtesse." The voice belongs to the theater director, who rarely ventures into the warren of corridors behind the stage these days. He sounds smooth and soothing, as if he is trying to persuade a child to relinquish a sweet. The director addresses my mother by her title only when he wants something. I am fascinated to know what it is he proposes. "Fanchette is not a woman; she is a simple girl. Why, your daughter, Madeleine—who has nothing like your talent—would be able to play her easily."

I hear a crash. *Maman has thrown something*, I think. It was because of the sound of my name coupled with a role she covets.

"My daughter, as you well know, is not healthy enough to play anything that requires speaking upon the stage." I can hear the blind fury in her voice. If someone doesn't prevent her, she might start to tear her gowns to pieces, as she did once before when a general she thought would marry her sent her a note saying that his wife required his presence in the country, and he would be unable to attend her that evening.

"My dear Gloriande," the director says, "I was not suggesting such a thing, only saying that perhaps you should play the countess, and another of our ingénues take the role of Fanchette." I can tell by his voice that he is frightened. Rumors fly around the small world of the theater that Maman was not thrown out, but that she murdered her husband and has been a fugitive from justice here in the Comédie Française. She has done nothing to contradict them, instead enjoying the gloss of mystery they add to her.

"Get out. Fanchette is mine." Maman's voice is controlled now, but her face must still be a frightening sight, because I hear the director's rapid footsteps. I slip around the corner just in time to avoid being seen.

Although I should be sad and sorry, I am not. I am elated. *The director thinks I can play the role of Fanchette,* I think. And I know I could. I know every one of my mother's lines from every play she has ever performed. If she died tomorrow, I could take her place without so much as a rehearsal.

But she won't die. She won't go away. This world is hers, not mine. It takes little time for the brief euphoria to fade, and once again I am just a lowly servant, sitting among the old ladies and Marianne and mending tears in cheap fabric got up to look beautiful from a distance.

I tidy Maman's dressing room, waiting for her to finish bowing to her adoring public. I can tell by the distant roar that the theater is full. She will be happy when she comes up, if she can put the director's inopportune suggestion out of her mind. She said nothing to me when I helped her dress, but

Marianne was there then, too. I've since sent Marianne to bed with a headache. I will have to prepare Maman for her evening assignation. I know she has one; I read aloud the note crumpled up on her dressing table, and a huge spray of flowers arrived just before she took her place in the wings for her performance.

Voices approach. It is Maman and a gentleman. *Merde!* I think. I hate it when her admirers come up and watch me help her take off the thick layer of white makeup to reveal her glossy dark skin and untie the laces that hold the costumes in place until she is wearing only her corset and chemise. Even though I am dressed, I always feel as if I, too, am exposed.

It is too late to fetch Marianne.

The door opens. Maman enters, followed by a tall, slender man with a thin mustache and sad eyes. His lips are red, as if he has been licking them over and over again. I try not to stare at him as I bustle around my mother. She, of course, does not greet me or acknowledge me.

"You say there is to be a change in the government?" Maman says, accompanying the words with her most winning smile.

"Hush, Gloriande! No one is to know! I told you in the strictest confidence." He glances in my direction.

"Oh! Don't worry about Madeleine. She is no one."

"It was said that the revolution itself could not have been so successful were it not for the treachery of ladies' maids." He nods in my direction. The nod is appreciative, I note.

Maman catches his look. "Ah, but Madeleine is not my maid. She is less than that. She is my daughter."

The words sting, and yet I am so accustomed to being treated this way that I shrug them off.

"Your daughter..."

The man approaches me and I shrink away. What I thought was sadness in his eyes now turns into something else. I try to meet Maman's eyes in the mirror, but she gazes steadfastly at herself.

"I must... excuse myself...." I can feel my face growing hot, my pulse racing.

"Unlace me!" my mother commands.

I don't dare refuse. My fingers tremble, and instead of accomplishing my task quickly, I take longer than usual. The man stands directly behind me and puts his hands upon my shoulders. The look in his eyes as he shifts his gaze back and forth between my mother and me sickens me. Maman's eyes are locked with his, which have glazed over into an expression of lust.

With all my strength, I shove my shoulder against him to free myself from his hands, and I run out of the dressing room.

Behind me I hear laughter.

21

For a moment after Joséphine's slap, we stand frozen in the autumn chill.

"Let us go indoors, Maman. You will catch cold," Eugène says.

From the expression on her face, I expect Joséphine to yell at him, or scream. But instead, she draws in a deep breath and stands up tall, turns, and walks gracefully back into her house.

Eugène gives me his arm again and leads me in. We stop in the vestibule and watch Joséphine glide up the stairs to her apartments.

"Forgive me, but I must go to my mother," Eugène says with a bow.

I wander into the salon after leaving my wrap with a servant, wondering whether I should go upstairs and write a letter to my mother. But Caroline is in the salon, standing in front of one of the long windows. She must have seen Joséphine hit her son. Something about the strange events I have witnessed here makes me bold.

"What did Joséphine want with you?" I ask Caroline.

She turns, her face radiant with triumph. "She takes my side! She will speak for me with Napoléon!"

At first I am confused. Speak for her about what? When she sees my confusion, Caroline wrinkles her forehead into a scowl.

"How could you forget? It's Murat, of course. She believes I should marry him, and soon."

I want to shake my head to clear it and put this news of Caroline's into its proper place, so that I can react and be suitably happy. But something is bothering me.

"That is wonderful for you, Caroline. But why is Joséphine so angry at Eugène?"

One corner of her mouth twists up in a mischievous smile. "I returned her favor to me by putting it in her power to prevent a most unwanted occurrence, which happens to concern her son."

"You'll have to explain yourself, Caroline. I cannot keep up with everything that goes on here." I sink into one of the soft upholstered chairs, suddenly exhausted by the strain of the currents and subtleties that make everything around me something other than it appears on the surface.

"I informed her that I heard—quite accidentally, on an

innocent stroll in the garden—that Eugène was likely to form a most disadvantageous alliance, one that would bring disgrace upon all the family."

So it was *Caroline who caused Joséphine's anger.* "I think I'll go to my room and read," I say, with a little curtsy to Caroline.

Now I am dressing for dinner, and I wish Ernestine were here. She would help me with my hair, which I see is very childish, just draping down my back. Why didn't I insist she come? I need help pinning my hair up, making those curls that frame a face. Perhaps one of the maids here will help me. Or perhaps not. I feel invisible in this place, surrounded by all these illustrious people who know so much more about the world. Even Hortense, Eugène, and Caroline are more experienced. My life seems so simple compared to theirs. What is being left alone at a boarding school in Saint-Germain while my mama goes back to America without me, compared to having to intercede on behalf of a mother so that her life will not be ruined? Or finding out that the person you have fallen in love with is completely unacceptable to your mother?

Something makes me think of Armand de Valmont. I wonder for a moment what it would be like to have a young man here who is close to my age. Not only that, but one who comes from the same background as many of the guests here and my hostess herself. I find myself remembering that Armand spoke to me kindly, if not warmly. He was also a very good dancer. I could have been stuck with someone infinitely worse. And he chose me. No one told him to come and speak to me.

Hortense says that he is not fond of Americans because he blames them for the revolution. But why did he approach me, knowing I was American? In fact, how did he know I was American at all?

I find myself now very curious about that student from the Collège Irlandais. He is an artist, so Hortense says. I should like to see his paintings. But perhaps there are none at his school, where doubtless he is being encouraged to study other things, subjects that will help him gain a post in the government, perhaps.

I wonder, indeed, what Armand would think of everything that has happened today, and I begin to wish I had someone outside of this cauldron of confusion to discuss things with. Someone ordinary, like me.

Of course, as a marquis, Armand can hardly be called ordinary. It must be difficult for him, having the title and the lineage but no money. I think I prefer my circumstances.

I decide, as I struggle to make my hair look more sophisticated, that perhaps being ordinary is not a bad thing. Being young and unimportant leaves me free to observe. I may learn much this way.

And now that Joséphine is against Eugène's connection with this actress, perhaps I will have a chance to make him notice me as someone more interesting than just his sister's young school friend. He would not have been so kind to me, surely, if he did not find me likable at least. I shall do my best to shine this evening. Perhaps I can comfort him.

I stare at myself in the mirror. My eyes are very pretty, and my nose is straight and fine. My cheeks are perhaps a little plump, but they are touched with a rosy color that is real, not painted on with rouge. I stretch my arms out. They are white, and not scrawny. And in this gown, my small bosom looks a little larger than it really is.

There is a soft knock upon the door. "Come," I call.

A maid enters with a tray bearing combs and some false curls the color of my hair. I smile.

"Mademoiselle Hortense sent me to help you," she says.

Hortense is so good and kind. I put myself in the maid's hands and know I shall look my best this evening.

22

Hortense

I do not want you to end up like me, always afraid that the world will come crashing down around you. My mother's words send a chill through me. She has told me this before, but somehow today it means more than it once did. She said it to me after I came back to her, when I was able to tell her that Bonaparte would remain with her, would not seek a divorce or parade her infidelities for the public to see.

He has been unfaithful to me, too, she said. For a moment, the look in her eyes made me think perhaps she knew something of my confusing feelings about my stepfather. But then she explained that she had heard reports of his adventures in Egypt—that he had philandered with the women who follow the army wherever it goes.

I lie on my bed, a damp cloth on my forehead. My temples pound from trying to understand all that has happened here, how it is that my mother knows I will do anything to keep our family with Napoléon intact, but does not know exactly why. And Eugène . . . Maman will stop at nothing to prevent him from being with his true love.

His true love. Can a humble actress be worthy of him? I am afraid that perhaps he simply pities her, and mistakes the feeling for love. From what little he told me, I understand her situation to be very hard. He says he plans to take her away from the theater, from the oppression of her mother, within the next few days.

But our own mother will stop him, I feel certain.

You, my children, will make great matches. I see it all. I know her desires for us come from love. She wants us to succeed where she has failed, to achieve the stature she has only been able to dream of. She has suffered so much in her life. I have witnessed nearly all of it, whereas Eugène was with our papa for many years, no doubt privy to other things, which have made him less forgiving of Maman than I am. I can only wonder what our father told him, what lies and distortions, about my mother's profligate ways.

But what if my life, my love, does not fall with some great man, as my mother wishes? I cannot help but think of Michel. He is humble, but talented and sensitive. I can so easily imagine a quiet future, making music together, our children brought up in a wholesome country cottage. It is a pretty picture. Would that not produce more happiness, more contentment than the glittering, perilous life my mother leads?

But how can I dream so! I do not know for certain that Michel truly wants me for his own. We have had too few moments together, and those either stolen from hours when we should not be together or carved out of times when we are surrounded by others. Perhaps he only sees a way to better himself through a connection to the family of France's greatest general. How can I know?

I must keep my dreams to myself. If Maman were even to guess at them, she would no doubt respond as she did to the intelligence about Eugène's *petite Madeleine.*

I met Maman at my door when she came back inside after confronting Eugène. "Did you know about this?" she asked me before I had a chance to say anything.

I am not accustomed to lying to her, just shielding her from painful truths. "Perhaps you will tell me what *this* is?" I said, knowing already.

"This . . . actress!"

I wanted to ask her how she found out. I cannot believe Eugène would have told her, after our conversation this morning. "I believe Eugène is in love," I said. "He only told me just today. You know I have not seen him for months."

"Why did you not tell me immediately? Why did I have to hear it from one of them?" She jerked her head contemptuously in the direction of the wing where Madame Bonaparte and Caroline are staying.

So it was Caroline. How could she have known?

Someone must have heard us. Eliza? I think not—she has hardly spoken to Maman. I didn't know what to say.

"You must find out everything you can about her, and we will make her go away. She probably only wants money or jewels."

"Hush, Maman," I said.

She stopped and lifted her chin. The excitement brought roses into her pale cheeks, and she actually looked younger. When she turned to me, she put her finger to her upper lip in a coquettish gesture, which I know hides her rotting teeth—teeth that give her much pain. She was herself again. I felt my shoulders relax. "Let us go down and join the others for luncheon," I said.

"No," she answered. "I shall ask for a tray to be brought upstairs. My head is aching, and I wish to be well for this evening."

"What is to happen this evening?" I asked.

"Why, Napoléon's brothers Lucien and Louis come to dinner tonight. Louis is but five years older than you are. Napoléon believes he will have a brilliant career, and there are plans afoot even as we speak."

Although I was relieved to see her back to her usual canny plotting, there was something in her voice and expression I did not like. I turned and put my hand upon the doorknob of my chamber, deciding I was not hungry and needed to rest.

"Try to look your prettiest this evening. The blue gown suits you, and your pearl cross." She touched her hand to her lips and waved it toward me in a kiss. Such a familiar gesture. Her eyes melted for a moment in an expression of pure love.

At times like those I could forgive her for anything. I fear that this evening I shall be forced to do just that.

23

Eliza

It is the hour before dinner. At this time of year, night comes early and everywhere candles shed their warm, inviting light over Joséphine's beautiful house.

We are assembled in the drawing room, waiting for all the guests to come down. I see that already there are several more people here than there were last night. Madame Tallien has arrived, perhaps to ensure that Joséphine knows her position in relation to Barras. If anyone could outshine Joséphine, it is Teresa Tallien. Her Spanish looks are not as refined, but she has a way about her that commands attention. She arrived in a pure white cloak of shimmering silk, draped in jewels of every color. Joséphine looks demure by contrast, with the simple gold-embroidered borders on the neckline and hem of her white gown. They greet each other like old friends.

"I thought Joséphine and Madame Tallien were ene-mies," I whisper to Caroline as we sip our champagne.

"They are. But they are also dearest friends. They were in prison together during the *Terreur.*"

I cannot imagine a world where two such women would be imprisoned just because of their aristocratic lineage.

No one is paying attention to Caroline and me, so I continue to question her. "If Madame Tallien and her hus-band do not get along and she has such an obvious liaison with the Vicomte de Barras, why do they not divorce?"

"Because it was Tallien who saved her from the guillo-tine. She owes him her life."

To watch everyone in this beautiful drawing room, chat-ting and flirting and drinking champagne, I would never know any of them had ever been in danger. But there is an undercurrent of something, beyond all the events of the day. General Bonaparte has not yet joined the company, and I see Joséphine casting anxious glances toward the door.

"Where's Hortense?" I ask Caroline, suddenly realizing that she has not yet come down, either.

"Perhaps she has returned to school. Her mother got what she wanted out of her." Caroline lowers her voice still more.

"What do you mean?"

"You saw as I did that she sent Hortense to talk to my brother. She has always been able to wind him around her little finger. Sometimes I wonder if she isn't a little besotted with him." She makes it sound like an insult. I ignore the comment, but I wonder if Caroline suspects something about Hortense's deep affection for her stepfather. Worse, is she implying that Joséphine is aware as well and knowingly sent Hortense in to achieve her own goals?

My thoughts are interrupted by a commotion at the drawing room doors. The footman flings them open and in marches Napoléon and two other young men. Both are equally small of stature but lack the commanding presence of Napoléon. One is positively unattractive. His nose dominates his face, which is sadly marked by pocks and pits.

Caroline turns to me with an unexpectedly gleeful smile. "My brothers! Louis and Lucien! I did not know they would be here!" She rushes over to them and flings her arms around her two brothers' necks like a child. The other Bonaparte family members come forward and cluster around the three of them. In all there are four brothers, with Joseph, who came with us yesterday, and Napoléon. To see them together like this creates an astonishing impression. They are like a country unto themselves, and yet dressed in French uniforms are so clearly of France. Individually they are distinct. Together they form a mass of people with the same eyes, the same expression, all smiling in the same way. And at the center is Napoléon.

Joséphine stands to one side of this family group, proud but meek. I have caught so many glimpses of her in these two days, but I cannot put her together into a single person.

I have seen her the loving mother, the angry mother; the devoted wife, the distressed wife; the hostess who dazzles everyone, and the outsider uncertain of her place in the world. Who is she?

As I watch, Napoléon takes hold of the ugly brother's arm and leads him out of the knot of their family toward Joséphine. She curls into herself, tucking her chin down and raising her fan to cover her mouth. I am dimly aware of an introduction—could this be the first time Joséphine has met this young man? She extends her hand, her delicate fingers and white skin making a beautiful shape. The brother bends stiffly over her hand and presses a smacking kiss on her fingers. Napoléon speaks. "Allow me to present my youngest brother, Louis Bonaparte."

The greeting is over. The members of the Bonaparte family disperse to speak with the others. Still Hortense has not come down. Napoléon whispers something into Joséphine's ear and a cross look darkens her features. Both of them glance toward the doors. The footman stands placidly by. Joséphine glides over to him and murmurs something quickly. He bows, slips out, and the door closes behind him. I wonder if I am the only person who has noticed this scene, and turn away, pretending to admire one of the paintings on the drawing room wall. It is of Joséphine herself, seated on a soft, cushioned bench, rich carpets beneath her feet. The artist is not very skillful. He has made the carpets more interesting than Joséphine, who is much more beautiful than she appears in the painting.

I hear the drawing room doors opening again, but I don't turn around. By the hush that descends on the company, I think someone important must have just arrived. Who could it be, though? Already the four Bonaparte brothers, Caroline, and Madame Bonaparte are here. Sieyès and Barras were standing stiffly by the fireplace the last time I looked. Captain Charles is nowhere to be seen. Madame Tallien is monopolizing Eugène. I cannot imagine who it would be, and so I turn at last.

It is Hortense. She looks so beautiful, so radiant, yet so sad that I stifle a gasp. I feel Caroline's grip on my arm. "You'd think she was being led to her execution, not paraded as a prize catch," she says into my ear, biting her words so hard that I feel a spray of spit on "catch."

A prize catch. What can she mean? Joséphine floats to Hortense and takes her hand, leading her through the guests over to where Louis and Lucien Bonaparte stand, deep in conversation about something. Everyone in the room is watching except for the two Bonaparte brothers, and Joséphine lays her hand on Lucien's shoulder to get their attention.

He turns and bows politely, and I see him cast an appraising eye over Hortense. Hortense looks down through it all. Louis, though, gives a quick smile and nod and tries to talk to Lucien again, but Joséphine gently yet firmly positions Louis so that he must pay attention to Hortense. A moment later, Joséphine takes Lucien's arm and leads him away to the conversation involving Barras, Napoléon, and Sieyès.

Hortense and Louis stand side by side, one looking as embarrassed as the other. *Heavens!* Joséphine is making a match between Hortense and her husband's brother!

24

Madeleine

Something important is happening. I can tell. First was the message two days ago from my beloved, just after the embarrassing scene in my mother's dressing room. I was in such deep despair, and the sight of a note in Eugène's handwriting made my spirits soar. Then I read it, and plunged again into a hopeless blackness.

My darling,

I know I promised I would come tonight, but I cannot, nor for several nights hence. Changes are afoot, changes I may not discuss. I believe they will result in my promotion, and therefore hasten the time that we may achieve our happiness. Know that I am thinking of you constantly, and send me your prayers that all will go as planned.

My mother, too, is in a foul mood. That night—that terrible night—was the last one in which the theater was full. We are performing a different play now, one where I have a small part as a poor urchin, as usual. Tonight, I could not help noticing that the stalls were nearly empty. Normally we look out over a sea of blue military coats, but this evening there was only a scattering of them.

Marianne and I help my mother undress after the performance. She has no visitors. "You odious child! It's all because of you. You coughed onstage when I was delivering my most moving line. It is that line, the way I deliver it, that brings them to my door night after night. Get out of my sight!"

I duck to avoid the shoe she throws at me. Then I place her glass of champagne on the nearest clear space—not easy to find in the tumble of paste jewelry, pots of rouge, combs, and wigs—and slip out the door before she gets drunk and becomes truly violent.

She is out of her senses, I know, and yet I cannot help having some sympathy for her. There is nothing more disheartening than hearing only lackluster clapping when I could see from the wings that she was pouring herself into the role.

I like to watch my mother act. She becomes someone else, someone better than she is. I always hope that this other person who is buried deep inside her will emerge when she is not onstage. She'd catch everyone by surprise.

When I watch my mother's glowing face in the light of the thousands of candles, I glimpse our life in Martinique, so long ago when I was just a tiny child. She used to pick me up and bounce me on her knee, feed me the sweet, ripe fruit that was always so plentiful. Papa, too, was a golden being. We were happy, the three of us.

Then we took the long voyage across the sea and came back to France, and everything changed. Papa was jealous— Maman gave him reason to be. He threw us out. We came to the theater.

But perhaps the final joke was on him after all. He went to the guillotine, like most of the aristocratic friends who persuaded him to give up his dark wife. Including the Vicomte de Beauharnais, my darling Eugène's father. They were friends, so I heard once. I have not told Eugène. He need not know—not yet, anyway.

I make my way up to the tiny room in the attics above the Salle Richelieu, this old palace where our world of the Comédie Française goes upon its constant, absurd rounds. My room is plain, my mattress only lumpy straw upon the floor. But I have a small window that looks out over Paris. Even at night when most of the streetlamps are extinguished I can see the ribbon of the Seine reflecting the moon, stretching away into a distant land I can only imagine.

Someday I shall sail away upon that beguiling water.

To my surprise, I find a bouquet of white roses on the little dresser where I keep my few items of clothing. They can only be from one person, and I rush to bury my face in their velvety petals and drink in their heady aroma.

The other actresses want jewels. "Flowers die," Maman said one day as I watched her toss a glorious spray of lilacs away. "Diamonds are as good as cash."

I don't imagine anyone would give me diamonds, and so I am quite content with flowers.

But that isn't true. I want more. I search through the stems and discover what I'd hoped for. A letter.

Ma petite! Ma cherie!

The day after tomorrow I shall come for you, in the morning. I cannot wait any longer, despite what I said before. Every time I close my eyes I see the bruise on your cheek, the one you could not hide when you were onstage the other night, and I know I must deliver you from that fiend you persist in calling your mother. We shall go away. It will be necessary to keep ourselves secret for a while, but we'll find a priest to marry us so we will not live in sin. You will not have to spend another night suffering upon the stage. Trust me!

Your beloved E

It is too much to hope for, and yet why would he lie? All the dark sadness drops away from my heart. Eugène will come for me after all!

He says it plainly: the day after tomorrow in the morning, he will come. I have preparations to make. What should I bring? Aside from the little parcel of belongings I have kept aside, my clothes are not worthy, not good enough to be seen in while arm in arm with him.

I have only one item of any value. It is the necklace given to me by my grandmother, who died before we left the island. A gold cross, with a tiny pearl at its center.

"This is for you, *ma petite*," I remember her saying. "Your life will not be easy. Your *maman* cannot know what awaits you should you ever go to France. I do not trust my son to be strong enough to overcome the gossipers and cruel ones. I wish you could wear this always, but you must keep it hidden away, or they will try to steal it from you. It bears our coat of arms on the back. Proof that you are of our blood."

I was only four years old, but something told me even then she was right. The world outside the plantation would destroy us. It has destroyed us. I kept the necklace in a box that I hid under a stone in the garden. Every day I checked to make certain it was still there, and when we had to flee for our lives, away from the slaves that were rising up against the cruel overseers, I tucked it into the middle of the pretty dresses the maid quickly packed for me in the middle of the night.

And it is still with me. My mother cannot even imagine that I have anything of value. She doesn't know about my most precious secret, my love, whose worth is beyond this tiny trinket that I treasure nonetheless.

He comes for me the day after tomorrow. Only two more nights, and my life can begin.

25

Hortense

Now I know for certain. She has not told me in so many words, but every action, every expression confirms it. She even sent me a beautiful diamond bracelet to wear.

She wants me to marry Louis Bonaparte, Napoléon's brother. I had to calm myself before coming down to join the party. The footman eventually sent a maid to fetch me.

"What is he like?" I asked her. The maid is a sweet young girl from the country.

"Who?" she asked in return.

Before I could explain, we were at the doors, and they opened. The most important people in France stood in small groups in Maman's drawing room, but I cared not in the least bit. Maman led me to Louis and Lucien, and now has left me here after taking Lucien—who, although not as attractive as Napoléon, is a little handsome—away.

"You are in school, I hear?" Louis finally asks me after an agonizing period of silence. I can tell by his restlessness—the way he first clasps his hands in front of him and then behind him—that he would far rather be with Lucien, Napoléon, and Joseph, who are deep in conversation with Barras, Murat, and Sieyès. I would like to release him, but fear my mother's wrath. She has asked him to take me into dinner and no doubt will seat him next to me. I have looked only once at his face, and it did not please me.

"Yes, in Saint-Germain," I say. "Do you know what the gentlemen are talking about?" I ask, thinking perhaps he will become witty and interesting at least.

"No. Yes." That's all he says.

I see Eliza and Caroline standing apart from the others by a window. Caroline bends toward Eliza, no doubt filling her head with lies. I cannot understand what I have done to deserve her cruelty! If I am forced to marry her brother, no doubt she will hate me all the more.

At last the drawing room doors open and the footman whispers to Maman. She turns with a smile to everyone and spreads out her arms. "Our dinner awaits us!" Then I see her walk through the room, pairing people. She has Napoléon take Madame Tallien in. That's a gesture of pure irony. Even I have heard the rumors that Madame Tallien had a brief affair with Napoléon when she was first with Barras.

She takes Eugène and gives him Eliza's arm. Ah, that

will please her. She is too young to hide the embarrassed delight on her face.

And now—she gestures to Murat and pairs him with Caroline! I cast a quick glance at Madame Bonaparte. Her eyes flash. But Joséphine is soon by Madame Bonaparte's side and hands her smoothly to Barras. Next, she looks in our direction and Louis obliges by giving me his arm. It is thin and wiry, and I stand a few inches taller than he.

Maman takes Lucien's arm herself.

It is like a ballet, or a pantomime. So much has been said without a word being spoken.

All through dinner I can barely eat. My stomach feels as if it is churning with eels. Louis says very little, and none of it to me. Perhaps he is as unhappy as I about this proposed arrangement. It is all I can do not to leap from my chair and run screaming from the room.

After what seems an eternity the dinner ends. The ladies leave the gentlemen to their smoking and brandy and retire to the drawing room.

I expect to be reprimanded by Maman for having had so little to say to Louis, but as soon as we are all there, she calls me, Caroline, and Eliza over.

"*Mesdemoiselles*, my dears," she says. "I ask for your indulgence in a matter of great import. I am afraid I have called my coach to take you all back to school this very night. It is the wish of my husband that you should remain there until you are summoned again."

"Sent back to school! What right do you have, madame?" It is Caroline. I understand her fury, but I feel only relief.

"It is not I but your brother who commands it, dear Caroline," Maman says, ignoring the insult.

To my astonishment, Madame Bonaparte joins us. "Yes, Caroline. Be a good girl. It is for the best."

Caroline whirls around and swishes out of the drawing room. I see her eyes glittering and know she is crying.

I take Eliza's arm. "Come," I say. "We can talk it all over in the coach on the way."

We discover that the maids have already packed our cases and have our traveling clothes ready for us. We wait in the vestibule for the coach to be prepared. The door of the dining room opens to admit a servant with a tray containing a new decanter of brandy. We hear Barras's voice sailing out through it.

"To the eighteenth of Brumaire!" he says.

A chorus of *"Vive la liberté!"* comes from the rest of the men.

I look at Caroline. "That is the day after tomorrow!" I say. "What can they be planning?"

She looks back at me and whispers, "I think I know."

At that moment the footman opens the front door and leads us out to the waiting coach. The air outside is cold but fresh. I breathe in deeply, not realizing until then how oppressive the atmosphere inside my mother's house has been.

We climb into the coach in our mantles and muffs, and

as soon as the footman shuts the door the coachman cracks his whip over the horses' backs and we start off.

Caroline sits opposite me with Eliza at her side. Eliza's eyes are like moist, purple grapes. Caroline's are as hard and brittle as jet.

She leans forward. "Are we going to allow them to send us away like children, when they are clearly planning something that will affect all of France?"

All I want to do is disappear into the world of school, and see Michel again. Now more than ever I hope that his regard for me is real, that there is a chance he could take me out of this confused mess of family relationships. But Caroline speaks with such passion, and I confess I am more than curious. "What do you suggest?" I ask.

"I propose that we meet them the day after tomorrow. Murat said something that I believe he was not supposed to, and I think I know where they are going."

"Yes!" Eliza says. "Eugène, too, said something mysterious, but now perhaps I understand!"

I lean back in my seat. "Very well," I say. "If you go, I go too."

Caroline does something I would never have expected. She reaches out her hand to me. I meet it. She grasps it, hard. "I know you do not want to marry Louis," she says. "I may be able to help you."

26

Caroline begins to speak, acting like a general consulting with her advisers.

"We must make our plan before we return to school, because there will be no time once we arrive." She turns to me. "Eliza, what have you heard?"

"I was seated next to Eugène, who was speaking across the table with Murat," I say. "He mentioned something about going to Saint-Cloud, but then, when he noticed that I was listening, dismissed it, as if he had made a mistake."

Hortense looks confused. "Why Saint-Cloud? If they are planning something with the Directoire, surely they would go to Paris."

Caroline speaks again. "I too overheard Murat and Barras talking at dinner. They thought I wasn't listening. They said they would have to get the Directoire out of Paris if the plan was going to work."

"And the Council of Five Hundred? What of them?" Hortense asks.

The Council of Five Hundred? I know little about them. "I don't understand," I say.

Caroline makes a clicking noise as though she is irritated with my ignorance, but she explains anyway. "You see, the Directoire, which is five men with different posts in the government, has made terrible decisions that have bankrupted the treasury. And the Council of Five Hundred, supposedly in place to ratify anything the Directoire wants to enact, is worse than useless. All they do is argue. There is no strong government."

Hortense interjects. "What can they mean to do—Bonaparte and the others?"

A slow smile spreads across Caroline's face. "I don't know for certain, but I believe the fortunes of my family are about to take another significant leap forward, and I want to be there to witness it!"

I shake my head. "How can we do that? We would have to leave school, we'll need a coach, and if anyone sees us they'll send us away."

"I think there is a way," Caroline says, "but we must be very clever, and very brave. We must disguise ourselves so that no one will recognize us." She looks back and forth between us. "No one must even know that we are women."

We sit in silence for a moment. I'm not sure I understand why this is so important to Caroline, and I doubt that Hortense—who is always so well-behaved—will go along with her.

"How does this make a difference to me? As you say, it is your family." I detect a note of bitterness in Hortense's voice, which surprises me.

Caroline draws herself up. "If we, the Bonapartes, are elevated to yet a higher position in society and the government, there may be no need for my brother Louis to marry for the sake of an old title."

That was unkind. I try to see the expression on Hortense's face in the dim light inside the carriage.

"We should dress as soldiers." It is Hortense. Her eyes are shining. Can it be that she agrees with Caroline? That she is not offended by what she said?

"How?" I ask.

Caroline grips my hands. "Eliza, your maid Ernestine is an excellent seamstress, is she not?"

I nod. "But where will we find materials? And how will we hide what she is doing?"

"I haven't worked out all the details yet, but are we agreed that we shall try?" Caroline asks.

"Valmont may be able to help," Hortense says. "Perhaps he can get us breeches to alter, castoffs from the Collège Irlandais."

Valmont? Why would he help us? I wonder.

"So let us make a pact. We vow to do whatever it takes to be with the army and the generals on the eighteenth of Brumaire. Agreed?" Caroline can hardly contain her excitement.

I look back and forth at my two new friends. What they are suggesting could cause serious trouble for me if we are found out, could result in having me sent back to Virginia in disgrace.

But their passion about the plan is irresistible. I take a deep breath. "Agreed."

Before I know it we are all clasping each other and laughing. I'm sure my mother never dreamed I would become involved in such an escapade. I silently ask her forgiveness, even as I look forward to our project with growing elation.

It is late when we arrive at the school. The night porter lets us in, explaining that Madame Campan is expecting us, that she received a communication earlier from Madame Bonaparte.

"And there is a letter and a parcel for you, Mademoiselle Eliza," he says, picking them up from the table inside the door and handing them to me.

I recognize my mother's handwriting, and suddenly I'm reminded that she has left Paris, and me, to return to Virginia. My heart sinks. "They're from my mother," I mutter. Tears threaten to overwhelm me, and I take a deep breath.

I feel Hortense's gentle hand on my shoulder. "Has something happened?"

I draw myself up. I will not let this disappointment infect my spirits. "No, nothing at all. My mother has simply returned to Virginia to be with my father when he runs for office in the government."

I can feel my lip quivering just the slightest bit and do my best to control it. I don't want them to guess how much I rely upon Mama still. I have seen the way they are so independent, and I want to be like them.

We go upstairs to our rooms. "Remember, ask Ernestine to help us," Caroline whispers before I close the door behind me. "I'll enlist the help of Hélène, too."

"Geneviève may also be relied upon," Hortense says. "If she has the time."

We kiss each other before parting. I am glad to see Hortense and Caroline showing affection. They are sisters, after all. I only hope that Caroline truly wants to help Hortense.

As soon as I am alone in my room, I break the seal on Mama's letter.

My darling Eliza,

Your papa has written to me and requests my return most urgently. I would have protested, were it not for the fact that I am feeling unwell in my present condition and long for the comfort of my own hearth.

But his news is quite important: he is called to

Washington, and there is talk of his running for governor of Virginia. I sent word to Madame Campan that I would see you, but she informed me that you had gone to stay with Caroline Bonaparte for a few days. That's as it should be; you must take advantage of the opportunities you are presented with.

To ensure that you do not lack for anything, I have given Madame Campan a generous bank draft, and enclose in this package some jewels and money for you. Use it as you wish, but I especially recommend purchasing gifts for your new friends.

Until next we meet, your loving mother.

I can no longer hold back the tears that fall on the paper that bears Mama's handwriting. Now not only am I in school, but she is far away, and I cannot know when she will receive my letters and share my adventures with me.

And there will be adventures. What does Caroline mean for us to do? At least there is one good thing: the money Mama sent will surely help.

I ring the bell on my dressing table. A moment later, Ernestine appears. She is wearing her nightgown and gives a very obvious yawn. I cannot help but wonder if she would do such a thing in front of a French mistress.

"We have need of your help, beginning early tomorrow morning," I say.

"Yes, Mademoiselle Eliza. But I hope not too early." She yawns again.

"As early as I say." I turn to her. I watched Joséphine and Caroline with the servants at Malmaison. They were calm but insistent. They expected obedience, but didn't order them the way we do our house slaves in Virginia. I fear I have been too informal with Ernestine, and she has taken advantage of my youth and inexperience by presuming too many liberties. That will change.

I see her expression freeze, the usual smile playing at the corners of her mouth stopped in an awkward place. "*Oui, mademoiselle,*" she says, and curtsies. If she dared, I think she'd stick her tongue out at me right now. But I have more important things to think about.

Tomorrow we will prepare to run away dressed as men. I understand why Caroline wishes to do so—I saw her with Murat, and she glowed with triumph. He is a very dashing man and clearly Bonaparte depends upon him. How did Joséphine manage to change Napoléon's mind so quickly?

A little thrill of excitement stirs me. When we go upon this adventure, I will see Eugène. And not as a polite young man in his mother's house, but as a soldier at the heart of action. I conjure up his face, thinking of all the expressions I have seen upon it in the brief time since I have met him, and I sigh.

It is silly of me to think of him, I know. But I can still feel his arms around me, protecting and comforting me. I will go on this crazy adventure of Caroline's not just because it will be fun to be with them, but for the sake of Eugène. I want to have another opportunity to watch him, to see him move about in the world of powerful men and hold his own, although he is but eighteen years old. He has that in common with Hortense: they both have eyes that are deep with experience. Their father was guillotined, their mother imprisoned. Their world has been upended and righted again so many times. I do not know if these were the lessons my mama wanted me to learn here, but, if nothing else, I begin to understand how small my existence has been so far.

Morning comes too quickly even for me. "Wake up!" Caroline shakes me.

"It's barely light outside."

"Yes, but we have so much to do." She takes hold of my arm and practically drags me from beneath my covers. "We must be well under way before Madame awakens."

I am alert enough that I know I will not go back to sleep, so I give in and ring for Ernestine.

She arrives surprisingly quickly, already dressed. She helps me into my gown and ties my hair back in a queue, positioning my blue ribbons exactly. It appears my tone has worked with her.

Caroline, Hortense, and I meet in the breakfast room.

"We need material. Is there enough in the sewing scraps, do you think?" Caroline asks Hortense. Is this new friendliness between them genuine? I don't believe Hortense would dissemble, but I am not so certain about Caroline. If they are truly to become friends, it pleases and disappoints me at the same time. Their friendship would rob my letters of half the content I was hoping to write to my mother.

"It depends on what sort of clothing we want to make," I say.

Caroline puts her hands on her hips. "We need to be soldiers."

This makes all of us stop what we are doing and stare. "How can we manage it?" I ask. A soldier's uniform is a very particular thing.

"If we could but purchase the jackets . . . ," Caroline says.

"I can help," I say, drawing my reticule out and opening it to show half the bundle of banknotes my mother gave me. I had the good sense to hide the rest.

"Where did you get so much?" Hortense says. I hear fear in her voice. Perhaps she thinks I have been dishonest.

"My mama left it for me. She wanted to make sure I didn't want for anything while she is away."

"Eliza, you are our savior!" Caroline leaps to her feet and throws her arms around me, then just as quickly sits back down and starts to rattle on about what we'll need.

Hortense looks at me with pity. I don't want to let my feelings show, to reveal that my mother's parting has had such a strong effect upon me, so I turn away from her.

"Now for the breeches," Caroline says to Hortense. "Do

you think Valmont could help?" She furrows her brow and purses her lips, tapping her chin with her index finger.

"He probably could. I shall send him a message. I expect there are students across the way who have outgrown their breeches, and they have to have white ones to wear for chapel. Many of the boys use the same ones when they join the army."

"But how will we get them here?" I ask.

"Valmont is a prefect, and sometimes he has to deliver messages here. I shall say . . . that the young ones need something to practice their mending on."

I have to admit, it could work. "And the jackets?"

"I have an idea about that, too," Hortense says, surprising us with how enthusiastically she is entering into the plan. "Eugène has grown so much lately," Hortense says. "Perhaps we can send Ernestine to Malmaison on the pretext that Eliza forgot something important. Maman will not rise until afternoon, with the gentlemen all gone. I'll write a note for the young maid there. I think she'll help us."

I don't know quite how, but we have concocted a scheme that has a chance of being successful. Even if it is foiled by circumstances, or we are found out, the thrill of attempting it is most diverting. Pity this is something I can never tell my mother. She would be horrified—and yet, she would probably wish she could have been with us, too.

27

Hortense

I have never done anything so deceitful in my life. Not only am I agreeing to help Caroline and Eliza with their scheme, but I am planning to deceive them as well. I shall find a way to ensure they are not blamed for my folly. But after these past few days at Malmaison, I realize I must grasp at a chance for happiness, if it exists at all.

I cannot bear the thought of the future my *maman* has planned for me. At least, not without knowing whether, in submitting to it, I will be turning my back on a true, genuine love.

Monsieur Perroquet comes today for my music lesson. Will he bring Michel with him? I must find out where he stands, what he intends—what I mean to him. Perhaps he was only toying with my affections. And yet, even as I think it, I believe the opposite. I believe he loves me. His soul is full of music. Surely that is evidence enough.

Everything I do for the next twenty-four hours depends upon whether I see any sign that Michel's love is true. If his intentions are as I suspect—*hope*—then he will take me away, we will marry in secret, and no one will be able to change it.

Caroline and Eliza have set their maids to working on the uniforms they shall wear. I cannot presume to occupy all of Geneviève's time in my service when she has others to care for, so I try to do as much as I can myself. Having once been apprenticed to a seamstress, I find I make good time. I am able to put my work away for a few hours during lessons and know that I shall be as prepared as the others.

I find it difficult to concentrate as Madame Campan drills us in etiquette and tests our ability to steer the conversation away from unsuitable topics, and I nearly allow a silence to elapse in our practice drawing room.

"Hortense, are you quite well?" she asks me, coming and laying the back of her hand on my forehead. "Perhaps the excitement of traveling to Malmaison has been too great for you. Or perhaps there is some other cause for your indisposition."

I am startled by her words. Has she guessed what we are doing? I force a smile. "No, madame. I am quite well.

Just a little tired from the traveling, is all." I do not want her to guess that there is anything else going on inside my heart.

She lowers her voice so that only I can hear it. "I have had a letter from your mother. I hear that, perhaps in not too long a time, we may have reason to congratulate you."

I wonder what else Maman wrote to her. How did she explain our sudden return to school after such a peremptory demand for my presence?

Madame Campan returns to her instruction, and I do my best to pay attention. But my heart quickens as the hour for comportment lessons draws to a close and I hear the bell indicating that Monsieur Perroquet has arrived. I strain my ears to discern if there is one pair of footsteps or two, but hear nothing.

A servant comes to Madame Campan and whispers in her ear. She looks around the room until her eyes alight upon Eliza. "Mademoiselle Eliza," Madame says, "would you do me the great favor of accepting a parcel that the Marquis de Valmont has brought over from the Collège?"

I try not to look at Eliza and see Caroline also turn away, as if she is occupied with pouring herself another cup of tea. But I can't help noticing that she turns a shade more pink than normal. I hope she won't give us away!

We continue the lesson without Eliza, and soon I hear the bell again. This time I am certain it must be Monsieur

Perroquet. When Madame claps twice to end the lesson, I prepare myself to take the next step in my daring plan.

Just as I am about to enter the music room, the score for the air I have been practicing tucked beneath my arm, Madame Campan comes forward from the dining hall. "Ah, Hortense. If you would give me just a moment alone with Monsieur Perroquet."

Her smile is inscrutable. What business can she have alone with him?

I wait as patiently as I can, casting my eyes over the molding that decorates the walls and converges in bouquets of plaster flowers in the corners. It is fortunate, I think, that the mobs did not consider this house important enough to ransack utterly during the revolution. One might almost imagine we are back in the time of Marie Antoinette and her court.

My ears are alive to every sound within the music room, and I distinctly hear the door on the other side open and shut. A moment later Madame Campan's voice approaches so that I just hear, "Thank you for your discretion, monsieur," before she opens the door and motions that I may enter. She passes by me and closes the door softly behind her.

Monsieur Perroquet is alone. My heart drops into my stomach. I notice that his face is flushed, though, and I see his hand tremble as he arranges the sheets on the desk of the spinet. I pretend not to see, and take my place at the music stand, looking down so that he can compose himself.

It is then that I see the note. A small, folded scrap of paper, left so that anyone might discover it. I don't know why I assume it is for me, but I cough and turn away so I can slip it into my bodice until later.

My lesson progresses as usual, although I find it difficult to concentrate. At its end, I curtsy in thanks to Monsieur Perroquet and turn to leave, but he stops me.

"It was my hope, Mademoiselle Hortense, that Madame Campan would allow you to share your gifts at a small musical event I am planning the day after tomorrow evening at my humble apartments."

I know he wishes to say more, but he pauses. I must act quickly. "And where, monsieur, might those apartments be? Did Madame give her permission?"

He squeezes my hand before letting it go. "Alas, Madame insists that you are too fatigued after your recent travels to attend me in the Rue Saint-Pierre, number thirty-six." Two round, red blotches appear on his cheeks as he says this. It is a message for me—I know it!

"Thank you, monsieur. I, too, wish I could form part of your evening entertainment. But alas, as Madame says, I am rather tired."

It is all I can do to walk slowly and calmly out of the music room and up the stairs to my bedroom. Rue Saint-Pierre is an easy walk from the Rue de l'Unité, where the school is located. If I have interpreted Monsieur Perroquet's unspoken message correctly, then the note I draw from my bodice once I close the door of my room must be from Michel.

I unfold it slowly, wanting to savor this moment, hoping to discover a confirmation of the feelings we began to express the other night, and a justification for all that I plan to do in the coming days.

Chère Hortense,
Dare I hope—

I can read no more. The door of my room bursts open to admit Caroline and Eliza, their arms full of the clothing their maids have attempted to make for them—and not quite succeeded. For the next half hour, I help them with the fitting. Both Ernestine and Hélène have made shoddy jobs of the alterations, but the damage is easy to fix.

When we finish, we agree to meet before dawn tomorrow.

"I can arrange for the coach," Caroline says. I do not ask her how she will arrange for such a thing, but by the look that passes between her and Eliza, I deduce that she is practiced in these matters.

They leave to dress for dinner. I immediately reach for the note so that I may finish drinking in the sweet sentiments it no doubt contains.

It is gone. I look around the floor, lifting the edge of the carpets to see if it was accidentally swept beneath one of them in the confusion. I reach into my bodice. Did I think to stow it away there? No, I would have felt it.

I open the door and look down the corridor. Eliza is gone. Quickly, I go to her door and knock. "Eliza!" I whisper as loudly as I dare.

She opens the door. "Hortense! What's the matter?"

"Where are the scraps?" I ask, too frantic to be polite.

"Here," she says, pointing to a pile in the corner of the room.

I rush over and dig through the bits of fabric, shaking each one out.

"What's the matter? Have you lost something?" Eliza asks.

It's no use. The letter is not there. "I thought I had, but it's not here," I say. "It's nothing."

Eliza's perplexed expression assures me that she has no idea about the letter. So it must be Caroline. How could I ever have believed she would change?

28

Eliza

I didn't know at first why Madame Campan sent me down to meet Armand. The message to him came from Hortense, whom he knows quite well. She would have been the logical person to greet him.

Yet I was nervous when I saw him in the entryway to the kitchens with his parcel tied up in a basket, its contents looking like a pile of odd rags rather than the garments that would soon let us three pass as young men in the world.

"Thank you, Monsieur de Valmont," I said, curtsying and trying not to look into his face. But he stared at me, hard. I could feel it. And so I eventually had to look up and meet his gaze.

"Hortense was very mysterious in her note. She can keep secrets. That's why I asked for you instead."

I had my hand on the basket handle and pulled it toward me. I wanted to end this conversation as quickly as possible. "I'm sure I have no idea what you're talking about."

"Is it a theatrical entertainment? Or something else?" He wouldn't let go of the basket. I felt awkward standing there.

"It's simply—sewing practice," I said, giving a tug that almost sent me reeling backward, since he let go as soon as he felt it.

Now I was furious. "I could have fallen!"

"Ah, but you didn't. And you've told me far more than you realize. What time do you three plan to steal away from the school?"

My mouth dropped open before I could stop it. I approached him so I was near enough to whisper. "This is none of your affair!"

"In fact, I would argue that it is very much my affair, since you have involved me in it. If I am thrown out of school for helping you in whatever it is you plan, I shall be on the streets. My family does not want me back. I'm not yet able to earn my own keep as a portraitist."

I took a long look at his confident stance, his smooth, calm face. Valmont might be poor, but he was every inch the aristocrat. Yet was he blackmailing me? Trying to get me to give him information that might incriminate us or allow him to spoil our plans? My father is a lawyer. I have heard him speak of such things.

"Monsieur le Marquis," I said, my voice as smooth and calm as if I were in the parlor still, going through the motions with Madame and the other students. "We are only school-girls playing an innocent game. I'm certain I don't know what you could be talking about." I tossed my head as I had seen Caroline do and turned away. But Valmont caught hold of my arm.

"This is no game," he said. "I know that Hortense and Caroline often hear things because of who their relatives are. Something is going to happen, isn't it?" His fingers dug into my arm.

"Ow!" I said. He let go, a look of genuine contrition on his face.

"I'm sorry. Only, you see, it could make all the difference to me. If there is a chance—even the slightest chance—that things will go back as they were, when people valued a title and a family history, I shall have a future."

He took hold of my shoulders and looked hard into my eyes. Only then did I see real sorrow, evidence of pain from difficult times, just beneath his elegant features. I realized that he did not intend to expose our plans. I took a chance. "It's possible, Armand. They think we are just silly girls, but we heard things that make us think tomorrow will be an important day."

"So you are going somewhere . . . in disguise?" He let go of me and tapped the basket. I felt a little cold without his hands on my arms.

"Yes. Before dawn. We hope to be back by nightfall. Please don't say anything!" It was my turn to be sincere.

He smiled. It was a warm, gentle smile, and I noticed his teeth were straight and white. I shook my head a little and forced myself to look away. He was not Eugène! *And besides, he doesn't like me,* I reminded myself.

Nonetheless, I could feel his gaze following me as I left the anteroom.

Now the day is at an end. It is hard to remain calm during dinner and afterward at our needlework. I keep feeling as if I need to get up and pace around the drawing room, but to do so would make Madame Campan suspicious, so I force myself to sit still and listen to Hortense read from a memoir. Her voice is very sweet, but when she reads the tender portions, where the lady recalls her first love, I hear her voice crack just a little. She clears her throat and takes a sip of wine. Madame Campan looks up at her without lifting her head, watching her as if she knows something.

At long last Caroline stands and stretches. "I am still fatigued from our traveling in the last few days. Might I beg leave to retire a little early?"

Both Hortense and I echo her sentiments and Madame Campan gives us permission to go to bed.

As we part to go to our separate rooms, we clutch hands together quickly. I look at both of them, but Hortense stares only at Caroline. Her eyes are beseeching. I have the impression that something has transpired between them.

I let that thought pass, and we part. Ernestine helps me undress and carefully drapes a shawl over the uniform I shall wear in a few hours. She drops a quick curtsy on her way out and puts her finger to her lips, indicating that she will say nothing.

I can hardly close my eyes. Tomorrow I will see Eugène again! And perhaps he has been persuaded by his mother to relinquish his love for this actress. I cannot help hoping for such a thing, as unlikely as I feel it is.

But even more than the fact that I will see Eugène, I find something utterly thrilling in the idea that I will enter the world of men, dressed as one of them. How strange it will feel! Caroline seem quite unperturbed by the idea. I wonder if she has done it before?

Yet I can't quite believe that Hortense has agreed to disguise herself as a man as well. She does not seem like someone who would consent to such a dangerous plan, especially one that involves escaping unseen from school.

She did not hold back, however, once the plan was made. Hortense is a very skilled seamstress. I don't know what we would have done without her. My blue uniform and white trousers fit quite wonderfully. It's very freeing to walk without a skirt, letting my legs stride out without the fabric catching between them.

Even Ernestine has gotten into the spirit of things. She

has agreed with Hélène to tell Madame that we are all indisposed and will remain in our rooms throughout the day.

Now I must try to sleep. I won't write to Mama this evening. I'm still very cross with her, and a little hurt, although she did try to tell me ahead of time that she was leaving. In any case, my letters won't reach her for weeks, so there is no hurry. I shall try to dream of Eugène. I imagine him standing out from all the others, a ray of light among a dark mass of men.

And I decide: I may not win his love—it may be too much to ask that he forsake another girl for me—but I will find a way to ensure that he will be the person who gives me my first real kiss.

I feel as if I have just closed my eyes, and here is Hortense, already dressed in her military garb, holding up a candle. Ernestine is behind her, looking sleepy but excited. She's enjoying this as much as I am.

In a flash I am wide awake, although my lack of sleep makes everything seem strange, unreal. I see my hands pull on the trousers and boots and fasten the buttons of the jacket, but they feel as if they belong to someone else.

We accomplish our transformation quietly and assemble in the vestibule.

I look at the two of them briefly. "This just might work," I say.

Caroline turns me around and then casts a quick eye

over Hortense. "We'll have to walk like soldiers, not dainty ladies." I can tell by the way she says it that she believes we can do it.

Hortense smiles. "I'm ready."

"So am I," I say, although my stomach is full of nervous jitters.

"Where is the coach?" Hortense whispers.

"We must leave the gates and walk a short way. I thought it best not to risk the noise of horses and wheels on gravel," Caroline says.

Caroline opens the door, holding the latch so it does not make a click, and we creep out as softly as we can.

The coach is down the street, just as she said it would be. It is the same one we took that night to the ball, with the same coachman. I still do not understand how she arranges such things, when she is always either at school or under the close observation of her family. Before I leave Saint-Germain I shall have to find out, or make her tell me.

"Are you certain Ernestine and Hélène will give the correct message to Madame Campan?" Hortense asks. Her hands are knotted into each other. She is more nervous than either Caroline or I. I still don't entirely understand why she has agreed to be part of this adventure. What has she to gain from it? Caroline has Murat, and I have Eugène. Hortense cannot wish to see Louis Bonaparte, who disgusts her—as anyone who saw them together the other night at Malmaison could plainly see.

"As certain as you are about Geneviève," Caroline answers. This silences Hortense.

We climb into the coach, but it is not empty.

Hortense gives a little shriek. Caroline puts her hand over Hortense's mouth. And I—I have to prevent myself from launching into an angry tirade.

"Good morning, citizens!" Valmont has dressed himself exactly as we are. Only he looks more like a soldier than we do.

"What is he doing here?" Caroline can barely suppress her fury.

"I don't know," I say, knowing that it's my fault, that my moment of weakness might possibly have ruined our entire plan.

"I am merely here as your protector," Valmont says, flashing his irritatingly lovely smile at us.

"There's no time to delay our plans," Hortense says.

Caroline shoots a look of absolute fire at me. I meet her gaze, trying not to give anything away. "Drive on!" she says to the coachman, who cracks his whip over the horses' backs and jolts us into motion.

It is not far to Saint-Cloud. Not even as far as Malmaison. We soon arrive at a town that has not yet awakened fully to the day, only farmers with their carts and shopkeepers unlocking their doors to prepare for the morning's business.

"How do we know where to go?" I ask. "Eugène didn't say anything beyond simply Saint-Cloud."

"You mean, that's all you know?" It is Valmont.

"We didn't ask you to come with us. If the situation doesn't suit you, please feel free to return to Saint-Germain." Caroline dismisses him with a wave, then turns back to us. "The château. It is the only building large enough to hold the Directoire and the Council of Five Hundred. But we cannot approach the place in this conveyance. . . ." To the driver, she yells, "Stop the coach!"

He draws the horses to a sudden halt. We four descend, Caroline first, then Hortense, then me, then Valmont. I catch my heel in the step of the coach and nearly plunge forward onto my face. But Valmont grabs hold of my coat just in time to prevent it.

"Thank you," I murmur.

In the dawning light I see the outline of a palace ahead of us, with the unmistakable contours of an army assembled around it.

"They are here already. We're none too soon," Caroline says.

"How will we know where to go, or what is happening?" I whisper.

"The directors and the council are not military men," Valmont says. "Most likely everything will take place within the château, and we will not be able to see anything."

Caroline glares at him. "Follow me," she says, as if she has carefully planned everything out beforehand.

Caroline may not have Hortense's grace and beauty but she makes up for it in courage. How can she be so brave? Now that I am here I am full of misgivings, and my hands are trembling. I cannot imagine that we will actually be able to pass as soldiers. I find myself suddenly grateful that Valmont has come, too. He is a little taller than we are and has the shape of a man. Perhaps we do not look so conspicuous with him among us.

Still, my heart is pounding. What seemed like an adventure yesterday seems more like folly today. I do my best to keep up with Hortense and Caroline, who march forward as if they belong there. Valmont stays at my side, although I flash him a haughty look. I imagine he wants to keep us all in his sights, that we may not evade him. I can't help but wonder how we must look to anyone who glances in our direction, our hair tucked securely under our tricorns, our breasts bound flat with linen wraps.

Soon we are among the other soldiers and I see that what looked like a uniform body of men is really a haphazard collection of young boys, older men, and even a few women who wear a variation of the uniform the rest of us are wearing, with a knee-length skirt and breeches beneath. They go from soldier to soldier with jugs of wine and water.

"Who are those women?" I ask Hortense.

"They are the *vivandières*. They keep the troops supplied with food and drink. They're part of the army."

"Do they go into battle, too?"

"No," Caroline says, "which is why we could not simply pretend to be of their number. They will remain outside the château."

To my shock, Valmont gestures to one of them, who comes over quite willingly. She pours a cup of wine out for him. He downs it in a single gulp and returns the cup to her. I catch the woman's saucy wink at him just before she turns away. He smiles at her retreating form, watching her hips sway invitingly as she goes to the next soldier who calls her over.

Before I can say anything to him, a murmur goes out among the soldiers, who until now have been standing about, not doing much of anything but talking quietly. Gradually all noise and movement cease.

From the distance I hear horses approaching and coach wheels squeaking. As they get closer, I can tell there are many of both. We are at the back of the château and cannot see what is happening at the front, where all these coaches are arriving.

Out of the corner of my eye I see Caroline sidling away. *She means to leave us!* I think, my heart racing. How will we get back without her? And yet, I cannot leave Hortense, who is standing by me, her hands gripped together.

Before I can think further, Hortense turns to me, grasping

my upper arms and staring into my eyes so that I cannot look away.

"What is it?" I ask.

"You must tell me honestly. Swear that you will!"

"I swear it," I say, not able to imagine what it is that she needs to know from me.

"Last night, when you and Caroline came to my room, did you notice a piece of paper anywhere about? On the floor perhaps?"

A piece of paper? "What kind of paper?"

"A paper with writing. A note. Addressed to me."

At least I can answer her honestly, although I doubt my answer will soothe her. "No, I saw no such thing."

She takes her hands from my shoulders and casts her eyes to the ground. I see the sparkle of tears in her lashes. "Then there may be no hope. I am lost."

I am about to ask her what she could mean when a wave of something goes through the assembled soldiers, making them snap to attention with their muskets resting upright on their shoulders.

Their muskets. *Of course!* I knew there was something that made me uneasy about our plan, something that would not let us blend into the crowd despite our uniforms and our careful preparation. We have no weapons! What kind of soldier walks into battle without even a dagger?

"Venez!" one of the soldiers nearby calls to us. "Get

your weapons and fall in before the sergeant gives you a whipping!"

I glance around frantically to see if there is somewhere we can go to arm ourselves. But I am too late. I look up to see a sergeant steaming over to where Hortense and I stand. But where is Caroline?

She's gone. And so is Valmont.

29

Madeleine

Today is the day that Eugène said he would come for me. He promised it would be early, before my mother is up and ordering me around.

"Marianne!" I call, running through the warren of corridors behind the theater, looking for my only friend.

"I am here," she says, tired as always. It seems not to matter when I go to sleep or when I get up; Marianne is always awake. She must surely sleep, but it's impossible to discover when.

"Help me find a dress that isn't too horrible to wear," I say, dragging her with me to the room where the costumes are kept. "Something for a peasant, say, a country girl, but not a beggar."

Marianne brightens up at the prospect. It's one of the things we enjoy doing together: sorting through the costumes on the pretext of mending them, but trying them on and acting out scenes of the lives we've always wanted but would probably never be able to live.

Today I begin a future. A *real* future. I shall live in a house, have children, go to parties.

"Have you figured out what you will say to your *maman* when you leave?" Marianne asks, pulling three or four dresses out of a heap in a large trunk.

"This one's not bad," I say. It's pale yellow with white trim. Not lace, but the cut is modern enough. "We can add a sash."

Marianne stops and looks at me. I don't want to answer her question. I don't want to tell Maman anything.

"You know she will do whatever is in her power to stop you," she says.

I pretend to be rifling through a basket of ribbons and laces, but really I'm pondering her words. "I must protect myself," I say. I knew it all along, that I would have to have some kind of weapon with me in case my mother sent someone after me, but a part of me wanted to pretend that I would just be able to leave, act as though my mother didn't exist.

"I'll make you a sheath for a dagger. You can wear it on your leg."

Marianne knows how to do things that make me shudder to imagine where she learned them. All I know is that she prefers this horrible place to wherever she came from, which is saying quite a bit.

We work fast—we have to. I am putting the final touches on my dress just as I hear the actors start yelling for Marianne to bring them coffee, to find their costumes, to hold the basin while they puke up the bad oysters they ate the night before.

I must go to Mother and pretend that this is the start of just another day.

My mother's room is a mess. I can see that someone was here, a man who must have left not long ago. "Ah, my precious," she says to me in a voice that contradicts her words. "I need you to fetch me something, from that gentleman in the Marais who always takes care of me."

She unlocks a cabinet where she stores everything she has of value: a few gold chains and the money she's extorted from her lovers, mostly. She holds out three gold *écus* to me. I stare at her hand.

"Don't just stand there! Be off with you! And get back quick or I might be tempted to thrash you."

I know she's serious, but all I can think is *What if he comes and I'm not here?* I can't send Marianne. She'd get a thrashing from ten people instead of just one.

My hand shakes a little as I take the money from her. I know the way to the opium seller well. I have had to go there myself ever since he was barred from entering the theater, when half the cast was too drugged to perform one evening.

Marianne waits for me outside my mother's door. "You must make him wait!" I whisper to her, clutching her arm.

She nods. "Don't worry. If he comes, he will stay."

I grab my shawl and run out the door before really hearing what Marianne said. *If he comes . . .* He *will* come! He promised. Only as I dash through the backstreets I begin to worry. He said he would be early. Yet I hear the bells from Notre-Dame. It is already ten. Perhaps that is early to a dandy, but not to an army officer, an aide-de-camp to Bonaparte.

My mind is so occupied I nearly miss the turn down the dark alley. The stink here is unbearable. Opium eaters too far gone to walk soil themselves in the gutter. I cover my nose and mouth with my shawl and knock the special signal on the small door. Three rapid taps, followed by two more widely spaced.

The peephole opens.

"It's me, Madeleine. I have money, for the medicine my mother requires."

I'm sure they know that I know it is not medicine, but we keep up the pretense. The peephole closes, and a moment later the door opens a crack and a hand reaches out for the coins. "Not until I have what you promised," I say. Once before, I gave the money and the door shut. No amount of knocking would open it. The beating I received when I returned remains a painful memory.

We enact a careful dance with our hands. I snatch the parcel that holds the soft lump of opium just as I relinquish my three coins. The door snaps shut. I hurry away, jumping over a man who is so completely motionless I think he must be dead.

My feet have wings as I run over the cobbles and rutted dirt of the Paris streets back to the Salle Richelieu. I don't dare seek out Marianne, but go to my mother's room straightaway. I find her pacing up and down, on the edge of that state of panic she was in when she threatened me before.

"Why have you been so long! Give me the medicine."

I know I must stay out of her grasp, so I toss the package to her and run. Fortunately, she is so desperate for the relief the drug gives her that she does not follow me.

Now to find Marianne.

She is not in her usual places. I see evidence of the work she has done in the tidy dressing rooms and the corridors that have been swept clean. But I do not find her. I call out, "Marianne!"

There is no answer. Then I hear the sound of a broom swishing across the floor. I rush around the corner toward the noise and see Marianne hard at work.

"Where is he? Did he come?" I ask, keeping my voice low.

"I . . . do not believe so."

I grab her shoulders. "He must be here! He said he would come!" I find myself shaking her, hard.

She takes hold of me. "He has not come. . . . He may not come."

I release Marianne and back away. I know she is right.

He is not coming, or he would be here by now. He promised, and he broke his promise. I must get away. I must go somewhere. I run to my attic room, the only place I feel at home.

30

Hortense

Eliza and I don't dare utter a word. Yet our silence only angers the sergeant more. He takes us into a nearby tent.

"What do you have to say for yourselves, eh? You were instructed to be ready for action, and you don't even have the basic equipment you've been given just an hour ago. What did you do with your muskets? Your daggers? Are you Jacobin sympathizers?" His voice rises with each question. I see Eliza's lower lip start to pucker and fear she will cry. I would squeeze her hand but I don't dare reach out.

The sergeant paces back and forth in front of us, covering the space inside the tent in three long strides each way. "You should be whipped. But I see you're young. Not even shaving yet! What do they mean, giving me mere boys to train? I suppose it's all these damned foreign wars. . . ."

He stops talking directly to us, instead fuming about

the army and Napoléon, wondering what the army is doing at a château that's perfectly peaceful when they could be out drilling for the next war. We must find a way to get out of here, and quickly. It is only a matter of time before someone discovers we are not who we appear to be.

Eliza jumps at the sound of a harsh command from right outside the tent. The sergeant stops his pacing and squares off to us. "I'll deal with you when this is over—whatever it is."

He turns smartly and leaves us alone in the tent. Eliza immediately runs toward the exit.

"No! We can't just dash out," I whisper to her, although my caution is unnecessary. There is such a noise of tromping boots on gravel that no one would hear us even if I shouted. The massed army is moving forward.

Although I cannot imagine that Caroline ever thought such a predicament would arise, this only compounds her misdeeds in my eyes. She must have been the one to take the note from me. She must have seen it—and seized the opportunity to torment me by taking it. I expect her to hold it over my head soon. If only she would tell me what it said!

And now she has left us alone in the midst of unfolding events that only she can understand, since she is the only one of us in a position to watch the proceedings.

My thoughts return to Michel. I badly need to see that note, to determine if my own actions later today will have the results I desire, or if Michel's intentions are not honorable.

But I can't do anything about Michel with Eliza to look after and no idea how we will get away. And if someone discovers that we are in disguise—it turns my stomach to imagine how we might be taken advantage of.

"Shh!" Eliza says. "I hear someone coming!"

Indeed, the march of a single pair of boots approaches, and we turn to face the entrance, dreading what will happen next.

The tent flap rises to reveal Valmont. He has a musket on his shoulder, which explains why he was not similarly hauled up for unpreparedness. He eases it off and lays it on the ground, shaking out his hand and rubbing his shoulder. "I'm afraid lifting a paintbrush is not so strenuous as this." Eliza runs toward Valmont and flings herself against him. He looks a little shocked, but I see him pat her kindly before he pushes her away.

"Hush! This is no time for tears. Come with me, and I'll show you what Caroline is doing."

"Thank you," I say. "Perhaps it's fortunate you are with us today." I look at Eliza as I say this. Since she was the one who met him to get the breeches, I can only imagine that her words gave our plans away.

"We don't have muskets," Eliza says.

"I know where to get them." Valmont gestures for us to follow him outdoors. "I'll explain what I've discovered on the way."

I see that now all the soldiers are closer to the château

and facing in one direction. I imagine that whether or not we are armed doesn't make a bit of difference now. No one is looking toward us. They are all concentrating their attention on a single door, as if they mean to march through it together.

"They have all arrived," Valmont whispers. "I followed Caroline and saw them enter. The Council of Five Hundred must already be inside the main château, but the Directoire is in this building here." He points. His words are clipped and efficient. I find myself a little irritated that he has somehow taken charge of our excursion. But I have my own plans, of which he knows nothing.

Although I know that what's happening beyond that door will change everything for the entire nation, right now I don't care. All I want to do is find Michel. I turn to Eliza. "I think we should not stay together. I'll see if I can spot another way into the building."

Valmont nods. "We need to get inside if we are going to discover what they are doing. But first we must furnish you two with Charlevilles, like mine." He pats the barrel of the rifle. "Then we can take our own separate ways. Eliza and I can try to find Caroline."

He leads us to a tent where a store of rifles lies stacked to the side. I admit, I am a bit puzzled by Valmont's consideration for Eliza. It continues in the tent, as he helps her hoist the rifle to her shoulder. I swing mine up with ease. My mother taught me to shoot during the *Terreur*, when we were all fearful for our lives.

Once we are equipped, we stride forth together as if we belong there. I nod to Valmont, who nods back. Swiftly, I turn as if I know where I am going and leave the two of them behind.

"I want to go with her!" I hear Eliza whisper just before I am out of earshot.

I glance behind. Valmont is pointing ahead and saying something to Eliza. He is distracting her from me. Does he know what I am about? Could that be why he has taken Eliza under his wing?

I see Eliza square her shoulders, trying to look as much like Valmont and the other men as she can. Her actions melt my heart a little. She is so young! I almost call her back to me, but then I realize I have no choice. The steps I have already taken have led me on from here. I turn away and leave them to their adventure.

31

Hortense

Forgive me, Eliza, I think as I watch her disappearing with Valmont into the columns of soldiers. She is concentrating on not faltering under the weight of the musket, which is indeed quite heavy. But I have other things to accomplish. My future—and my future happiness—depends upon what occurs in the next few hours.

No one is looking back. All eyes are forward on the drama that is taking place within the château. I take my chance and lean my musket against a stone wall, then follow the trail of horse droppings to what I hope is a stable.

How will I dare? I cannot permit myself to imagine. I must simply act, and hope that what follows justifies the means I will have to employ.

To my satisfaction I see that I have located the palace stables. With most of the activity centered on laying siege to the Directoire and the Council of Five Hundred, no one is taking much notice of the courtyard or the stable building.

I enter the dim, warm space. The smell of horses has always soothed me. The sweet hay mixed with polished leather reminds me of happy hours riding over country fields and through the woods. When I was young, I would jump upon whatever beast I found in the paddock, my bare legs against the smooth barrel of the horse. I did not mind, then, about propriety.

It wasn't until I went to school that I was forced to ride sidesaddle like the others.

But now, that early freedom will stand me in good stead.

A stable boy starts to his feet when he sees me. I can tell that he has been napping on a bale of straw. Imprints of it are still upon his cheek. I have to think fast, before he has a chance to question me.

"I must take a message to Malmaison," I say, not able to think of any other place within easy riding distance that might be believed. "Saddle that mare for me, lad."

Either I am more convincing than I feel or he is simply accustomed to following the orders of anyone wearing a uniform, because in a matter of moments he leads the chestnut mare I spotted out of her stall and brings a mounting block to her side. I step upon it and swing my leg over, urging her forward with a twitch of my muscles, and we soon leave the stable boy behind.

I am not certain of the way, so I stop at the first cross-roads, where I see a peasant driving his donkey cart to market.

"*Excusez-moi,*" I say, aware that I am perhaps more polite than the fellow is accustomed to. "Can you direct me to Saint-Germain-en-Laye from here?"

He takes off his cap and slowly points along the road. "Take that way; then, when you see the tavern, turn right. It's only four kilometers from there."

I thank him and continue.

This is the first moment I have had since everything began yesterday to consider what I am about to do. Without having had the opportunity to read the note from Michel, I cannot be certain that it was a proposal. And yet, everything in his face, and in the attitude of Monsieur Perroquet's words to me, convinces me that it can be nothing else.

I know with every pound of my horse's hooves on the packed dirt road that I am certain to alienate myself from my mother forever. I have always tried to protect her in my way, to be loyal to her whatever others are saying. Much of what she has done since being released from prison has been for the sake of Eugène and me. She does not want me to suffer the deprivation and degradation she suffered at the hands of my unfaithful father.

Yet by pushing me into the arms of a man I do not love—just as she was sent to be a wife at the age of fifteen to someone she had never before met—she does exactly that. I am convinced it was the lack of affection between Maman and Papa that led to her troubles, nothing else.

Sooner poor than miserable, I repeat to myself, making a rhyme of it and then a tune, and then imagining the evening hours when Michel and I will sing together, our children fast asleep in their beds in our small but comfortable house. His father, Monsieur Perroquet, makes a good living as a music tutor, after all. At least he appears to. He arrives at the school in a coach and dresses in silks.

By the time Saint-Germain comes into view it is full day. Even though I am disguised, I must avoid the street where the Académie is located. It would not do to make liars of all three of us. We are supposed to be in our beds, nursing illness from eating something spoiled at Malmaison.

I slow my horse to a walk and meander through the back streets until I reach the Rue Saint-Pierre. I wish I could make myself invisible, but a lone soldier on a horse is not the most common of sights in this quarter, and I soon find I have an assortment of children following along, singing bits of the "Marseillaise."

"Allez-vous en!" I say, hoping my voice sounds sufficiently gruff. The smaller ones back away. I feel wretched that I have frightened them. One of the older boys remains where he is and casts me a defiant stare.

"You!" I say. "Which one is number thirty-six?"

He steps forward and salutes me. "I shall be a fusilier one day, like you. My name is Hippolyte."

"Well, then, Citizen Hippolyte! Can you direct me to the house I seek?"

"Is the music master in trouble? I should like that. He is such a fop."

I cannot help the flush that floods into my cheeks and must make my voice harsh to convince the boy that it is anger, not embarrassment. "That is no affair of yours. I merely pay a social call."

His shoulders droop and he points to a modest house diagonally across the street.

"Be a good lad and look after my horse for me?" I say, swinging my leg over and dismounting. Instantly Hippolyte's face is transformed and beaming with pride.

"Yes, sir!" Another salute, which I return, and then I walk to the door of the house where my fate awaits me.

32

Valmont and I keep pace with each another, although his strides are much longer than mine. We are almost at the front of the columns of soldiers, when suddenly a sergeant I cannot see cries, *"Avant!"*

I feel everyone around me step forward like a single creature, musket barrels like trees pointing into the misty air. I glance around me to see if I can tell where Hortense has gone, but I cannot find her.

The rifle is so heavy it makes my arm shake. I don't know how much longer I'll be able to hold it like this, and then I will be certain to give away that I am not as I appear. I don't want to look weak in front of Armand, who—for a painter—makes a very convincing soldier.

I catch quick glimpses of the men's faces. They are all concentrating on what is happening ahead. There is no mirth, no softness in them. They would have little sympathy for a young girl who is on a silly adventure just for the sake of chasing after a young man who probably thinks no more of her than a pet dog.

I struggle not to let the sudden realization that I am on a fool's errand overwhelm me, but focus on finding Caroline again.

"There she is!" Armand whispers. I feel his breath on my cheek and follow his gaze. She is right at the front, near the door to the gatehouse. How did she manage it?

"How will we reach her?"

"Stay right next to me," he says. I confess, I'm glad he's here. With Caroline and Hortense off on their own, I'm not sure how I would manage.

Staying as close to Armand as I can, I begin to march as if it is my duty. To my surprise, the men seem to sense us coming and step aside so we may pass.

Soon we are nearly level with Caroline, but just as we start to move toward her she darts into a passage between the two buildings: the smaller one, the gatehouse, where she said the directors are being held, and the main château, where the Council of Five Hundred wait, all unsuspecting that something dramatic is about to happen.

I start to follow Caroline, but Armand puts his hand on my arm to stop me. "Best to leave her to it," he says. "I think we might be able to see something this way."

The door of the gatehouse opens, and I see a tight-knit

group of men in uniforms covered in braid and ribbons marching around the side from the front. It is the generals, being led by Napoléon. He is noticeably short among the other men. I watch as one by one the leaders of the French army enter the building. I see Louis and Lucien with Napoléon, as well as Caroline's Murat. Where has she gone? *"Hmmph!"* I say.

"What?" Valmont says.

"Oh, nothing. I just noticed Murat."

"Caroline's beloved," he says, surprising me. I wonder how he knows. But of course, he and Hortense spoke for quite a long time at the cotillion. Perhaps she gave him a lot of information.

We have gradually moved forward, pushed by the press of men behind who want to see what is happening. Armand nudges us into a better position to get a glimpse through the door.

At first, all I can see is the backs of the generals and their aides-de-camp, still clustered inside the gatehouse. I wonder why I have not seen Eugène, who would surely be by Napoléon's side. A sentry stands with his musket stock resting on the ground, looking straight out over the heads of the massed army.

"Now just follow me," Armand says.

Before I can ask what he is doing, he steps smartly forward to the door. I do as he does, summoning all my courage.

"Halt!" the sentry says. "Only the generals and their ADCs are permitted within."

We stop. What now? I hold my breath, wondering if Armand will say anything.

He salutes in a crisp gesture. They must teach them at school, I think. "I have an important message for Lieutenant de Beauharnais," Armand says.

The sentry looks us up and down. "You won't find him in here! He's gone off in that direction." He points away from everything.

This time we both salute, and step a little back.

"Now what?" I ask, trying to speak without moving my lips. Why on earth did he ask for Eugène? Perhaps Hortense told him something else.

Armand doesn't respond, and there is an uncomfortable pause while we stand where we are.

The sentry continues to glare at us. "Please rejoin the ranks, soldiers," he says.

I am about to turn away, assuming Armand will do the same, but something happens inside and all attention is suddenly focused there.

I feel Armand's hand on my arm again, and he pulls me past the distracted sentry. We slip into the room, standing with our rifles as straight and tall as we can, trying to blend into the walls.

For the moment, no one is paying attention to us. Armand is so close I can hear him breathing. The generals and the five directors stand in the center, facing each other. I recognize Barras and Sieyès from Malmaison, but not the others.

"What right! What right, I say, do you have to impose your rule upon the French people, who democratically chose a directorate and a council as their form of government?" It is one of the men I do not recognize. His reedy voice trembles. Hardly surprising, since he is unarmed and facing the bold Napoléon and his generals with their swords at their sides.

"When a government has effectively become inoperable," Barras replies, "steps must be taken. Bonaparte has the hearts of the people behind him. With the three of us as equal governors, we can at last undertake the necessary reforms and bring France back to glory. Surely you must realize this is essential, Ducos!"

"A consulate? You propose a consulate?" The man I now know is Ducos darts his gaze from one person to another. "Let us see what the Council of Five Hundred has to say!"

With that, Ducos strides toward a door that I think will lead to the main château, followed by all the others. I gasp as a soldier throws the door open. There is Caroline, where she must have been hiding all along. We see each other, but she does not signal to me.

Without thinking, I follow the general movement through a passageway, heedless of whether Armand is with me, trying to catch up to Caroline without drawing attention to myself. I notice that Murat has not come with the generals, though, but quietly steps out into the courtyard, where the army waits.

Soon we are in a vast hall where the Five Hundred are gathered. Barras strides to the front and addresses them. I glance behind. There is no sign of Armand.

"The Directoire has agreed upon the establishment of a consulate, consisting of myself, Sieyès, and Bonaparte," Barras says.

He can't say anything more because the roar of anger that greets him drowns out every voice. The council and their guards surge forward. All at once, Napoléon is surrounded!

I see Lucien draw his sword, but not before one of the council's guards raises his and lunges toward Napoléon. He is wounded! Caroline screams, but no one pays her any notice. I try to rush over to her, but the crush of people prevents me, and only then I realize that Murat has returned, with the soldiers from the courtyard behind him.

Will I be caught in a battle? If only Armand had not been left behind! It occurs to me in that moment that he would protect me.

And then, suddenly, it is over.

The council—all businessmen and tailors, merchants and doctors—is too frightened to press their advantage against Bonaparte's army.

I start to breathe again, realizing that I have not been doing so for some time. Dots of light dance before my eyes. Where is Caroline?

I see her moving through the crowd. She is heading toward Murat.

Everyone else is clustered around Napoléon, ushering him out another door.

Murat alone remains. Caroline approaches him. He doesn't notice her, probably assuming she is nothing more than a common soldier. Caroline reaches out to touch him.

"Good God! What the devil are you doing here?" I hear him all the way to where I stand, and start to back out, hoping he won't notice me.

Murat grabs Caroline's elbow and steers her away from the center of things. I can no longer hear them, but I see that they are talking and gesticulating at each other.

I'm not sure what I expected Caroline to do, but to my horror she rises up on her tiptoes, puts her arms around Murat's neck, and kisses him. At first he staggers a little backward; then he wraps one arm around Caroline, practically lifting her off her feet with the force of his embrace.

Suddenly I hear laughter. I look to the side and realize that several soldiers have turned their attention away from the departing council and are watching Caroline and Murat.

What must they think!

Caroline looks around, confused. Then I see her realize what's happened, and before I have time to register what she is doing, she takes off her hat and let her dark hair tumble over her shoulder.

Now I know I must get away, instantly. But before I turn and run headlong out of the door, I see Armand appear from nowhere, running toward Caroline and Murat.

I back into the courtyard, where most of the army still stands, wondering what will happen next.

33

Once outside, I stride without really looking where I am going and am suddenly confronted with a soldier standing directly in front of me who looks very familiar.

It is Eugène. I realize that he was not with the generals, not even inside the buildings. I see him put his hand up to shade his eyes, or perhaps just to focus them out over the troops. He calls out, his voice sailing into the muted atmosphere like a clarion call.

"I need a courier! Someone to carry an urgent message!"

Before I have a moment to doubt the wisdom of my actions, I answer, "Here, sir! I will take the message!" I march forward to Eugène, wondering if he will recognize me.

Eugène's face has lost all trace of softness and kindness, and he drills me with his eyes, his teeth gritted. He holds out a folded piece of paper to me. I grasp it, but he does not let go. "This is a confidential assignment, soldier. I must tell you the address in private."

He doesn't know who I am!

He leads me around the corner of a building, where we are out of sight of the others, who in any case are still concentrating on what is happening inside the château.

Eugène removes his cockaded hat and expels a long breath. His expression changes, as if he has removed a mask. "Look, good fellow, I'm in a bit of a bind here. This business is going to take all day, and I have an important appointment—"

Something about the way he is speaking makes me decide I had better interrupt him, let him know who I am. I fear a confidence that I won't want to keep. "Eugène," I say, making no attempt to disguise my voice and touching the sleeve of his blue jacket.

He stops, his lips parted, brow creased, and peers at me. "What the . . . ?"

I can feel myself going crimson with embarrassment. "I'm sorry. It's a long story, it's—"

"Mademoiselle Monroe? What is the meaning of this subterfuge?"

For a moment I hesitate. I was Eliza to him two days ago. I suddenly feel very small, very stupid. I don't know how much to tell him, or even whether any of it matters. "We—that is, Caroline, Hortense, and I—"

"My sister? Is she here?" He grips my shoulders hard. He is angry.

"Please! It was Caroline's idea."

"*Sacré coeur!*" Eugène mutters. "Well, I suppose you had better tell me what this is about. But quickly! I'm expected back at any moment."

I recount our adventure in as few words as I can muster, barely pausing for breath.

"Where are they now?"

"Caroline went forward, to try to get inside so she could see what was happening. Hortense...I'm afraid I don't know. She was waiting at the back. And—" I am about to mention Valmont, but something stops me.

Eugène looks up at nothing in particular, tapping the almost forgotten note against his gloved palm. "What will happen to you, do you suppose, if this ruse is discovered?" he asks.

I hadn't really thought about the possibility that we would be found out, only trusting that Caroline and Hortense wouldn't let me come to any harm. "I suppose...I will be expelled from school and sent home to Virginia."

"Would you like that to happen?"

I want to say, *And never see you again? Never watch how gracefully you move and see the depths in your eyes?* But I can see that Eugène does not think of me as an object of love. At least, not yet, not now. "No, I would much rather stay here." I cannot meet his gaze. Shame over being so foolish suddenly overwhelms me.

"Then you must do as I say. Take this note—" He hands it to me, letting me keep it this time. "Take this message to Mademoiselle Madeleine de Pourtant, at the Comédie Française, and make sure you tell her it comes with my most sincere compliments."

Madeleine de Pourtant. The Comédie Française. Who else could it be? I am to take a secret message to his mistress. To the woman Joséphine objects to so strongly, the cause of much family strife at Malmaison. What if she finds out? After all I witnessed the other day, I have no doubt that Joséphine could be a more formidable enemy than Napoléon himself, if she chooses to be. Yet how can I say no to Eugène?

"All right," I say. "But how shall I get there?"

"You can ride, I presume?" Now he smiles.

I return the smile. "Ever since I was a tiny tot."

"Let's go find you a horse."

He marches off and I follow in the direction of the palace stables.

The stable boy is sweeping bits of straw around, clearly avoiding other work. If he'd been one of our slaves I would have told Papa. Most slave owners would have him whipped, but Papa is too kind, Mama says.

"A horse for the soldier, and be quick about it!" Eugène commands.

"There's only the old gelding left," the boy says. "The other soldier took the mare."

Eugène and I exchange a glance, and in that moment we both suspect who the "other soldier" was. But there isn't time to consider why Hortense would have taken a horse.

"It will do," Eugène says, softening his angry edge by tossing the boy a coin.

In no time I find myself seated atop a swaybacked bay gelding whose head hangs down as though he has no more interest in leaving his comfortable stall than climbing to the moon. "I'll need a crop," I say. The boy fetches one with two strands of knotted leather at the end.

"Follow the main road until you get to the crossroads. There will be a sign to Paris. At the gates, simply say you are on Napoléon's business. They won't question you." Eugène gives me the instructions as he checks to make sure the saddle is secure.

"What shall I do when I'm finished?"

"Ride the horse back here, if he's still alive. I'll make sure you are returned to school without anyone knowing what you've done."

For just a moment he covers my hand with his. I bend forward, not really knowing what I expect.

He kisses me, lightly, on the lips. I do not move away from him, but reach closer. Our lips touch again. I feel the soft warmth of his mouth and close my eyes. For just a moment, he returns my kiss.

Then abruptly, he pulls away and gently but firmly pushes me upright upon the saddle. "Thank you, Eliza," he says, his eyes full of gratitude, and perhaps something else. Then he steps back, tips his hat to me, and slaps the horse's rump to get him going.

34

Madeleine

I don't know how much time has passed since I shut myself in my attic room. I am surprised that my mother has not come with an ax to break down the door. Marianne must have done a great deal to keep her at bay. Marianne, and the opium.

If my mother were awake, no doubt she would be ranting, calling for me, demanding that I come and help her. She is doubtless still sleeping off her drug-induced dreams. Once she awakens, she will commence her torments, and I will have to leave this place.

How differently I thought this day would go! I shouldn't be here anymore. I feel like an in-between creature, not real, not imaginary. Half white, half black. Part educated, part ignorant. I am not whole, I am in pieces, and if I sit here long enough I will disappear.

"*Pssst.* Madeleine!"

The voice is quiet, but it pierces my awareness. It's Marianne. What has she come to tell me? I open my mouth to try to speak, but all that emerges is another strangled sob.

"I have heard something. Something that may explain why he is not here."

There can be no explanation. He promised. But I listen anyway.

"The Directoire and the Council of Five Hundred have fled to Saint-Cloud—supposedly for their protection. But a courier came by the theater and said that the army was there, waiting for them. It seems that several of the actresses expected callers who wouldn't be able to make it today."

I try to still my weeping. "Th-the army? Why?"

"The government is falling. They are getting rid of the Directoire. They say Bonaparte will be in charge one way or the other."

It would have to be something that important, I think, *to make Eugène break his promise to me.* "So, what happens next?" For me, hope blossoms again. Perhaps he is not faithless after all.

"No one knows. But you see, Beauharnais has not broken faith with you!"

I am silent. Whatever the reason for his absence, the fact remains that I am still here, and now my mother, who surely has discovered that I had plans to run away, will make it impossible to go. "Why could he not send word himself?" I say, the heavy feeling pressing down on my chest again all the harder for the momentary relief I felt.

"Where is that wretch!"

My mother. She has awakened.

"I—I don't know, madame," Marianne answers. But she is not a good liar.

"She's up there, isn't she? Hiding!" My mother's voice somehow manages to be harsh and slurred at the same time.

I hear her angry footsteps below and she mounts the ladder to the locked hatch into my sanctuary, pounding and pounding on it until my ears want to pop open. "Trollop! Minx! *Putain!* You thought you could get away, didn't you? I'll send for the director. He will get a carpenter. You'll have to come out, and then you'll feel the imprint of my anger!"

I must keep away from her! But how! If she beats me, I will have bruises.

"Madame, you must not exert yourself. You perform this evening. Let me massage your shoulders. . . ."

Dear Marianne. She knows better than anyone how to placate my mother when she is in such a state. I wish I could do something for her. I don't know why she has taken my side so completely.

However she manages it, Marianne succeeds in leading my mother down the ladder and toward her dressing room. The banging and shouting cease, and I am again free to close my eyes and imagine Eugène coming for me. I hear the pounding of his horse's hooves, see the smile on his face as he rides up to the theater, carrying a warm cloak to throw around me. He strides in. No one dares stop him! Right past my mother, whom he pushes aside to reach me. I open the door and fall into his arms. He sweeps me off my feet and carries me down the stairs, past Gric, who stares and drools. I am gone! Away from here! To a new life . . .

"Madeleine—someone is here. With a message!"

Am I still dreaming? No; it's Marianne. "Find out who it is!"

She runs off. I hear my mother somewhere below, laughing.

35

Hortense

I know I have arrived at the correct house when I hear scales on a pianoforte, interrupted every now and then with a flourish of an arpeggio. A maid opens the door to my knock and looks startled at seeing me. For a moment I have forgotten my disguise in the anticipation of seeing my love.

"Is Monsieur Michel Perroquet at home?" I ask, trying to be gentle and carry authority at the same time.

She curtsies as she opens the door wide and lets me step into a small, tidy vestibule. She has been taught well, I see. And I see as well that the house is commodious enough to welcome prestigious students.

"Who shall I say is calling?" she asks.

She reaches for my hat. The jolting of the ride has loosened the pins that held my hair in place, and when I remove my tricorn, it unleashes my long blond hair and sends it cascading over my shoulders. She takes a step backward, her eyes round and frightened. I smile to reassure her. It is too late for subterfuge now. "Just tell him a friend awaits, who received his letter and is ready to do his bidding."

Understandably, the poor woman is beyond speech. She scampers into the room where the music is coming from.

The scales cease as soon as the maid enters. I hear firm, rapid footsteps cross the floor to the door, and in a moment it is flung wide. There is Michel.

I want to throw myself into his arms, to let him take the matter where it must go from here. But his expression—his eyes brim with tears and yet he appears nervous, uncertain. He turns his head just slightly in the direction of the room behind him, and I see beyond to the figure of an attractive young lady seated at the pianoforte.

The maid hangs back, no doubt waiting to see what will happen next.

"Did you not receive my letter? I explained everything in it."

It is as I feared. The letter Caroline stole contained vital information that might have made me act differently. "I received it, but it was . . . mislaid . . . before I could finish reading it."

"Corinne, take Mademoiselle Hortense up to my sister's room so that she may refresh herself." He must sense my confusion. I am a contradiction. A freak. A stupid, stupid girl.

I manage to hold myself together all the way up the

narrow stair until after Corinne closes the door behind her and I find myself in a small but pretty bedchamber. Unable to do otherwise, I throw myself upon the carefully made bed and let myself sob into a stranger's pillow.

I don't know how much time has passed, but my tears have ceased. I hear a gentle knock upon the door. *"Entrez!"* I call out, hoping I do not sound as though I have been weeping.

The young lady I saw at the piano enters the room, closing the door behind her. "My brother has told me a little about you."

She approaches and sits on the edge of the bed. "I am sorry to have intruded upon your household," I say. "I had no idea Michel had a sister." And, I must confess, I am very relieved to discover it. My imagination leaped immediately to the conclusion that the lady I saw at the pianoforte must have been his love, his true love, and that he must have written to tell me he had been mistaken about me after all. Curse Caroline for stealing that letter!

"Michel is very distressed. I can hardly console him enough for him to tell me the entire story. Perhaps you could enlighten me as to why such a famous young lady as yourself, Hortense de Beauharnais, stepdaughter to our country's greatest general, has arrived at our door, dressed in such unconventional garb."

I can't quite discern what she thinks about me. She has sympathetic eyes, but she does not smile. "You have the advantage of me," I say. "You know my name, but I do not know yours." I am reluctant to unburden myself to Michel's sister, who is after all a stranger to me. And I know how protective sisters can be of an only brother.

"Forgive me, of course. I am Louise Perroquet. There are only three of us, with Papa. Our mother died when we were both children."

"I'm sorry," I say, a little ashamed that I know so little of this man I love, who I am ready to elope with this very minute if he will have me. "I believe I may have misinterpreted something. Your brother and I . . . we love each other. But he sent me a letter through your father, and I began to read it, but was interrupted. The letter vanished before I could form anything but a vague impression of what it said."

I don't want to tell her more. I still don't know how she feels about Michel and me.

"It is unlike my brother to enter into a secret correspondence. Still more strange that my father would have permitted it. I wonder why it is that my brother has not mentioned you to me before today. We share all our secrets. He is devoted to the family." Her eyes shine with pride. I realize then that she considers me an enemy, a rival, someone capable of undermining the security and safety of their family. I understand how that feels: not wanting anyone to upset a fragile balance of affection. "Such an omission would indicate that perhaps you *have* misinterpreted his intentions."

The words hit me like a slap. *No!* In the times we have

been together I cannot have mistaken his feelings. Something else is going on; I know it. I can say no more to Louise. "Where is Michel? I must speak with him."

"He has left the house to give a music lesson to the daughter of a wealthy merchant. She is a dear friend of mine, and I have long cherished the hope that she would one day be my sister."

Clearly, Louise will do everything in her power to obstruct Michel's and my love for each other. "I must return to the Académie. I fear I . . ." I look down at my uniform, now splotched where my tears have fallen.

"Please select one of my gowns to wear. Corinne will help you do your hair. I'm sorry not to invite you to stay for a dish of tea, but I have calls to make." She stands. She is very pretty, but there is an edge of sadness around her eyes. She curtsies, no more than a dip, says, "Good-bye, Mademoiselle de Beauharnais," and turns away from me.

"I must know something before you leave," I say.

She stops and looks over her shoulder at me, not willing to interrupt herself for more than a moment. "Yes?"

"We have never met before, so how can you dislike me so?"

She takes a deep breath before speaking. "With a father and a brother who are both musicians, it is left to me to take care of the practical matters of the household. I know what kind of woman my brother must wed to ensure his happiness and the security of my father and myself. And that is not someone like you."

"How can you know what I am like?"

She flares her nostrils. I can see she wishes she could say what is in her heart, but will hold something back, out of respect for her brother's feelings. "One need only reflect upon your mother's life, her blatant disregard for economy and desire to be admired by all men, to have a sense of what a man like my brother might suffer at your hands."

She turns and walks away quickly before I can say another word.

36

I am quite astonished at the freedom of traveling dressed as a man, and on horseback as well. At first when I started to gallop away from Eugène, I felt exposed, almost naked. Sitting like that atop a horse, my legs free to move without skirts clinging to them, seems almost indecent. That and the lingering memory of Eugène's kiss combine so that I am no longer certain who I am. Am I a young American girl on an adventure? Or a boy soldier who has just witnessed the making of history? Am I a foolish young lady with hopeless dreams? Or did I just receive my first real kiss from someone I love?

The events of the morning have become more and more unreal as I ride, yet I became more and more accustomed to sitting astride. I stopped wondering, after a bit, where Hortense had gotten to, and what happened with Caroline and Valmont. Everyone I pass takes it as a matter of course that a young soldier would be riding a horse on the highway to Paris, looking as though he is on some urgent business or other.

Even the sentry at the city gate did not question me further when, as Eugène suggested, I said I was on Bonaparte's business.

Now I find myself walking my tired mount through the streets. He hangs his head, foam dripping from the corners of his mouth near the bit. Poor beast. Before I deliver Eugène's message I must find a place to give him water and food. The actress can wait.

I see a stable and deposit my horse there with a groom, tossing him a coin and telling him I will return. I find my way to the nearest fiacre stand, climb like a schoolboy into the first empty one I find, and ask the driver to take me to the Comédie Française.

He cracks his whip above the horse's flanks, and we trot off for about a minute, if that. Then he stops.

I look out the window and call up to him. "*Qu'est-ce que c'est?*" I ask, now irritated at the fellow.

"*Ici la Comédie Française,*" he says with a mischievous shrug, pointing to the building to our left, with its columns along the facade and an alley beside it.

My face burns. How was I to know I was close enough to walk here? My mother and I took carriages everywhere when we were in Paris together, so I have no idea what is where.

I step down and fish in my pocket for a coin, but the fiacre driver, perhaps thinking he's taking pity on a green young man going to pay court to an actress he admired when he was among his comrades, waves me off and walks his fiacre forward, where it's quickly engaged by someone else.

Brushing some dust off my sleeve, I go toward a door where I see men entering, most clutching bouquets of flowers. I assume because it's easy for them, it will be easy for me to get in.

At first, all is well. The door is not locked, and I step through it into a dim interior that smells of perfume and sweat.

"What do you want, soldier?" says an old man in drab clothing who is seated just inside. He sticks a leg out to prevent me from climbing the stairs.

"I have come with a message for Madeleine de Pourtant," I say, mustering all the authority I can.

He looks me up and down, an expression on his face I can describe only as disdain. What disdain! No one has ever glared at me like that! "Mademoiselle de Pourtant is not receiving visitors." He points to the door I came through.

"My message is most urgent," I say. I ought to be glad not to be able to deliver Eugène's words of love to his mistress, but I am furious at being treated like this by a mere servant. I will not be denied. "I am under strictest orders by my officer to see that she gets it."

"I'll take it to her," he says, reaching out his hand and grinning, revealing several gaps where teeth should be.

I don't know what to say to this, and am about to protest, when a head peeks through the door at the top of the stairs. "*Alors*, Gric, what is all this fuss? Has Adèle's gentleman arrived yet?"

"Only this little cub here who insists he has a message for Madeleine."

The lady steps through and gasps. "Come up quickly, young man! She is waiting most anxiously."

I can't resist looking down my nose at the surly Gric as I pass him and take the stairs two at a time.

The lady who saved me grabs my hand and pulls me through a maze of corridors. I hear snatches of voices practicing songs, the beat of a cane against the floor as dancers rehearse, and a deep male voice declaiming some lines I recognize—from a play by Molière my mother and I saw together before she left. It's as if the magical world one sees on a stage has been shaken together and tossed on a table like dice.

Before I know it we have entered a room so chaotic and colorful I don't know where to look. Candles burn even at this time of day, before mirrors that reflect their points of light and make everything glow. Heaps of gowns in vibrant colors hang from hooks and strew the floor. Before each mirror are pots of white lead, red lip stain, lapis blue powder for around the eyes. A lady looks up at me with half her face painted and the sight frightens me. The contrast between the white of the lead makes the other half of her face appear dark as night. She laughs. There is something familiar about her.

"Is Madeleine still up there?" my guide asks, ignoring her.

The half-painted lady sucks on the end of a pipe and blows out a plume of aromatic blue smoke before answering. "Yes. Crying. I'll show her why she should cry soon enough!" She jerks her head toward the ceiling.

Suddenly I recognize this lady. She is the very same one Caroline and I saw at the masked ball! The one who tried to engage with Eugène, but was spurned by him. Swathed in dirty robes, her face so strangely made up, she looks like a different creature.

I make a move to leave the dressing room and seek out Madeleine, but the lady at the dressing table stops laughing and leaps to her feet, grabbing my arm. Her eyes roam over my entire body. I swear it feels as if I am meat hanging in a butcher's shop and she's looking for the most succulent bit to have sliced off. "What's your name, lad?" she asks, her voice now sweeter than I would have imagined possible.

"Madeleine! Madeleine! The messenger is here! You must come down!" I hear my guide outside in the corridor.

I want to listen for a reply, but my attention is dragged away again by the half-painted woman. "I asked you a question. It's impolite not to answer. I am Gloriande," she says, blinking rapidly in a coquettish gesture and putting out her hand to be kissed. I cannot ignore this gesture, so I take her hand. I notice it is well veined, that of someone much older than her face appears.

I bow over the hand, not intending to actually kiss it and hoping my trembling from the strain of keeping up my disguise isn't too obvious. But who am I? How can I answer her question? I never planned on having to give a name! I seize upon the first man's name I can think of. "Émile," I say. "Émile Gouin at your service." I hope I'll be able to remember what I've told her in case I need to repeat it.

"How old are you, Émile?"

I realize I am very small and there is no trace of a beard on my face. She must believe I'm just a boy and is trying to embarrass me. If only she realized how wrong she was!

But I am saved. A sound draws our attention to the door of the dressing room, where I see a girl standing, a defiant look on her face. She appears not much older than my fellow Blues at school. Her eyes—a beautiful deep brown, impossibly large and rimmed by long, dark lashes—are red and swollen from crying, and her hair is disheveled. This must be Madeleine, the object of Eugène's love. I am surprised, and somehow touched.

"Marianne says y-you have a m-message for me." She is hiccuping still. She must have been crying for hours. I am frozen in place. She reaches her hand out to me, and I quickly find the folded and sealed paper Eugène gave me. I walk to her and give her the note.

Suddenly she takes my shoulders and plants two wet

kisses on my cheeks—wet mostly because of the tears still streaking her face. "I'm to wait for a reply," I say. Seeing how sad she is makes me want to cry, too.

Madeleine tears open the seal and unfolds the letter, her eyes burning into the page as she reads as if her life depends on it. When she gets to the end, she sinks like a wilted flower to the ground and presses the letter to her chest.

"Are you ill?" I ask.

"Yes, she's sick. Sick to death!" Gloriande's voice is harsh once more. "She has conspired against me. She wants to leave the theater, she says. Why? Because of her precious Eugène, whose mother spends so much money on herself she can give him none of his own for presents that he might shower upon Madeleine."

"Maman, tais-toi!" I'm shocked to hear Madeleine address this woman as her mother.

It's almost impossible to believe that this dark, deep-voiced creature is the mother of the woman Eugène loves. I cannot help myself. My mouth drops open.

The older lady gives a snort of laughter. "I can read, can't I?" She fishes in the pocket of her gown and pulls out a filthy scrap of paper.

"Ma chère Madeleine. Words cannot convey my feelings for you. I hope to carry you away soon, but first I must satisfy your mother's carnal wants...." She is not reading, I realize, but making up the words.

"How dare you! You don't know what he says—you

can't read!" Madeleine leaps toward her mother, but Marianne stops her.

In an instant Gloriande is on her feet. She raises her hand and slaps Madeleine hard, leaving a red handprint on her cheek.

Without thinking, I step between mother and daughter. Marianne has shrunk back out of the way. I don't blame her; I'm not certain myself what will happen next.

Something shifts inside me. All at once I realize that Eugène has not been ensnared by a scheming actress, but genuinely loves this young girl who, I imagine, has been thrust upon the stage for her mother's sake. I feel the horrible difference between her situation and mine, and I want to help her. I must think fast.

"Stand away, Gloriande," I say, feeling brash to address a woman my mother's age by her first name. "Madeleine is coming with me."

I feel Madeleine's delicate hands grasp my shoulders and she breathes into my ear. "I cannot! She will send them after me. But thank you."

"We are going to leave now, and Madeleine will not return." I say it as if I can really make such a thing happen. I wonder, briefly, if the courage comes with the uniform.

Before I realize what is happening, I feel Marianne press something into my hand. It is a dagger. I hold it out menacingly toward Gloriande, who takes a step back.

I reach back with my other hand and grasp Madeleine's

hand firmly. Keeping her behind me, I make us back away from Gloriande. When we reach the door, we turn and run. It is my turn to lead someone quickly through the maze of corridors above the Comédie Française.

Once she realizes I am serious, Madeleine does not resist, but helps me find a different way out that will avoid the nasty gatekeeper, Gric.

Soon we are out on an unpaved Paris street. Madeleine throws her arms around me and says, *"Merci, merci, merci!"* planting kisses on my face between each word.

I gently push her away from me, holding her off so I can look in her face. "I am not who I seem," I say, "but you can trust me."

"Where will we go? Where is Eugène?" she asks.

"We'll go to Saint-Germain-en-Laye," I say, knowing I must return to school. "Eugène is still at Saint-Cloud."

The excitement fades from her eyes. "So it was true. About the coup. But his mother, Joséphine. How will we ever...?"

"I don't know. But we can't stay here. I'll tell you the rest on the way."

I decide it's best for us to go in a closed carriage rather than try to make the broken-down horse bear the weight of two. Soon we are on our way back to Madame Campan's. I have no idea how I shall explain what I have done, who Madeleine is. What is more, I have no idea where Caroline, Valmont, and Hortense have gotten to by now.

We sit in silence part of the way. Once the gates of Paris

are behind us, Madeleine turns to me. "You're a girl, aren't you?"

I nod, thinking I may as well start the tale then, but she puts her hand on my arm to stop me.

"And you're in love with Eugène."

Now it is my turn to weep. Madeleine comforts me the rest of the way to Saint-Germain.

37

As I put the finishing touches on my retransformation into a young lady who attends Madame Campan's school, I still feel the sting of Louise's comments about my mother.

There is some truth to what she says, and yet... Louise—like the rest of the world, it seems—does not know the full horror of everything my mother has been through. Maman clings to luxury as a way to stave off want, and she does it not for herself but for us, for me and Eugène. I know this. I see it with my soul.

And yet... Surely we would be as happy if she could simply have wed any of the soldiers or merchants who have fallen in love with her? We could live in peace and security, and Eugène and I could both marry whom we want, rather than have to live up to her idea of who is worthy of us.

A timid knock at the door. *"Entrez."*

It is Corinne, the maid, come to see if I need help with my hair. I decline politely and descend to the front door.

The house is clean and simple, but not without its touches of luxury. A painting hangs on the wall of the vestibule, a pastoral scene. A shepherdess brings a basket of fruit to a shepherd. I can tell by the light that it is evening, implying that the two are lovers. For a moment I imagine the pair is Michel and me, and soon my view is misted over with tears I must try to hold back.

"Shall I summon a fiacre?" asks Corinne.

"No. It is not far. I prefer to walk."

Besides, I have to find a way to return the mare I arrived on to the barracks at Saint-Cloud.

The boy I asked to tend her is still standing across the street, a small circle of younger children clustered admiringly by. He allows them to pat the gentle creature's nose in a constant rotation. A natural leader, I think. *May he never rise to greatness, and know the unhappiness that goes with it.*

As I approach him, he looks up and I see dawning confusion on his face. He recognizes me but sees I am not the soldier who engaged him to undertake the task. As soon as I am close enough, I open my mouth to begin my explanation.

But I am stopped when Michel suddenly steps out from behind the mare. "I'll manage from here," he says to the young lad, giving him a few *centimes* for his trouble. "Run along, all of you."

Michel may be the son of the music master, the fop my

makeshift groom made such fun of, but he speaks with authority. Reluctantly, they scatter, the more curious among them going not too far away.

"Shall we walk together a little?" Michel says.

I am too overcome with sorrow to do anything but nod.

"You must understand that my feelings for you are no different than I expressed before. I am sorry if my foolish actions have caused you any pain." A trace of a smile plays at the corners of his mouth. "My sister is a very determined person. She has managed our household since Mother died five years ago, and will not give up her position lightly."

We are walking so slowly that the horse has time to snatch at bits of grass growing between the cobbles on these quiet streets. "I am not certain exactly what you mean, monsieur," I say.

Something about the way Michel speaks annoys me. He does not appear crushed, defeated, the way I felt after everything Louise said. How I wish I had that note!

"I mean, foolish Hortense, that simply because Louise says it must not be so is no reason to give up hope."

"For me to give up hope, or for us?" I ask. Suddenly I feel as if he has taken the position of a typical man to whom the pursuit is everything. Now that I have shown myself willing to act in the most desperate manner to be with him, he has power over me. I shudder. I am behaving exactly like my mother.

He turns toward me and we stop walking. "How much

of my letter did you read? You must have read some of it, because I cannot imagine what else would have brought you here. I meant to counsel patience. I wanted to introduce you to my sister tomorrow, at our soirée."

Patience? Was it simply a written invitation for an innocent evening? Now Michel is implying that I've ruined everything. What good is patience in our circumstances? "I have exercised patience all my life," I say. "I learned it at the feet of two very cruel masters, whose names are prison and threat of death." I spit the words at him.

Michel looks down at his feet, kicking at a loose stone. After a long silence, he speaks. "I am not free simply to run away and wed. My family depends upon the income from my students as much as from my father's. I could not establish my own household. Not yet."

I want to scream to the heavens. *Money!* Why must it govern everything? I was so certain my affection was returned, that our passion was pure. But once more, money is a barrier to love.

Something digs its claws into my heart and I cannot help what I say next. "You believe I came to throw myself at your feet. But that is not true. I came because I had to tell you something before you heard it by general report."

I start walking again, keeping myself just a little ahead of him.

"Such an elaborate plan simply to tell me something?" He smiles. It's not an unkind smile, and I can see the love behind it, but still it vexes me. "I must admit, you were quite fetching in your uniform—"

"I am to be wed, but not to you." I blurt it out, interrupting his pretty speech.

The color drains from Michel's face. Instantly I want to swallow the words back in, but I cannot. And besides, in the eyes of my mother at least, they are true.

He gulps once. "I see. Why did you not tell me your affections lay elsewhere? That is a cruel joke to play upon me."

How I wish we were not standing in the middle of the street, no doubt watched closely by prying eyes from most of the windows. "It's not a joke. Or if it is, the joke is not on you, but on me." I reach out and touch Michel's cheek softly. "It is my mother's wish. She has arranged it."

"And you?"

It's my turn to look down. I don't know what to say. I am no longer absolutely certain of Michel's love, and now I am ashamed of my actions today. "I had better return to school. The mare came from the barracks at Saint-Cloud. Can you take her back? Say that a messenger from Louis Bonaparte borrowed her and asked that you ensure her safe return."

That's as much as I can say. Nothing has been decided or settled for me yet. I have placed everything back in his hands now. If he truly wants me, he must decide.

"Will you still come to Father's soirée and sing?" he asks. For a moment I cannot imagine what he is talking about.

Then I remember. Monsieur Perroquet's invitation. "I think that would be unwise," I say.

The look on his face stabs my heart.

Michel bows and kisses my hand, then leads the mare away. I continue to the school, wondering if I shall find Eliza and Caroline already there.

38

Madeleine

If I could have died from weeping this morning, I would have. I did not want to face a future in that depraved theater, fetching drugs for my mother and avoiding beatings, living half starved and unhappy.

And now, here I am, rescued. But not by Eugène. How curious indeed that my savior should be a girl with a foreign accent, dressed like a soldier. She has told me little, other than that she knows about my love for Eugène. And I can see that she acts not for my sake, but because she cares about his happiness. She is in love with him, in her way, although I think she is very young.

"I have never been so far from Paris," I say. "At least, not since I first came here when I was a small child." I want her to speak; I want to know who she is, why she has taken such a risk for Eugène's sake and mine. "Where are we going? To Malmaison?" I only know that it is west of Paris, and that is the direction we are headed.

"We go to Saint-Germain. I am at school there."

"Ah, at the Académie Nationale. Madame Campan's establishment."

"You know it?" She seems very surprised. But, then, I suppose a lowly actress would not be expected to know of such a genteel institution as that.

"I have heard of it. Some of my mother's... friends... have spoken of it as a place where they send their daughters to become true ladies. What is it like there?"

She thinks for a moment, then looks at me, curiosity in her eyes. "You ask me about my school, but not why I happen to be wearing a soldier's uniform in the middle of a day when I should be attending lessons."

"Would it be more normal to be wearing it in the evening?" I ask.

"That's not what I meant," she says, but I see I have made her smile.

Then I think to say, "Well, I suppose you might be dressed like this if you were going to a masked ball."

"I have only ever been to one ball, and no one knew I was there," she says. "I saw your mother before I knew who she was, though. And Eugène, too."

What can she mean? I decide not to question her about it—I laugh instead. "You sound a little like me. I was at a ball once, too. Only not as a guest. My mother blacked my face and put me in an exotic uniform, made me carry a feather fan behind her. She was dressed as though she had just left a pasha's harem, and I was her little slave boy."

Now her smile turns into a laugh. It makes me realize how young she must be. Her feelings for Eugène must be naive. I doubt he has kissed her.

Not as he has kissed me. All at once I can hardly catch my breath at the thought of his arms around me, our lips touching first, then tongues. I took him to the room below the stage, where trapdoors let actors down when they disappear as if by magic. It was the only place I knew no one would watch us after the performance was over.

"Ginger," I say aloud, remembering the moment.

"What?" The girl is confused.

"Oh! I was just thinking of my favorite scent," I say, hoping she does not notice my blush. What really went through my mind was the taste of Eugène's kiss. He must have eaten a sweet before coming backstage to find me.

"We'll be there soon," she says, casting a worried glance out the carriage window.

"Did anyone follow us?" I ask.

"I don't think so. The army is at Saint-Cloud. There were no soldiers or guards near the theater."

Eugène mentioned Saint-Cloud in his letter, and Marianne told me the government had been taken there.... "What is happening today?"

"The government is changing. I saw Napoléon and the

generals overtake the Directoire and the Council of Five Hundred. And Caroline—"

"Who is Caroline?" This girl intrigues me.

"Again you ask the strangest things! Not 'How did a few men managed to vanquish five hundred?' but 'Who is Caroline?' Caroline is—"

She stops herself.

"Is she your friend?" I ask. "Is she the one who persuaded you to dress like this?"

"No one persuaded me!" She is angrier than the question warrants, which makes me feel I have hit upon something. "I chose to participate in a grand adventure. Besides, if I hadn't, where would you be?"

Where indeed? What she does not know is that despite her bold gesture, I will undoubtedly end up back at the Comédie Française, where I'll be greeted with a beating that will keep me in my room for a week. Unless Eugène is waiting for us in Saint-Germain. . . .

"Will Eugène meet us?" I ask.

"No. We've reached the village. We must walk from here."

She knocks on the carriage roof so the driver will stop, and pays him—from a very well-stocked pocketful of coins, I notice. The flash of gold catches my eye. Perhaps even without Eugène I can release myself from perpetual slavery on the stage.

And yet, I know the thought is unworthy. I decide I must trust this girl a while longer, Eugène or no Eugène.

My life has been full of unfortunate accidents so far. May-hap it is time things combined in my favor at last.

She stops in the middle of a street, clearly undecided about what to do. "I cannot return to school dressed like this," she says. "I shall have to send word for my clothes."

A fine drizzle has started to fall, the kind that feels wel-come on a hot summer's day but that stings like tiny needles on a cold autumn day like this.

"Let's see if we can get inside the château," my new friend says.

Together we walk to it, not far from where we descended from the fiacre. But the few doors we try are locked, and it won't do to look as though we are seeking a hiding place—especially in a deserted château.

"There's shelter here," I say, pointing to a deep porch that shields the door to what looks like a chapel.

It's dry but still cold. I do my best to smile at the girl. One way or the other she will be my salvation. Best to make her believe she is also my friend.

39

The château of Saint-Germain is deserted. No one lives here anymore. I try several doors but none are open.

"Here's a dry place," Madeleine says, pointing to a covered porch where we can be sheltered from the light rain that has started to fall.

Madeleine shivers. "You cannot know what you have done. But I am grateful. Perhaps now is the time to ask how you come to be dressed in this manner."

I don't really want to tell her my story. It seems so unimportant compared to hers. "That explanation must now wait. I should get word to the others. Stay here."

"What others?" she asks.

"Caroline Bonaparte, sister to Napoléon, and Hortense de Beauharnais, sister to Eugène." Something makes me resist telling her that there was a fourth, a young man.

She opens her mouth to speak, but closes it again.

Across the street is a ribbon vendor. I buy a length of purple silk from him and ask to borrow a scrap of paper and something to write with. All he has is a bit of chalk, so I make the message brief. Hortense and Caroline must help me. I pray they, too, have found their way back to Saint-Germain. I don't know what I shall do if I must remain out here with Madeleine all night.

I send a young boy to the school, telling him to ask for Ernestine; then I return to find Madeleine humming to herself, very quietly, but I can hear that she must have a beautiful voice. Having walked away from her and seen her from a distance, now I cannot help noticing how very thin she is. Her wrist is like a bird's. "How old are you?" I ask.

"Sixteen," she says, which surprises me. I am much bigger than she is, and two years younger.

"You are so frail."

"Maman . . . I play the orphans in the theater, and I must look like a child. But I am not."

I cannot help thinking that she would be extraordinarily beautiful if she had some flesh on her bones. "How did you and your mother come to be in the theater?" I ask, looking for a way to pass the time. The damp is icy, and Madeleine shivers like a birch leaf. "Here." I take off my uniform coat and give it to her. Even without it, I don't feel the cold as she does.

"Maman and I came here with the Vicomte de Pourtant.

He found her in the islands, when he was there tending to his interests in sugarcane. I was born there."

Madeleine stops, as if she has told me enough. But I want to know more. "He did not marry your mother?"

Her large eyes open wider than ever, and it seems almost as if she will laugh. I don't know what I said that was so funny.

"So he claims, although my mother says otherwise. *Vicomtes* do not marry their slaves! Even when they are all freed by decree. And even when the *vicomte* has fathered a girl child," Madeleine says and then laughs, the notes of her mirth tumbling about like tiny silver bells.

The realization hits me as hard as the slap Madeleine received earlier. Gloriande is a Negro slave—or was! And Madeleine is the daughter of the liaison between a *vicomte* and his slave. Whether or not her mother and Pourtant were ever married, she is a mulatto. A half-breed.

I have taken someone who might be working in the fields in Virginia into my protection. I have befriended someone who should be a slave herself.

What can I do? I cannot turn her away, tell her to go back to her cruel mother and her half-starved state at the Comédie Française. She is a girl like me.

Only not like me!

"Ah, you did not realize . . . ," she says, calmly now. "You speak with an accent. Where are you from? I don't even know your name."

"I am Eliza Monroe, daughter of a man who will soon be a member of the government of the United States of America. We have a plantation in Virginia, with many slaves to work the land and serve in our house. I am here attending school so that I may acquire the polish of a French lady."

Madeleine is silent. I wish she would turn her enormous eyes away! Her skin has the palest tint of light caramel. Why didn't I see it before?

"Mademoiselle Eliza, you need not protect me any longer. I have survived so far, and will make my own way. I may look delicate, but I am very strong. Thank you for what you have tried to do."

She removes my blue jacket and hands it to me. I take it without thinking, dazed. She steps out into the rain, which has become heavier. Already I see her slender shoulders outlined by the thin fabric of her dress, which soaks through quickly even though it is just drizzling. And her slippers—made of cloth and suitable only for stepping on the boards of a stage, not sloshing through muddy streets—are completely drenched.

"Wait!" I call out.

She turns her head only, casting me a sad glance over her shoulder, but my voice has stopped her progress.

"You must stay. Nothing can undo what I have done. Please let me help you."

She smiles. Her teeth are very white against her skin. Soon she is back underneath the porch with my jacket warming her again. *What if,* I think, *all our slaves are like this? The same as we are?* They don't look as much like us as Madeleine does. But in her past are those who must have been every bit as black as the foreman on our plantation.

My thoughts are swirling and confused. Since I was tiny I have thought of people with black skin as less than we are, as property. I was taught not to be cruel to them, as one might be taught not to be cruel to a pet. I never imagined our slaves could be the same as I am, with the same feelings and ideas. And yet here is Madeleine, whom I would never have guessed had Negro blood in her veins, and not only is she like me, she is in love with someone I thought I was in love with. What is more, he loves her in return. If he—the noble Eugène de Beauharnais—does not think she is unworthy because of her ancestry, what right have I to think so?

Madeleine is dear to Eugène. And so she must be dear to me.

My note brings help, but not in the form I wished for. I don't know what to say when I see not Hortense and Caroline, but Hortense and Valmont appear from around the corner that leads toward the Académie and the Collège.

"You must be Madeleine, if I am not mistaken," Hortense says, stepping ahead of Valmont. I wonder how she can know. I said nothing about it in my note.

"Yes," Madeleine answers. "I am the one who might spoil all your mother's wishes for your brother." Madeleine's eyes flash. How does she know it is Hortense? Can she have seen her before? Or perhaps she just recognizes her because of Joséphine, or a family resemblance with Eugène.

Hortense reaches her arms out to Madeleine. "I want only my brother's happiness."

After a moment's hesitation, Madeleine rushes forward into Hortense's embrace.

Valmont approaches me. "This is all very touching," he says, "but you look cold." He starts to unbutton his own coat to give to me, but Hortense stops him.

"I have brought her clothes, including a warm cloak," she says, handing me the basket she was carrying. I glance around. How can I change? I look at Valmont and blush. He has the good grace to turn away.

"How are you going to explain this person?" he says, looking down his nose at Madeleine, who is indeed very much smaller than he is.

"Hortense, we need to find Eugène," I say, ignoring him.

"That won't be possible," Valmont says. "All the generals and their aides are occupied in Paris."

"Then Madeleine must come to school with us," I say.

Valmont shakes his head.

"Well, she cannot remain out here, nor can she return to where she came from!" Hortense puts her finger to her lips. I drop my voice. "There must be a way. Just for a few days, until Eugène can come for her."

"Perhaps she can pass as a boy and return with me," Valmont says, but I can see by his expression that he is joking.

"She can be my cousin!" Hortense says, lifting her chin and gently separating herself from Madeleine. "She is visiting from Martinique, and her parents would like her to spend some time with me at school."

"Perfect!" I say. "Madeleine is an actress. She can play the role, I'm certain. Now I have to become myself again." I cast a pointed glance at Valmont, who sweeps an ironic bow in my direction.

"I gather my protection is no longer needed," he says.

"I have only these clothes to wear," Madeleine says, looking down at her dress, which is obviously ragged in the daylight.

"I am certain we can think of something," Hortense says.

"None of us will be worth trusting if we don't return to school soon," I say. "And now, I must change." I look around. The shops across the street are all closed for business now.

"Stand in the shelter there. We'll shield you," Hortense says.

Again I glare at Valmont, who suddenly shakes himself out of his stupor. "I'll fetch a fiacre."

I have never felt the cold air against my base skin. It's a peculiarly vulnerable yet free feeling. It doesn't last long. Soon I am dressed as the genteel young lady my mother is determined I shall be—and no doubt assumes I have been during these days since she departed for Virginia.

I finish very quickly, wanting to ensure I have transformed myself by the time Valmont returns with our conveyance.

Hortense has just tied my sash and I stuff my uniform into the basket as a fiacre approaches us from around the corner.

Madeleine, Hortense, and I climb in. Valmont tips his tricorn to us. "Aren't you coming?"

"That would be a fine thing! No, I shall sneak back into the College grounds on my own and reappear in time for afternoon exercises," he says, nodding to the driver.

I turn and watch him. I don't understand why he has done any of this. What can we matter to him, really?

My attention is diverted by Madeleine. "I've never been to school," she says, breaking the silence we have fallen into as we roll along the cobbled streets.

"How do you learn your lines?" I ask.

"I can read, of course!" she says, and I remember her reaction to Eugène's letter.

"In a week, you'll be walking with a stack of books on your head," I say. "Now *that's* what I call education!"

We all laugh, relieved, I think, that the day's extraordinary adventures are at last concluded—whatever happens next.

40

Hortense

When I saw Eliza with Madeleine it was all I could do not to stare. This is the object of my brother's affection? She is barely more than a child and looks so frail that someone like Caroline could easily crush her. Seated pressed up next to her in the fiacre I am aware only of the sharp points of her elbows, the way her dress hangs off her shoulders rather than clinging to the plump outlines of a bosom as it should.

Why did Eliza bring her back? At Malmaison I was certain my American friend had begun to form an attachment to Eugène, futile as that would be. Perhaps she thinks to ingratiate herself to him by helping him achieve his object.

On reflection, though, Valmont has become oddly attentive to Eliza since he discovered our plan. I wonder if her girlish affections have been swayed by his actions.

We soon arrive at the school and my thoughts are interrupted.

"We'll all go in the back way, Madeleine, and you come to the front and ask for me. Say you have just arrived from a long ocean voyage," I say.

"I have no luggage," Madeleine points out.

Of course. I hadn't considered that. If she is my cousin, she would have some means, surely.

Eliza speaks. "Say your trunks will arrive soon. Then we can claim they have become lost at sea."

"Yes! That is a perfect plan." I am relieved, but also surprised that Eliza might have thought of such a thing.

Eliza and I sneak in easily enough the back way. Geneviève is there to ensure that we are not seen.

Eliza and I descend to the parlor, finding Caroline already there.

"Some broth? Or warm milk?" Madame Campan asks.

Although I have not eaten all day and my stomach is hollow with hunger, the idea of food makes me feel queasy. I don't have to pretend to be unwell, I am so anxious about what is to come with Madeleine.

"Perhaps just some dry biscuits," Caroline says, placing her hand over her stomach in a rather melodramatic way. We had already agreed upon the story that something we ate at Malmaison made us unwell.

Poor Eliza eyes the sweet biscuits hungrily, but she, too, abstains. Soon we are all settled in the parlor, sipping tea and talking quietly when I hear the bell tinkling down in the kitchens announcing a visitor. I listen to the footsteps of the maid who answers the door, and it is only moments before the serving girl appears in the parlor.

"Mademoiselle Hortense has a visitor," she says with a curtsy.

"At this late hour?" Madame Campan is not pleased. "And she has not been well!"

"She says she has come from very far away and begs to be admitted to see her cousin."

Caroline almost spoils everything by looking very confused. We have not had time to tell her about Madeleine. I prevent her from asking an awkward question by exclaiming, "She is come—at last! We have expected her these few months now, but the weather has been so bad for sailing."

I rise and go to greet Madeleine, whose surname we decided would be Mornay—just in case Madame Campan is familiar with the theatrical family and their dubious history.

I bring Madeleine in on my arm, and I feel her trembling. Surely such a consummate actress cannot be nervous in this small theater of our school. It makes me pity her more, knowing she is.

I introduce her to Madame Campan and the rest of the girls—the ones who are old enough to sit up after dinner, that is. For a moment, I am afraid Eliza's propensity for nervous giggling might give us away, but she controls herself, turning her reaction instead into an expression of delight at meeting someone new.

Madame Campan calls for more tea and sandwiches for the traveler, and some broth for those of us who have spent the day in bed. I confess it pains me to have deceived her in this manner, the lady who has taken me in for less than the accustomed tuition as a favor to my mother—and never spoken of this arrangement to anyone. But we really have no choice.

"Tell me, Madeleine, why did you not go directly to Malmaison instead of here?" Madame Campan asks once we are all settled again.

I hold my breath. We didn't think of that!

"It was my mother's express wish that I be permitted to remain at your school, madame." As she delivers her line, Madeleine's voice begins to tremble, until by the end two tears spill over the barriers of her lower lashes and make their way down her cheeks, as if she is capable not only of controlling when her tears fall, but how many and how quickly.

"Was?" Madame Campan's face, normally so placid, becomes the picture of concern.

Madeleine sets her teacup down on the table and starts searching in her pockets for a handkerchief, which she does not find. In the meantime, tears continue to streak her face.

To my amazement, Madame Campan reaches into her own pocket and produces an exquisite lace-edged square with her initials elaborately embroidered on it. She goes to

Madeleine and kneels down by her, dabbing at the now sobbing girl's cheeks.

Madeleine shakes her head prettily, but takes the handkerchief she is offered nonetheless. Madame Campan gets up off her knees and brings her chair over to Madeleine's side.

"There now, *ma petite*. Tell me what happened."

Madame looks up at the rest of us and signals that we should take everyone away. It is nearly time for us all to retire anyway, but I desperately wish I could stay and hear the tale Madeleine is about to spin.

Once upstairs, the three of us gather in Caroline's chamber, the largest. Eliza and I quickly explain everything to Caroline, who now strides up and down, wringing her hands.

"What will she say! She could put us all in danger. I blame this on you, Eliza!"

Eliza recoils as if Caroline has slapped her. I go to her and put my arm around her shoulder. "It is not her fault, Caroline. Remember, we each left Eliza to attend to our own affairs."

To her credit, this elicits an apology from Caroline, who then continues, "The fact remains that we now have a problem. Madeleine cannot stay here. Who will pay her tuition? And if she does not stay here, where will she go?"

Caroline seems so distressed, I sense that something is wrong beyond any concern over Madeleine's tuition. "Caroline, is something the matter?" I ask.

Her eyes begin to fill with tears. "It's nothing, really. I know he is fine. It was just a scratch."

"He? A scratch? What is it?" I ask. Eliza and I each take one of Caroline's hands.

Eliza whispers to me. "It's Napoléon. He was wounded today at the château. I saw it." Caroline is now crying in earnest.

The news shocks me. I have not even thought about the outcome of the day, only assuming it was completed to everyone's satisfaction. "Oh, Caroline! You must know how I can sympathize with you. I was so distressed when my own brother was injured. . . ."

She shakes her head and frees her hands, rubbing them together as if they are cold. "He is well. He must be, or I would have heard. My brother is stronger than that. He can withstand a superficial wound."

We are silent. I am thinking how selfish I am, to worry about the state of my heart when the future of France is at stake, when my stepfather may be mortally injured.

But I cannot forget Michel. And I suspect Caroline is still desperate for Murat. I wonder if she saw him? Perhaps that, too, weighs on her now.

Added to everything, downstairs is a young actress who could destroy not only my brother's life, if she chooses, but could expose all of us for the frauds we have been this past day.

We each recognize that we have inadvertently entrusted

our most cherished secrets to someone about whom we know almost nothing, except that she has captivated my brother.

"Bonaparte will survive, and Eugène will make everything right," Eliza says.

I don't have the heart to tell her that my mother will use all her powers to prevent him from doing any such thing.

41

This morning, the news is all over France.

"Caroline! Hortense! Eliza!"

Madame Campan calls to us and I can hear her running up the stairs. I have never seen her run before. She usually chastises us if we move too quickly, so at first I imagine there has been some terrible catastrophe.

Hortense and I meet in the corridor. She is neatly dressed in a white gown with a dark blue sash, her hair done simply but perfectly. I am dressed but my hair has not been arranged. A moment later, Caroline emerges from her room still in her dressing gown. We all three are gathered just as Madame Campan reaches the landing.

She is out of breath and must stop before speaking to us. While she composes herself, she opens the *Gazette* and waves it in our faces.

"Bonaparte," she finally gasps out. "Bonaparte has been made first consul of France. It is only a step, but an important one."

"A step?" Hortense says.

"Toward a monarchy! And toward a France as glorious as she has ever been."

Her eyes are shining. At first I am confused. Then I recall that she was mistress of the bedchamber to Marie Antoinette, and that apparently she had a great fondness for the queen. Of course she would welcome a return to something closer to a system that was so kind to her.

And then I think of Armand. This was what he wanted. He, like Madame Campan, is eager to see things go back to the way they once were.

Madame Campan takes Hortense's hand and then Caroline's. I stand a little aside. She seems to have forgotten me. Her eyes are moist with tears. I have never seen her display so much emotion.

"I beg you finish dressing and come down to breakfast. We have a great deal of work to do."

"Work?" Caroline says.

"These events call for a celebration. With both of you here at my school, we must show our loyal support for Bonaparte and the consulate."

"So Bonaparte is not injured?" I ask, then immediately regret it when Caroline glares at me.

"Injured? Why would he be injured?" Madame Campan looks back and forth from me to Caroline.

"It is only that so dramatic a change—can it have occurred without bloodshed?" Hortense says.

I relax when I see that this explains my comment to Madame's satisfaction. "I see. Of course. But it was all quite peaceful, apparently, although the army was ready in the event of trouble." She turns her attention away from me and focuses once more on Caroline and Hortense. "We must plan a celebration. We shall have music and dancing. Do you think, Hortense, your mother would grace us with her presence? And of course we must have the students from the Collège here too."

Hortense blushes and casts a quick glance at Caroline, who has pressed her lips together. I don't really blame her. Napoléon is her brother, after all, and she should have a bigger role to play in any celebrations that have to do with his new role in the government.

Hortense is quick to soothe her. "I'm certain that a celebration at the school will bring all our relatives, if they are not otherwise occupied with important matters of state," she says.

Madame continues as though she hasn't heard her, though, her mind racing ahead to the next matter. "I have sent word to Monsieur Perroquet to attend us this morning. We will have just enough time to rehearse some patriotic songs. I do hope there are some boys who can sing."

She rushes away as quickly as she arrived, leaving the three of us staring after her.

"What next?" I ask.

Before either of them can answer me, Madeleine appears. I permitted her to sleep in a truckle bed in my chamber. Hortense's room is too small, and Caroline, still angry that she was here at all, did not offer to accommodate her. Madeleine slept restlessly, tossing and turning and occasionally calling out in her sleep. At last she lay still, so I did not wake her early. She was still asleep when I came out. Now I see she has dressed herself and her eyes are bright and wide, so that she looks as though she has been awake for hours.

"What next?" she echoes.

"How much did you hear?" Caroline asks.

"Enough to know that there is to be a celebration, and that guests will come." She smiles and takes hold of Hortense's hand. "Do you think Eugène will be among them?"

Hortense looks puzzled, and I realize her mind has been far away.

"If Napoléon attends, Eugène is sure to follow," Caroline says, not entirely kindly. But her comment appears not to have any effect upon Madeleine.

"Excuse me," Hortense says, then turns away from us without a further word and goes back into her chamber.

I cannot imagine what upsets her so. Perhaps she is truly distressed about her brother's love for Madeleine after all. Or perhaps she is worried about Napoléon, and not because he suffered a wound at the hand of one of the council members. I shiver.

"I must make some preparations and write to my mother," Caroline says. She, too, is preoccupied. I thought I was in their confidence, but suddenly, this morning, I am no longer certain.

Madeleine and I continue downstairs for breakfast. Neither Hortense nor Caroline appears, but they both arrive as the entire school gathers in the ballroom.

"Caroline, you must take charge of the costumes. Everyone should wear white, which we will decorate with red and blue." Madame is already lining us up by size, deciding how we will stand in the old ballroom to perform our tribute to Bonaparte, the new first consul.

"Eliza, I shall need your assistance planning the menu for the reception afterward. Kindly go to the kitchens and see what we have, and what we must send for."

The kitchens! For a moment I am so taken aback that I find myself fixed to my spot. Just as I recover from the blow of being assigned to the lowest of the tasks for the celebration, Madeleine stops me with her hand.

"Please, let me go," she says, casting a quick glance at Hortense before turning her eyes to Madame.

"Very well," Madame Campan says. "What is important is that it is done, whoever does it. I must meet with the headmaster of the Collège, who will be here any moment."

I think we are all ready to go and scurry about, preparing for the event, when Hortense steps forward. "If I may, madame," she says, hesitating.

Madame Campan looks up from the red and blue ribbons she is showing the younger ones how to fashion into rosettes. Her face softens. "Yes, dear Hortense?"

"I have composed an anthem, to honor Bonaparte and his victories. Might we not perform it today?"

How wonderful! Hortense composes music? Every time I see her, I learn something new about her talents. I cannot help admiring her above Caroline, who seems only able to scheme and deceive—and dress beautifully, of course.

But Madame hesitates. Something passes between her eyes and Hortense's, and Hortense looks down first. She is feeling guilty about something.

Suddenly I realize that Hortense never said where she went while Caroline, Valmont, and I were still in Saint-Cloud. And I have not had a moment to question her or Caroline about when they arrived back at the school, before Madeleine and I appeared. What secret can she have?

"When Monsieur Perroquet arrives, I shall show him your composition and let him decide." Madame turns away and Hortense nods in acceptance.

Does it have something to do with the music master? The music master! He is such a dandy, and so old. I must ask her about it later, and take my place next to her, joining the group that is already busy turning snaking lengths of silk into stiff, ceremonial flowers to wear in our hair and on our dresses.

Everyone chatters excitedly about the news. But Madame Campan doesn't complain once about the noise. And no one complains about the work, either. Even the ladies' maids happily join in, fetching scissors that drop to the floor, threading needles for the younger ones. . . .

Before long all the younger boys from across the street arrive, scrubbed and dressed in their best. Valmont is not among them. Was he discovered? Is he in confinement? Being punished?

The master from the Collège takes his charges into the ballroom, where they rehearse a recitation. I hear their high voices, one at a time, reading the words of a long poem by Racine, originally intended to glorify King Louis XIV. I think perhaps it is a little hasty. Napoléon isn't a king, after all.

After half an hour of this activity, Madame claps her hands. "Come with me, Hélène, Ernestine. Let us confer about the dresses."

I would far rather have to do with the costumes than the decorations. I clear my throat. "I beg your pardon, madame, but might I also assist with the costumes? I may have some ornaments that you will like to use."

I can see that she doesn't much care, but she is in too jubilant a mood to disappoint anyone, I think, and she lets me follow along.

We go up to the top floor near the dormitory, where a room has been set aside for all the gowns. A smell of singed fabric and starch greets us. This is where the maids iron and mend the clothing. There are long racks lined with dresses in different shades of white. Who would think such a bland color could vary so widely? Madame sets me to pulling out the whitest of them.

Caroline is already here, with one dress spread out on a table. She takes a few ribbons, places them against it, then discards them. I keep one eye upon her as I quickly accomplish the task Madame requested of me, and see her expression gradually change from vexation to triumph.

"Ernestine!" Caroline says. I am surprised she calls my maid, but then Ernestine knows a great deal about fashion.

"Yes, Mademoiselle Bonaparte," she says with a curtsy.

"Do you think we can transform this gown into a Grecian style, like the ones on the statues in the hall? And these others, too?" Caroline gestures toward the ones I have just finished pulling from the rack.

Ernestine expertly fingers the different weights of fabric. The silk, the cambric, the voile. She purses her lips and closes her eyes, then says, "Yes. I think it can be done."

"Excellent!" Caroline says. She turns to me and Hélène, who looks undeniably put out that Caroline has asked my maid and not her own to help her. "We shall present a *tableau vivant*. A little dramatic scene. Let those who wish sing some insipid ditty. The rest of us shall be the Sabine women, an allegory for the strength of France."

Wonderful! Although I want to sing Hortense's anthem, the idea of a tableau is much more exciting.

Ernestine claps her hands with delight. "Let us begin immediately!"

42

Madeleine

Yesterday, when I waited for Eugène and he didn't come, the last thing on earth I expected would be to find myself here, today, with another opportunity ahead of me. Another opportunity to be with him, for him to take me away and make me his.

I feel a little guilty for playing on the sensitivities of Madame Campan and the others, but I do not have the luxury of time and resources on my side. They can spare a few tears for me, just as the audiences at the Comédie Française do. And here—my performance is free.

I think Caroline is aware of what I am doing, but perhaps that does not matter. We are alike. We are ambitious. Perhaps...

I must first ensure that I distinguish myself in the performance later. Eugène has heard me sing, but his mother, the formidable Joséphine, has not. Although she regularly attends the theater, I have not been permitted to raise my voice on a stage where I might outshine my mother, the great Gloriande de Pourtant.

"Monsieur Perroquet has arrived!"

Hortense is breathless when she bursts into the room where I have been pretending to sew sequins on white ribbons, having already instructed the kitchens and discovered that there will be ample delicious food. I have spent so much of my life hungry that I find it difficult not to steal buns from the kitchen, just so I have them to eat later. But I do not want to arouse Madame Campan's suspicion. So far she seems quite happy to accept Hortense's story about me.

Hortense comes to me, making an effort, I notice with gratitude, to be kind and accepting. "We must leave what we are doing and go to the music room to rehearse."

Her eyes shine. Hortense was evasive yesterday when the others asked what she had done. She said only that she left them to try to be certain of something, and that now she was. I see by her expression that the arrival of the music master carries some import for her. Could she be in love with him? It is dangerous for one who will occupy such an exalted social station to be so obvious, so easy to read. I smile, let her take my arm, and together we go back to the ballroom.

The boys—all young—have been cleared out, leaving only a faint smell of sweat and shoe polish, to go back and have some dinner at their school. I discovered from listening to the prattle of the girls that it is directly across the street. I take my place among the forty or so girl students. How strange it is! I have never been among so many my own age. And yet I feel so much older than they all appear to be.

"Monsieur Perroquet is a very able musician," Hortense whispers. Her voice is calm. I would almost say she sounds disappointed. Perhaps it is not this music master who interests her so deeply. Indeed, I would be surprised if it was. Monsieur Perroquet is a dandy if ever there was one, with his powdered wig and patches, all vestiges of an earlier time. I cast my eye around the room. It, too, is an echo of times past.

The music master wanders among us, moving us about, arranging us by height. This places me in the front, since I am small for my age, suiting my purpose quite well.

"Let us warm up our voices first," he says.

Until now, the seat at the pianoforte has been vacant. Then a young man enters, head bowed, trying hard not to look at anyone. I steal a glance at Hortense. Her cheeks are bright pink and she clutches her hands together to keep them from trembling.

So that is the way of things! Not the music master, but his assistant. I take a closer look.

He is not bad looking, but in an effete sort of way. His hair is reddish, and his eyes clear gray. I prefer someone with more defined looks, like Eugène. But the young fellow's hands are very fine. Similar, in fact, to those Monsieur Perroquet is waving in front of us, pointing and rearranging us in our rows.

The young man plays the chords that set us off on our *vocalises*. *He must be the son,* I think, and then it takes very little imagination to see how unsuitable Hortense's attachment to him is.

Madame Bonaparte faces the possibility, I realize, of having her daughter elope with a poor musician, and her son with me, a starving actress. It would be enough to horrify any mother. But I shall do my best to change her mind.

At first, I keep my voice small. I don't want to call attention to myself until the right moment. Just blend into the inferior voices around me—that's all that is required right now.

After a while, Monsieur Perroquet lets his arms drop to his sides in frustration. "Come, *mesdemoiselles*! I have heard you sing much better than this. I am given to understand that we will have some very important guests for the performance."

"Monsieur Perroquet?"

The voice I recognize as Caroline's comes from the last row, since she is one of the oldest and tallest girls. I did not realize she was there. She must have come from elsewhere, as indeed Eliza did, who stands two rows behind me. The music master bows his head slightly, giving her permission to proceed.

"A number of us will not be able to sing in your chorus, for we are to form part of a tableau instead."

A murmur of delight and excitement ripples through the schoolgirls. I see that there is little enthusiasm for a musical ensemble compared to the opportunity to be seen in costume in a tableau.

Monsieur Perroquet tries not to look cross. "Very well, Mademoiselle Bonaparte. Will those who will be in the tableau please make yourselves known to me?"

All the girls in the white ribbons raise their hands, except for Hortense. All the Blues raise their hands as well. I imagine these are the poor Perroquet's strongest singers. All the better for me, but I must not appear too delighted.

"Might we be dismissed to attend our own rehearsal?" Caroline asks, no doubt already assuming consent.

Monsieur Perroquet gestures grandly in the direction of the door, setting off a chorus of giggles.

Once they are gone, we are a very pathetic group, I see. Hortense is much taller than the others. I wonder how Monsieur Perroquet will handle this disruption of his plans for a uniform chorus of girls' voices.

"Perhaps, Mademoiselle Hortense, we can have you sing a solo? Is there a solo passage in your anthem?"

Hortense brings the music forward. "I regret not, monsieur," she says, handing him the score. I see the slightest flick of her eyes toward the young accompanist, but he stares steadfastly at the empty desk of the pianoforte.

"I have taken the liberty of copying out the parts,"

Hortense says. She must have done this days ago, I think, as I watch her distribute a few sheets of music to us.

I accept mine from her hand graciously and cast my eye over it.

It is surprisingly good. I can hear the melody in my mind—and words that embody the ideals of the new France. So Hortense has more talent than one might think for a girl brought up with few meaningful skills. I will be sorry to take her brother away from her, but so it must be.

"How many of you can read this music?" Monsieur Perroquet asks.

I wait to see which of the others indicate that they can do so. Only two. I raise my hand to make it three.

"Please take those who cannot read the score to another room and teach them their parts, Mademoiselle Hortense," he says.

The young ones follow her like lambs. Clearly she is a favorite with them.

"So, we are left with you three. I know you, Mademoiselle Sylvie, and you, Mademoiselle Jeannette. But I do not believe we are acquainted, Mademoiselle..."

He approaches me. I curtsy, making my speaking voice small and timid, like the orphans I so often play onstage. "I am Madeleine Mornay, cousin to Mademoiselle Hortense. I am visiting from Martinique."

"*Eh bien*," he says, obviously not expecting much. "Michel, the introduction, please."

The young man at the piano begins to play. I let my throat relax and imagine the first note I must sing, so that when it emerges I have hit it exactly. And then I allow my voice to unfold in all its strength. It feels good to do it, as if I have kept a little songbird in a cage and finally open the door so it can fly free.

I hardly notice when the other two stop singing and there is only me. I pour my feelings into those patriotic words, imagining the love for my country is really my love for Eugène.

I hold the final note, gradually letting it die away to a whisper.

Monsieur Perroquet's eyes glitter with tears. I have had the effect I desired.

Yet I feel another pair of eyes upon me. I shift my gaze a little, just enough to see Michel, the music master's son, piercing me with his gaze.

Someone has opened the door and now I feel the weight of many watching me. I turn. It is Hortense, and behind her are the rest of the students.

She looks at Michel and then at me. I want to make her understand that I have no designs on the accompianist. But there won't be time. The drama must be played to its conclusion.

43

Hortense

Who is this creature my brother has fallen in love with?

Her voice—it is beyond beautiful. It is unearthly. I should be thrilled that my humble composition will receive such a magnificent performance, but something holds me back.

"Hortense! I need the young ones as well for the tableau."

Caroline interrupts my thoughts. She has been sly, but what else would I expect? This tableau—she invented it on the spot so that she would not have to be part of a chorus. She hates to blend in, and doesn't do it well. "But what about the chorus?"

"Monsieur Perroquet has decided that Madeleine will sing alone, so the rest of us can concentrate on my project."

I knew somehow this would be the result as soon as I heard Madeleine sing one note. "If I am to help with the costumes and the movements, I must know the theme," I say. I wonder if she actually has one.

"The theme is the intervention of the Sabine women. You know the painting, by David?"

Her words shock me. I know the painting, and I know Jacques-Louis David. He came to Malmaison while I was there this past summer to apologize to my mother. It was he who signed my father's death warrant during the *Terreur.* Surely Caroline cannot be ignorant of that fact.

I must keep my opinions to myself, though. Madame Campan has entered the salon.

"Ah! A tableau! Wonderful idea, Caroline. And Monsieur Perroquet tells me that our chorus has become a solo. I must admit I am relieved. The fewer who are required to learn words and melodies the better." She touches my cheek affectionately as she passes. "I shall send Geneviève to Malmaison with the invitation to your mother. Have you any word to add?"

In the flurry of preparations I had not considered the coming scene very carefully. My mother will be here—she would not refuse an invitation from Madame Campan, to whom she owes so much—and she will doubtless be enchanted by Madeleine. Will she recognize her from the stage? It is risky for Madeleine to take such a chance. Risky for my brother to allow it. But of course, he does not yet know Madeleine is here.

The girl my brother loves is either very certain of herself, or very desperate.

I dare not think about my own situation. "No, I have no word for my mother. I parted from her just three days ago." Best simply to concentrate on the task at hand. Perhaps all will go smoothly, and no one will be upset.

"Hortense! My bow has come undone!"

"I can't hold my arm like this for hours. It hurts!"

"Ouch! Christine keeps stepping on my toe. You have to move her."

I cannot believe how difficult it is to get forty girls to strike three different poses at the same time and remain motionless long enough for someone to understand what their frozen actions are intended to convey.

And what a message—Caroline has chosen with care. It is the moment when the Sabine women come to the defense of the men, saving them from bloodshed and destruction. Although I harbor deep hatred for the artist whose painting our scene is modeled after, I approve of the point, and so I do as I am instructed to try to bring this feat of concentration to pass.

Caroline keeps me so busy helping her manage the restless younger ones and arrange the decorations for the tableau that I do not realize until nearly teatime that I have been left without any role to play in the actual celebration. Even Eliza has been given a prime spot in the tableau, on one knee next to Caroline herself, who is of course the center-piece.

And the whole time, from the music room I hear the words and tune I poured my heart into issuing from the throat of the undernourished actress who wants to marry my brother.

Worse, I saw how Michel looked at her.

I am suddenly seized with an idea. If Louise Perroquet considers *me* unsuitable, she would be devastated at the idea of Madeleine as a match for her brother. I know Madeleine is in love with Eugène, but what if he rejects her after all, and she turns to Michel for comfort? I am jealous, I admit, but I cannot help myself. Even if Michel and I can never be together, I do not want to hand him to this strange creature. I quickly scribble a note and ask a servant to take it to Michel's house. And then I write another, to Armand de Valmont. He must have some sympathy for my predicament. And he knows so much already.

Of course, I cannot help thinking of my brother. When he told me of his passion a few days ago in the garden at Malmaison, I never thought I would actually meet Madeleine. I simply assumed his infatuation would spend itself in a few flowers and assignations, and he would end up marrying the woman my mother chose for him. Such is the way with many young men.

I was prepared to sympathize with him, to let him cry on my shoulder, but not to help him.

Now she is here, and I, in pursuing my own desires, made their meeting—and possibly their marriage—possible.

As recently as this morning I still held myself apart from the reality of everything. I thought only of my composition, and the idea that Michel would understand the message buried in the words, knowing how much of it was meant for him. It speaks of love for my country, of loyalty and sacrifice. But the words can easily be construed to mean love of a different sort, loyalty to a beloved individual, and sacrifice of safety and comfort for that person. I cannot help sighing. I imagined an altogether different outcome. I pictured myself singing among the pure, sweet voices of the still artless students at the school, with Michel accompanying us. Imagined him hearing only me, the chords anchoring me and supporting my song.

But Madeleine has succeeded in taking the song over completely, and with it—I fear—Michel. I hear him at the keyboard, altering the simple underpinnings I created, adding a counterpoint now and again to make the most of Madeleine's supple voice, or supplying the melody while she soars into flourishes that wind around it.

The anthem—and its message—is no longer mine.

After two hours of effort, at last the tableau is achieved. Caroline has created three different poses, progressing and building in complexity to the ultimate one that places

Caroline at the center. I have to admit, it could be quite affecting. She has a natural dramatic flair.

Now all attention is on the costumes. I am relieved to sit. My body is still sore and tired from yesterday's exertions. But I cannot rest for long.

"My mother has sent word that my brothers and all the generals will attend the performance," Caroline whispers.

"What!" I exclaim. This is not welcome news. "Are they not still at Saint-Cloud?"

"I have asked Madame Campan to change the hour of the entertainment to eight o'clock this evening so that they may all come from their different locations."

I wonder how Caroline managed it. I know my mother would not have insisted that men with more important things on their minds come and see a gaggle of schoolgirls bestow naive admiration upon them. Her presence would have been more than enough.

That means not only Bonaparte and Murat, but Eugène, Lucien, and Louis will be here. Madeleine will have quite an audience.

And I... Perhaps that is how Caroline persuaded my mother to exert pressure on Bonaparte to make the trip to Saint-Germain. Maman sees another opportunity to throw me together with the dull-witted Louis. Now all at once I am relieved that I shall not be paraded before them, displayed like a prize hen. I can stay safely in the background, observing everyone else.

Yet I know I must do more. I cannot simply let matters take their course, but must act to bring about the best outcome. What is the best outcome? I am faced with a dilemma. If I help Madeleine flee with Eugène, there will be no danger to Michel. But then Maman will be furious, and I will have no hope of avoiding Louis's suit.

If I prevent Eugène from taking Madeleine away, I fear she will persuade Michel to step into the breach. And so I will still be left with no other option than Louis Bonaparte.

Neither of these scenarios can occur. Madeleine must leave, and she must do so alone. There is no other way. As soon as her song is finished, she must reveal who she is and return to the Comédie Française. That is where Valmont can help, if he is willing.

Valmont, and Louise Perroquet. She will assist me, but she will exact a condition.

Another deep sigh escapes me.

"Is something wrong, Hortense?" It is Eliza.

"No," I say. "I'm just a little weary."

How can I explain to her what she has done? She did not know of my love for Michel. And she will never know that her actions have taken all my hope away. Because I realize that I must relinquish him in order to save Eugène.

44

Eliza

Hortense looks so sad. If she were someone else, I might think she was sorry about not being in the tableau. But I can't imagine she's very concerned about being excluded from Caroline's presentation.

But she's also no longer singing the anthem she composed. More likely that is it. She has a beautiful voice, too. Not as rich and strong as Madeleine's, but still lovely. Perhaps there is a way for me to do something for Hortense. If I talk to Madeleine, she might consent to have Hortense sing with her in a duet instead. She owes me that, at least. I went to a great deal of trouble to take her away from the theater—even if it was because of Eugène.

Yes, I shall ask her. I shall insist!

Madame Campan enters, clapping her hands to get the attention of the young ones, who are so excited they are giggling and shouting. "Dinner is a buffet this evening, so that you may all finish quickly and prepare for the performance," she says.

Rather than quiet everyone down, her words have the effect of launching a fresh burst of delight. I expect her to stand still and give an icy, disapproving stare, but instead she smiles and leads the way to the dining hall. "Pearls first, then Blues, Pinks, and Greens last."

"All the sweets will be gone before we get there!" I hear one of the youngest protest under her breath.

Madame Campan hears her. "I expect everyone will exercise restraint. There is ample refreshment for all." She flashes one of her quietly disapproving stares at the little girl, whose name is Yvette. It is enough to silence all the youngest ones, and Yvette's lip begins to tremble.

I am not the only girl who has noticed her distress, though. Hortense slips out of her place in front of us Blues, pretending she has forgotten something. She goes straight to Yvette and stands by her in line for a while, whispering something to her that not only makes her forget about crying, but brings a smile to her face. A moment later Hortense is back, helping herself to dainty portions of the cold meats, pickles, and vegetables, not even touching the beautiful display of cakes and pastries.

Caroline and I follow Hortense's example. One by one, all the girls in the upper levels fill their plates with savories but hold back from taking the sweet treats, which have no doubt been specially prepared for the occasion.

When the greens reach that spread of desserts, all the best treats are still there. *Now*, I think, *a plague of charming little locusts will descend.* I am certain the young ones will be unable to exercise restraint when faced with those trays of iced cakes and crisp, flaky pastries filled with sweet cream and drizzled with chocolate.

Yet the example set by Hortense makes its way through even the youngest of the students. Each girl takes one or two desserts, leaving the trays still quite full when Madeleine enters the room.

I didn't actually notice her absence before. But once she arrives, she commands everyone's attention. Perhaps it is the way she walks. Her movements are not as refined as Hortense's, or as commanding as Caroline's, but every step or gesture is carefully calculated. Her head of dark, curling hair sits atop a slender neck, perfectly balanced on her shoulders. She looks as if she could have spent her entire life in a school like this, learning to be what she is.

Madeleine has not seen everyone else pass along the buffet, but she takes a plate with confidence and begins helping herself to food.

The rest of us are seated by the time she finishes. Her plate positively teeters with the best bits of everything she finds, all mixed up between sweets and meats, vegetables and pickles and sauces. She takes the empty seat next to me, still unaware that all eyes are staring at her mountain of food. Or perhaps not unaware, only not remarking it because she is so accustomed to being looked at by strangers.

She reaches for her knife and fork, but I cannot let her commit such a breach, and snap myself out of the fascination of watching her.

"Ahem," I cough politely, placing my napkin in my lap and nudging her at the same time. She looks up, sees that no one else has touched their food, and leaves her silverware by her plate.

As the oldest, it is Caroline's duty to signal when we may begin eating. She is across the long table from us, seated next to Hortense. I see Hortense training her eyes on Madeleine. I wonder what she is thinking. She gives her head the minutest shake, as if willing herself out of a trance. At the same time Caroline lifts her fork, and everyone follows suit.

Immediately the room echoes with the tinkling of silverware against china, and the silence is broken by excited whispers that grow to conversations and then laughter.

Yet none of us at the top of the table has said a word. Hortense picks at her food in small bites. Caroline eats slowly, methodically, until her plate is nearly clean. The other Pearls watch them, eyes round, deciding which one they will mimic and settling upon Caroline as the most appealing.

Madeleine eats as though this will be her last bit of sustenance on earth. She knows how to comport herself, but clearly she has never seen so much food in her life. She cuts large pieces of meat and somehow fits them into her dainty mouth, managing to chew and swallow without opening her lips.

The tension among us subsides a little as we become sated. "Madeleine, might I have a word with you in private before we go to prepare for the evening?" I whisper to her. Remarkably, she has finished everything on her plate and shows no sign of discomfort.

"Of course, Eliza," she says. No more "Mademoiselle," I see.

I take Madeleine to an anteroom, near the ballroom where our guests will come to watch and listen to our performance. The servants have already set up gilt chairs in rows, and the gardeners are hammering together a platform to raise Caroline's tableau a foot above the level of the floor. We did not practice on a raised stage, and for a moment I am worried. But I must return to my task. "I think Hortense should be allowed to sing her anthem," I say to Madeleine, taking hold of her shoulders so she has to look directly at me.

"But Monsieur Perroquet and Madame Campan have agreed that I am to do it," she says, surprised.

"Yes, but can you not see how sad she is not to have any part in the presentation? Perhaps you can sing a duet. Her voice is nearly as good as yours."

Madeleine's face clouds. "It will not do."

"Why not?" I ask. Perhaps it is impertinent of me, but since I have been the one to rescue her from her life of near enslavement at the theater, I decide I have a right to press her.

"You are a clever girl, Eliza, but you apparently have not seen things that are right before your eyes."

I know Madeleine is older than I am, but something about the way she says this annoys me. "I believe I have at least as much insight into the workings of my friends and this school as you do, who have only just arrived here yesterday."

She smiles. "I may have only just come here—thanks to you, dear Eliza—but I am more acquainted with the ways of the world and the heart than you are.

"I must sing alone because my plans demand it," she continues. "I'm sorry for Hortense, but she will have many other opportunities to show herself to advantage, while I have only this one."

"Now that you are no longer at the Comédie Française I'm certain you will be welcomed into society," I say, not entirely believing it myself. What will she do? If Eugène does not take her away this evening, where will she go? I had not considered these things in the excitement of taking her from the clutches of her mother.

All at once I feel less like someone in the process of arranging things than like someone who is being acted upon by everyone else. It was all right with Caroline and Hortense. I want to be like them. But Madeleine—she is such a mystery.

And her circumstances are so dire there's no telling what she might do.

"You're planning to make trouble, aren't you." I don't mean it as a question, and she doesn't answer me.

"Don't worry about yourself," Madeleine says. "Even though your family keeps slaves, I have nothing against you." She draws herself up to her full height, which brings only the top of her head to my eyes. "I must go and prepare my costume, and I suggest you do the same."

Madeleine dips the smallest of curtsies to me and walks calmly away. Her words have left me stunned, and for the first time, I am aware of the deep, burning anger within her. She may never have been to school, but her knowledge is greater than mine, and more dangerous.

Someone will be hurt this evening. But I must warn Hortense.

I intend to go and find her immediately, but when I pass through the ballroom and then back through the dining hall on my way to the stairs, I notice someone standing at one of the long windows that face the gardens. I stop, not wanting to announce my presence, and proceed on tiptoe.

But I am too late. He has heard me.

"Mademoiselle Eliza," Armand says with a bow. He is dressed in his finest, and I have to admit looks very handsome.

"You're early," I say, making no move to approach him.

"The others will be here soon. The headmaster sent me

over in advance to discuss a few arrangements with Madame Campan."

"What arrangements?" I ask. It sounds to me like an excuse.

"I overheard what you were saying to the actress."

Armand walks toward me until he is standing only a few feet away. Something about his presence, about the two of us standing alone like that, brings a flush to my face. "It seems only fair that Hortense should also sing," I say. "But if you heard it all, you also know that she is determined not to give in."

"Yes, I know. But the important thing is that you suggested it." He is now only an arm's length away from me. I feel like backing up, but something tells me it would be rude, and so I stay put. "I've been trying to discover what took you to the Comédie Française at such an odd time. And why did you come away with Madeleine de Pourtant in your keeping?"

"That is my affair. I don't see that it has anything to do with you." Indeed, why should I tell Armand? I hardly know him. Although he was kind to me when we were in Saint-Cloud, and he helped Caroline get back safely to Saint-Germain.

"Actually, it does. You see, Hortense has asked for my help. But before I do as she requests, I want to make sure I won't be hurting you in the process."

"Why would that matter?" I ask. "I'm just a girl from

Virginia who, according to you, is personally responsible for fomenting the French Revolution!" Truly, I am confused. But he appears sincere. He has not taken his eyes from my face, has not acted at all like someone who is just saying something false to make a good impression.

"I was rude, wasn't I? I'm sorry." He drops his eyes now and reaches for my hand. "Will you forgive me?"

"I . . . Yes, of course . . . but . . ." I don't know what is wrong with me, but I can hardly put two words together and make sense.

I hear footsteps approaching.

"I must go, or I will not be ready for the tableau," I say, pulling my hand away. He bows, but I cannot interpret his expression. Is he sad? Angry? Disappointed?

There is no time to worry. I must run. I hear his footsteps leave the dining room through the door that leads to the kitchens, and decide that after the performance I must seek him out, try to discover what he was trying to tell me, and why.

45

Eliza

But the strange revelations of the evening are not over for me, apparently. As I dash across the vestibule to the sweeping staircase, I catch sight of Hortense going the other direction, toward the ballroom. She has already changed into evening dress. I think of stopping to say something to her, but I realize she hasn't seen me and am afraid I might startle her. Instead, I watch her continue toward the ballroom, open the door, and shut it softly behind her, as if she doesn't want anyone to know she is there.

Perhaps because of what Armand has just told me, her actions make me curious. I stop, tiptoe back across the vestibule, and stand near the door, debating whether to follow her in.

I have almost decided to leave and dress for the

performance when the sound of voices stops me. I lean in closer to listen.

"I only suggested my anthem because I thought we would have a chance to be close, if just for a few moments this evening." Who is Hortense speaking to? Armand? He could have returned through the dining room. But what would her anthem have to do with being close to him?

"Hortense, mademoiselle...I am so sorry for what happened yesterday. I wanted to spare you that hurt, that humiliation—"

I recognize the voice, but it takes me a moment to realize that it is Monsieur Perroquet's son, Michel, the young man who will play the pianoforte to accompany the anthem. How bizarre!

"I can never be humiliated by love!" Hortense speaks with such deep emotion, she almost does not sound like herself. She mentions humiliation—I wonder, suddenly, if she's talking about what happened yesterday when she was separated from us.

"Nonetheless, you see now that I should never have confessed my feelings for you," Michel responds. "My circumstances do not allow it. I feel so wretched. I don't know how I dared. You are so far above me that I might as well try to love one of the seraphim."

There is silence between them for a moment. I am eavesdropping, but I cannot tear myself away. A quick glance around assures me that no one else is nearby, and I lean closer to the door once again.

"It must have been a very feeble kind of love, to be so dependent upon circumstances." I hear a trace of tears in Hortense's voice.

"Hortense!"

"*Shh!*" she says. "I—"

She is stopped in midexpression. How I wish I could see what is going on!

A moment later, I hear the sound of a small struggle. "No!" Hortense says. Then her footsteps approach quickly, as if she is running to the door. I back around a corner out of sight. I hear another stifled exclamation, and then silence.

I have tempted fate by staying to listen. Whatever they are doing, whatever is being said, I must leave them to their own thoughts and actions. I take a step toward the stairs, but stop when I hear them begin speaking again, this time more intimately. They are just beyond the door, and clearly very close to each other.

"Perhaps it is not hopeless," the young Perroquet says. "My sister may marry well. There are several wealthy citizens who court her."

I see how it is. They are poor. His family needs him to marry someone of fortune, not simply someone famous whose real family doesn't have two *centimes* to rub together, according to Caroline. Yet couldn't a match with Hortense bring fame, and a great deal of business among wealthy daughters? I don't see why it must be impossible.

Suddenly I hear Madame Campan approaching.

"Have the flowers been delivered?" she asks the housekeeper, who follows her into the vestibule from the parlor. When she sees me, she says, "Eliza! Why are you not preparing for the tableau? Our guests will arrive within the hour."

Beyond the door to the ballroom the voices speak again, but more quietly.

"We must go!"

"No, I shall not abandon you again. You're right—I was cowardly."

"Not now!"

Madame comes closer. I hope she was too far away to hear what I've heard. "Are you quite all right, Eliza?" She reaches out and touches my forehead.

"Yes, madame," I say, and curtsy. "I was only pausing to consider the stillness I must achieve in the tableau. I have never taken part in such a thing before."

She seems relieved and looks away, clearly wanting to continue with her other preparations. She turns to the housekeeper, who is still awaiting her orders. "We must ensure that all the best chairs are in the ballroom for our guests. Call the groundsman and the gardener." She motions me to step aside so that she can pass through the door into the ballroom.

My heart leaps into my throat. What if they are still within? And in each other's arms! I must prevent Madame from entering, at least for a moment so they have an opportunity to escape out another door.

"Madame, might I see which flowers you have chosen?" I ask hurriedly. "I should like to take some to Caroline, to thank her for her hard work arranging the tableau."

She smiles at me. "You have already come along so well here," she says. "It is very sweet of you to be so thankful of the advantages you reap in being among the first young ladies of France." Instead of opening the door to the ballroom, she leads me toward the conservatory, through the parlor.

As soon as we pass through, I am certain I hear the ballroom door open and Hortense's light steps as she runs to the stairs. I don't know what happened to the young accompanist. I half wonder if he has encountered Armand. Perhaps that is the favor Hortense asked of him. Perhaps they are planning to elope! If Eugène succeeds in carrying Madeleine away and Hortense becomes betrothed to the young Perroquet—oh, dear. Joséphine won't be at all happy.

Moments later, I bring a small bouquet of lilies up to Caroline, who hardly glances at them for a moment, all her attention focused on a mirror, where she watches her maid Hélène put the finishing touches on her hair. "You had better hurry," she says to me. "Everyone else is ready. We are about to descend to take our places in the dining room."

"Do you not want me to help you with your gown?" I

say, hoping to keep her upstairs a little longer, to protect Hortense from Caroline's curiosity as well.

"No, Hélène can manage." She turns to me and waits for me to leave.

Caroline—could she have a secret, too? How can that be when I have spent so much time in her company as well as Hortense's in the last few days?

I go to my room and Ernestine helps me don the gown that has been altered enough to suggest a Grecian theme. Just as we finish, the excited babble of boys' voices rises from the voices courtyard. As soon as they are inside, I hear the sound of carriage wheels on gravel.

"Our guests are here," I say, waving Ernestine away and standing in front of the mirror.

I am quite surprised by what I see. Something about me has changed. I look... older. Or perhaps I just feel older. I have certainly learned much in these past weeks that has opened my eyes. Paris is a great deal bigger than Virginia.

I wait until all the others pass by my door before I emerge. Somehow, I feel the chatter of the little ones will distract me. I know Caroline is the centerpiece of the tableau, but she has given me a very good place in it. Eugène will see me. He may be in love with Madeleine, but that doesn't mean I don't want him to admire me. He kissed me, after all.

He kissed me. In all the excitement since yesterday, I almost forgot that. I succeeded. It was a real kiss. I now have something against which to compare all other kisses.

But it is not Eugène's face that comes to me as I prepare to go downstairs. It is Armand's. *Armand?* It seems he doesn't dislike me as much as I first thought. And I liked it when he took my hand. He said he didn't want to hurt me by doing what Hortense asked of him. What did he mean by that? I imagine that the next few hours will reveal much. It nearly makes my head burst to think of it all.

I take my time walking down the hallway to the stairs, reflecting on all that has happened in so short a time. I shall write a long letter to my mother about this evening.

Just as I am about to turn the corner I hear a voice.

"One moment, my dear! I forgot a detail of my costume."

It is Madeleine. What is it about her voice that is so distinctive? Now that I have heard her sing, I hear that potential when she speaks. But there is something beyond that. It is as though everything she says is for the benefit of an audience. I admit she has captivated me.

As quietly as I can, I tiptoe around the corner. Madeleine is in one of the guestrooms and the door is ajar. I could announce myself and we could walk downstairs together. But I don't. Instead I step quietly to a place where I can see her but she cannot see me.

I watch her lift her skirt to reveal a sort of long purse, strapped to her leg, with a flap that buttons it closed. She unbuttons the flap, then reaches for something she has hidden behind the mirror on the dressing table.

I catch just a glint of steel before she puts the object into the clever hiding place beneath her skirt. I gasp, nearly betraying my presence.

There is no mistaking it. Madeleine still has the dagger we took from the theater.

46

Madeleine

I suppose what I am planning to do this evening will only confirm what everyone probably already thinks of me. But if Eugène doesn't take me away tonight, there is only one course of action for me. Returning to the theater is not a possibility.

The excitement of the evening sends a crackle through the air in this quiet place. Even when we all stand in the drawing room completely silent, Madame Campan facing us in her black silk gown with the white lace, I feel a thread of tension binding us all together. Someone on the other side of the group need only take a deep breath, or raise a handkerchief to dab her eye, and I can feel it.

They don't know it yet, but they will all participate in my drama. I have written these lines for myself—an impromptu ode that takes advantage of the moment. Years of being in the theater has given me insights to people, ways of knowing how to predict their emotions.

I turn. Eliza is staring at me. Her eyes are round, questions behind them. What is it? I have tried only to be kind to her, to be grateful for her help. Perhaps she still has hope that I will consent to sing with Hortense instead of alone. I smile. She looks away, guilty. Or is it fright?

The boys have already trooped noisily into the ballroom and will soon start their patriotic recitation. They will join the audience for our selections when they are finished.

I seek out Hortense, who stands meekly in the background, making little adjustments to the young ones' costumes. She is beautiful; there can be no denying it. But sad. How can she be so sad? I do not believe that, even with everything her mother went through during the *Terreur,* she has any cause for sadness now. Could she really imagine that the son of a music master is the match for her? She will undoubtedly do much better. By captivating the young Michel—for I know I have—I perform a great service for her. I intend to use him in a way that will expose his lack of real love for her. It will hurt, for a while. But she will recover.

Over there is Caroline. She, on the other hand, looks triumphant, like her brothers, I imagine. I admire her for it, but I do not like her.

Not as I like Eliza, despite her family's unfortunate habit of owning slaves. If she were not so young and foolish, I might be friends with her. But she knows that African blood flows in my veins and she cannot forgive the color of my skin, pale as I am. She has been brought up to expect that such a person like me is less than human. She will think differently by the time this brief performance is over.

"Ladies!" Madame Campan hardly needs to raise her voice. Only one or two whispers break the silence. "As you know, our guests are now seated. Among them—I can hardly believe how honored we have been at this time—are the first consul himself, with his mother, his brothers Lucien and Louis, his aide-de-camp Eugène de Beauharnais, and General Murat."

This makes the entire room erupt in chatter. I feel it needling into my neck, the sound. How does no one understand that in order to give one's finest performance, complete stillness and concentration are necessary?

The tableau is to follow the boy's recitation. I think Caroline thought her masterpiece would be the climax of the evening. I wonder if the sound of the boys' monotonous voices droning through the door irritates her as it does me.

Yet not all of the schoolboys are on the stage. The older one, the one who seems to have a penchant for Eliza, is standing over by the door. He has been given the task of holding it open for all the performers, I see, when it is their turn to enter the ballroom.

"You go and sit with your mother and brother," Madame Campan says to Hortense, who has no role on the stage. She nods her head meekly and leaves by the door that leads to the vestibule, so she can enter at the back of the audience.

I confess, I am envious of Hortense. She possesses the kind of beauty that is not merely lovely to behold, but which radiates from her and encompasses everyone in its magic. I see how many eyes follow her out of the room, and without her here our costumes appear a little more drab, the level of excitement dims.

"Remember, we must walk in quickly and quietly, in the order I told you." Caroline instantly takes charge. "And our changes of pose must be made with as little noise as possible."

She would be furious if anything disrupted her tableau. I cannot entirely imagine why she has chosen this particularly inactive entertainment. Surely a dance would have achieved her object better. There is someone sitting out there whom she means to captivate—that much is perfectly clear. With a little more time I will discover who.

"We can view the tableau through the back," Madame Campan whispers to me while the others file obediently through the side door into the part of the ballroom that is behind the makeshift curtain. Polite applause greets the end of the boys' recitations, and the movement of thirty or so of them, followed by forty girls in Caroline's tableau, creates quite a din.

I don't see him, but I hear the young Perroquet playing some music on the pianoforte to hide the inevitable shuffling and nudging, at least one *"Ow!"* and a stifled *"Merde!"*

Madame Campan takes my hand and pulls me to the door behind the guests. One of the maids—the one called Hélène, who seems to belong to Caroline—opens the door silently for us.

In the moments before the curtain slides to the floor like a silken waterfall, I am transfixed by what I see. I have never stood thus, behind an audience, where I can view the backs of their heads, the parts of their bodies they don't even notice when they peer in the mirror.

As still as an ice statue, Joséphine sits not in the center, but a little to the side. She perches, one leg out slightly farther than the other, and from here I see that the fan she uses to hide her mouth trembles just a bit. It must be difficult for her to sit so that her head is lower than Bonaparte's. What a study she has made of success! No wonder she will not give her children away lightly. If only she knew that I could make more of Eugène than any of the fine ladies of Paris. . . .

Next to her is the great general himself, sitting erect and as posed as the tableau we are about to see. His hat in his lap, he taps the fingers of one hand against its brim. He is impatient. Indeed! How must it be to go from the events of the past two days to these meaningless displays?

The other generals, two of them his brothers, sit in more or less the same pose, and all either tap one foot, or look up at the ceiling, or stifle yawns. *Yes*, I think. *You want to go and find your mistresses, let them tell you how brilliant you are and how much your dangerous exploits have aroused them.* I wonder, fleetingly, if any of these generals will find their way to the Comédie Française, perhaps even ask for my mother's company for the evening.

Only one of them does not betray boredom. It is Murat. He is a handsome fellow. I have seen him once or twice at the theater, and always with a different lady. What could be his interests here? Surely not Hortense, who has her eye upon the insignificant young music teacher.

Then it hits me. *Caroline!* What a match that would be. And the fact that he is here explains her determination to be the brightest star in the performance.

A tutor stands eyeing the unruly boys. He walks behind the last row, where one of the lads is about to drop something down the back of the fellow sitting next to him. The master grasps the boy's hand and the unsuspecting fellow yelps, making everyone turn for a moment.

I catch Joséphine's eye. She looks at me vaguely at first; then I see comprehension dawn in her expression. It hardens. I smile a little and nod to her. She shifts her glance slightly to Madame Campan, who is next to me. Something passes between them.

Hortense has taken a seat next to another young lady, not one from the school, nor even anyone I recognize from the theater audiences. She looks a little familiar, though, so I am not entirely certain. I see Hortense incline her head to the lady and speak quietly into her ear. I wish I could hear what they are saying, but instead my attention is diverted by a voice much closer to me.

"You are very fortunate, mademoiselle, in having so influential a friend as Eliza Monroe," Madame Campan whispers in my ear. "She is naive, but I am not. Listen very carefully to me."

I try to edge away, but Madame Campan has a tight grip on my arm.

"At the end of this performance, you will plead a head-ache. I have already summoned a carriage, which will be waiting to return you to the theater whence you came. The driver will have money for you—more than enough to compensate you for this evening's performance."

How did she find out? My performance has been flawless. Was it Caroline? Eliza? Caroline is too absorbed in her own matters to care much about me. And Eliza—no, I think she would not try to undo her one act of heroism for the sake of Eugène.

It must have been Hortense. How could she? I thought she wanted her brother's happiness. And ensuring that happiness would leave the blushing teacher, Michel, for her. Suddenly the game has changed. I will not be undone by Hortense.

Madame Campan's words cease with the end of the introductory music. Someone yanks the cord with a flourish and sends the curtain tumbling to the ground.

The first pose is quite perfect. A flutter of polite clapping goes through the audience. Then the schoolgirls move to the next, which is almost exactly right except for the youngest girl, who teeters a little. More applause, mixed with a stifled laugh.

After a moment, it is time for the final pose. The young girls must turn away, kneel down, and lean in a dramatic gesture, leaving Caroline and Eliza alone in the center of the stage. But they have not rehearsed on the raised platform, and as they adjust their position this upsets the balance completely. I watch openmouthed as two of the girls topple off the platform and end up sprawled on the floor, their gowns showing indecent stretches of leg.

47

Hortense

At first, I am not certain what has happened. What was initially a well-ordered assemblage of costumed girls becomes a mass of flailing arms and legs. But that is not the worst of it. The boys seated behind me naturally start to howl with laughter. And our guests...

I sense rather than see several men rise and charge toward the stage. Eugène does not, but Napoléon and his brothers and Murat— Before I have a chance to make sense of the situation, they climb over the young ones, trying not to step on their hands and feet, but almost all of the girls are now crying loudly. Murat has removed his jacket and has thrown it over Caroline's shoulders.

I caught only a glimpse, but I saw that Caroline's torso was covered only by the sheerest of fabrics, revealing quite clearly the shape and outline of her body. She might as well be naked.

"If this is meant to be a genteel entertainment, then I must wonder about this school!" Louise hisses in my ear. She shifts, as if to rise.

I grasp her arm and keep her where she is. "Please stay. I need your help. Michel needs your help."

She relaxes and remains seated, but keeps her eyes averted from the stage.

Caroline wears a curious expression. I'm not certain whether it is triumph or shame. Her tableau is a disaster. I should go and help the young ones, but I don't dare leave Louise's side. I am depending upon her to get Michel away immediately after the performance, before any damage can be done. Armand is in the dining room, ready to draw him away from Madeleine if need be, and at the same time prevent Eugène from getting to her, either. I hope he performed the first favor I asked of him: to deliver a message to Madame Campan that would reveal Madeleine's identity.

I glance at my mother without turning my head.

She is laughing. Her close-lipped laugh, the one she reserves for important social occasions, when she will not reveal her teeth to anyone.

I am tempted to laugh myself. Poor Caroline! Whatever she planned, it cannot have been this. Just behind me sits her mother. I pretend to cough and steal a glance at her. Madame Bonaparte is as red as a beet.

Madame Campan comes running up from behind and together with the maids manages to clear the stage of sobbing girls. I wonder what she will say when this is over?

Murat leads Caroline out of the ballroom into the dining room almost tenderly. So he really does love her. I feel a pang of envy. How wonderful it must be to have one's head and one's heart in the same, safe place.

All the Bonaparte brothers return to their places. I see bright spots of color on their cheeks. I steal a look at my own brother. I have caught him just looking away from me. I don't like his smirk of satisfaction. Does he think to consider himself above the Bonaparte clan because I have more sense than to display myself for all to see?

If only he knew that I am like Caroline at heart. I have done everything I could today to ensure that Michel will not bestow his affection elsewhere. In fact, the only difference between Caroline and me is that she has chosen someone to whom her mother cannot object.

For a moment I hope that the disaster of the tableau will curtail the evening's activities, and we will go directly into the parlor for the light refreshments and champagne Madame Campan has planned.

But then, once the stage is cleared, she stands in the middle of it as though nothing at all has happened.

"If you would be so kind, we have a much more suitable

entertainment yet to come. Please take your seats for an anthem, composed by our own dear Hortense de Beauharnais in honor of the occasion. . . ."

Polite applause. Everyone is bored already after the momentary excitement. Madame Campan motions me to stand and take a bow. I oblige. I see my mother's questioning look; she would naturally expect me to sing it. I turn my eyes away. Let her discover for herself.

"I did not know you wrote this anthem," Louise says. I sense an ounce of admiration, and look at her.

"I exist for music. It is the only thing I care about. That's why I am going to help your family."

She looks puzzled. I don't bother to explain.

With becoming modesty, Madeleine walks out from the dining room and stands in the center of the raised platform, her eyes cast to the ground. I cannot help looking directly at Michel at last. How I wanted it to be me up there next to him! What a fantasy I had, to prove to my mother that, despite our difference in status, he and I were meant for each other. Now, instead, I plot his removal from the scene, and prepare to betray my own brother's love.

My view of the stage mists over as Michel plays the introduction.

It's good, I know. I am not unaware of my abilities, small though they are. I notice even the generals sit up a little straighter at the stirring sounds.

Madeleine starts to sing.

For such a slight creature she has surprising power. I can hear it more readily now that I am not separated from her voice by a wall. Not only does everyone listen, but all inch forward in their seats.

I wonder about Eugène, how he feels to see his beloved here, and turn to look for him.

He isn't there. When did he leave? It must have been just as Madeleine appeared.

My mother. Could she know? How? And yet the look on her face—rigid, expressionless. She can't have said anything to him.

Madeleine is soon completely absorbed in her performance. She does not look at the small group in front of her, but reaches out with her voice and her emotions to some audience far beyond. The words I meant to convey so much to Michel she now gives to Eugène. And yet—he's gone.

At the shrine of Mary,
They both make their vows,
This desired union
That will make them happy.

A union, I think, that both Madeleine and I have wanted. She clasps her hands together and holds them out beseechingly, then opens them as if she is letting a songbird go free.

Everyone in the chapel
Says, when they see them:
Love to the most beautiful,

She looks at me, but not with love. I see something in her eyes that disturbs me, but do not know how to interpret it. I feel not as if she is singing my song to the crowd, but *at me*, as though it is some kind of weapon she will use against all of us.

She pauses before the final line of the anthem. Michel inserts a flourish at the pianoforte. They have practiced this moment.

Madeleine kneels down, her fingertips brushing the floor as she catches the hem of her dress.

Honor to the most valiant.

After Caroline's daring gesture, I thought the evening would be calmer. But I am badly mistaken.

As Michel plays the final chords, Madeleine reaches beneath her gown and pulls out a dagger, brandishing it high in two hands, its tip pointed down toward her breast.

Everyone gasps. There is a rattle of metal as the soldiers in the room reflexively reach for their swords. The entire front row stands, a wall of blue coats and white breeches.

Silence. Or near silence. Madeleine breathes hard, her

chest heaving. She takes a step toward my mother. Napoléon plants himself between them.

"You think, all of you, that love is simply another game to be played on the board of life. You think that a broken heart is no more deadly than a piece of chipped crockery."

Madame Campan, who had taken a seat at the front but slightly to the side, makes a move toward Madeleine. "My dear, no one—"

"Taisez-vous!" Madeleine commands, changing her stance. Now she crouches, the dagger in one hand out in front of her, directed toward Madame Campan. She slowly arcs it across us, aiming it from person to person. When the dagger is pointed at me, I swear I can feel its tip graze my cheek, although it is two meters away.

"I did not plan to be here. I should have been many miles away from this place by now," she says, with a slight shake of her head, her eyes now unfocused, combing the small audience for Eugène.

She does not see, as everyone else does, that he has entered behind her through the side door, his pistol raised and aiming at her heart.

I grip the edge of my chair. Michel! Surely he will do something?

He has left his seat at the pianoforte and now cowers behind it. My heart drops like a stone. Is this the man I thought I loved? First his sister has the power to prevent our union, then he becomes enthralled with a stranger because of her beautiful voice, and now he is not man enough to leap forward and wrest the dagger from a delicately built actress's hands.

I flick my eyes over to Eugène. He has taken a few noiseless steps toward Madeleine so that he is almost close enough to reach her.

"Now you shall allow me to leave with my beloved in peace. He is here. I know he will come for me. He promised. . . ."

Tears wash down her cheeks. Her nose starts to drip. These are not stage tears, I realize. She is desperately in love!

I must help her after all. I can't deny Eugène such happiness. "Eugène, no!" I cry.

Madeleine whirls toward him. The dagger catches his hand, but no blood flows. In his shock, his soldier's instinct faultless, his finger squeezes the trigger.

Madeleine falls to the floor. A pool of blood quickly forms around her.

This time, no one moves.

48

Eliza

Sitting here, in my room, the whole day seems like a dream—or a nightmare.

After the disaster of the tableau. I waited in the drawing room with the others, embarrassed for Caroline, who appeared not to be in the slightest disturbed by what had happened. But she and her General Murat were simply standing to the side as if nothing had happened. He held his uniform jacket closed across her ample bosom. She looked so happy. It was a daring gesture on her part, and it appeared to have worked.

The young ones were buzzing with excitement, clearly wanting to talk it over. They seemed torn between disappointment that the tableau was over, and thrill that something so scandalous had happened in their very well-behaved school.

Of course, they didn't know what we three have been up to in the past few days. Nor did they suspect that something even more scandalous would occur only a few minutes later.

I wanted to listen to Madeleine sing. I felt I had been uncharitable toward her, ever since I discovered where she was from, what her background was. Clearly, I thought, she is talented and feels deeply. She has also suffered abominably at the hands of her mother, and has had the kind of life I would not wish on an enemy.

Besides, if Eugène had fallen in love with her—the most noble, handsomest gentleman in France—then surely I could accept her.

And of course, I could not restrain my curiosity concerning the dagger I saw her hide under her skirt. I assumed it was simply there in case she needed it when they ran away together. I was certain that was her plan. Eugène would hear her sing, fall even more deeply in love with her, and together they would flee the school and run away to be married. The idea was so very romantic, if so very sad.

As I crept around to the door at the back of the ballroom to hear Madeleine's performance, I had almost decided that if she could not manage to get away with Eugène, I would bring her back to Virginia with me. Perhaps, I thought, she could help me persuade my mama and papa that we should free our slaves and give them a wage for working in our house and on our land. After all, Mama wanted me to gain a French education, and the French have decided that slavery is evil. I wondered how many of our slaves, given a chance, might be like Madeleine—talented and intelligent.

But as I started to make my way to the other door, Eugène walked through. He saw me and bowed in a friendly way.

"Eugène," I said. I wasn't sure what to say next.

"I see you delivered my message to the Comédie Française. I confess, I did not anticipate that it would have such an outcome."

Of course, he had not asked me to take Madeleine away from the theater. I was a little ashamed. I felt my face go hot. "Her mother was so cruel, and she is so unfortunate. I could not leave her there to suffer."

He touched my cheek. I felt the touch tingle through me, and once again recalled the soft feeling of his lips. "Do not distress yourself," he said. "You have a good heart. Madeleine is extraordinary, and deserves better than she has had so far in life. But I received a disturbing message some hours after you and I parted, from the servant Marianne at the theater."

He reached into his pocket and pulled out a scrap of paper. In very shaky writing, it said:

Forgive me, Vicomte, but I fear my mistress, Madeleine de Pourtant, is not safe or sane. When you didn't come, I

*thought she would take her own life. Now she has gone
away with a strange girl dressed as a soldier, and she has
taken a weapon with her. Please find her before something
bad happens.*

A weapon. "We had a dagger when we left. The servant
gave it to us. She seemed to think Madeleine would need
protection if her mother sent someone after her." I couldn't
understand why she would now be concerned about what
Madeleine might do with it.

Before he could speak further, the opening strains of the
song stopped him with their exquisite beauty. "What does
my sister think of her?" he whispered, his eyes misted over
with emotion.

I didn't want to tell him what I believed was true, that
Hortense had decided that his love for Madeleine must be
thwarted. Why else would she not have sent word to him
right away, to tell him that Madeleine was at the school?
Since I could say nothing, I put my finger to my lips, and
we moved toward the ballroom door in order to hear Madeleine better.

Eugène was enthralled from the first note. I couldn't
help sighing.

"He is too old for you."

I jumped. I had been concentrating so hard on Eugène,
and on Madeleine's song, that I did not notice Armand. He
had left his post at the door to the ballroom and come up

behind me. "I don't know what you mean," I said, although I knew perfectly well.

"Would you prefer it if I wore a uniform? You seemed not to dislike me so much yesterday, in Saint-Cloud."

"Shh!" I said. But I had to admit, he was right. I think I hadn't really looked at him properly until I saw him in his blue coat and white breeches.

I was about to make a conciliatory remark when, on the last line of the song, just when I expected that everyone would begin to applaud wildly for Madeleine's beautiful performance, I heard instead a gasp and the rattle of swords.

In an instant, Eugène sprang forward and, noiseless as a cat, opened the door. I took a step toward him, but Armand held me back. "Don't!" he said, then nodded toward the young ones. The two of us shepherded them back and silenced them with a fierce look.

One of the youngest, a member of the Pink class, broke free of the group and stood where she could see through the door. Her mouth opened wide. She turned and said aloud to everyone, "She has a dagger! She is threatening Joséphine!"

My God, I thought. My first instinct was to run to Eugène, but again Armand held me back. I felt cold, as if someone had put ice on the back of my neck.

I watched as Eugène crept forward and drew his pistol from his belt, holding it out in front of him as he moved farther into the ballroom.

It all happened so fast, and yet when I think about it

now I see everything slowly, in every detail. Madeleine whirling around with the dagger, her eyes shining, hopeful. The sharp retort and flash from Eugène's pistol. Her body crumpling to the floor and blood flowering around it. All the young ones screamed, and I felt an ache in my heart so intense that I couldn't even cry.

Horrified, I turned and buried my face in Armand's shoulder. He wrapped his arms around me and stroked my hair.

I didn't want him to let go, but the sound of the door slamming made me push myself away. Madame Campan had rushed through and locked the ballroom door. Her face was as white as the lace on her sleeves, her lips drained of blood.

"You must all go to your rooms. At once!"

I had never heard her speak harshly before then. Everyone was so frightened they obeyed immediately.

All except for me—and Armand.

I looked up at him. "It's all my fault," I said. I knew it was. Would any of this have happened without me? If I hadn't brought Madeleine back to the school?

49

Hortense

I run to my mother's side. She leans forward, a handkerchief pressed to her closed eyes. Napoléon, Lucien, and Louis form a tight group, standing away from the stage. Madame Bonaparte sits erect. I catch sight of her expression, which is a curious mixture of horror and triumph. I wonder, briefly, how much blood she has seen shed during the course of her life.

"Fetch me my salts," Maman says to me, but I cannot obey her. Instead, I am drawn to the stage, where now Eugène kneels by Madeleine, who lies in a crimson pool, her life draining away. I join him, not paying attention to the scarlet stain that seeps into my white gown. I pick up her hand. Her eyes are staring and her mouth opens and closes. She lives!

"Madeleine! Madeleine! We have sent for the doctor."

She does not appear to hear me. And her hand is so cold it chills me through.

"It's no use," Eugène whispers.

I cannot believe she will die. I lift her arm and put her hand to my cheek, rubbing her wrist, trying to keep her from fading away. I feel as if she is attempting to say something, but cannot speak. I lean forward.

More people throng the stage. I am aware of Caroline, with Murat at her side. I look up and see pity in her eyes. She must realize all too clearly that my brother, my dear Eugène, has accidentally killed the woman he loves.

"Come, Eugène, you can do nothing here." It is Murat. He is a good man, I realize. I raise my eyes and see that his and Caroline's fingers are intertwined. Now everyone will know that they are in love. A pain stabs my heart, as though the dagger Madeleine brandished has found its home.

Madeleine stirs a little. She tries to lift her head. Eugène leans closer, mingling his tears with hers. No one breathes.

"It . . . wasn't . . . ," she starts to say, but the effort costs her too much, and she falls back again before summoning the will to speak once more. "I would never . . . I only did it . . ." Then louder, her eyes fixed upon Eugène's, she says, "I love you."

Her body relaxes completely, her head tipping to the side. The hand I hold slips out of my grasp.

Eugène's tears flow freely as he shakes his head slowly from side to side.

I sit up and cast my eyes around the room, a familiar place grown strange. Michel and his sister are nowhere to be seen. They must have run out in the confusion.

Beyond the pianoforte, I see Madeleine's dagger. It's near the wall beneath the long windows, where it must have flown when Eugène's bullet hit her tiny frame. Without thinking what I am doing, I stand and walk over to retrieve it. No one pays attention to me, because the doctor has arrived. I watch from a distance as he kneels by Madeleine, feeling her pulse, confirming she has indeed passed beyond the reach of his arts.

"Her mother must be informed." It is my mother, the beguiling Joséphine. She stands, dry eyed. I see she is relieved to have such a troublesome situation resolved so absolutely. Yet I also see that her heart aches for Eugène, to have his dreams dashed so violently, and at his own hands.

As everyone backs away, clearly wondering what to do next, I weigh the dagger in my hand and notice something odd about it. The blade feels much heavier than the handle, as if the handle is hollow. I turn it this way and that, and notice a tiny button at the point where one's thumb would rest. I press the button down. Nothing happens. I test the sharpness of the blade. It is quite dull. So dull that I can push on the tip of it without pricking my finger at all.

Something makes me decide to touch the blade's tip at the same time as I press the button with my thumb.

I move the blade into the handle until it disappears completely.

"Look!" I say to everyone. All eyes are upon me as I repeat the action.

Maman approaches. "It's a trick dagger," she says. "I have seen them used upon the stage. To make it appear that an actor has plunged it into his adversary, the blade retracts smoothly into the handle."

"That's what she was trying to say," I murmur. I cannot help meeting Eugène's eyes. "She meant no one any harm."

One by one, everyone leaves. Eugène lifts Madeleine's body and carries it out to a waiting wagon. The doctor must have sent it.

At last only Caroline and I remain in the ballroom. I am too weary and sad to say anything to her. When she breaks the silence between us, it startles me.

"I shall leave school tomorrow. My education is finished. My life as a married woman will soon begin."

She is triumphant but subdued.

"So tonight will be the last you ever spend at the Académie," I say.

Caroline nods and leaves. I am alone in the room where so much has happened today.

Love is a strange and dangerous thing. Eugène came so close to finding happiness, and an accident destroyed his fate. Caroline has triumphed, discovering a mutual love that will make all her family rejoice in the end. And I? How foolish I was to think that Michel and I could ever marry! I let my passion for music confuse me, seeing something that wasn't really there because I wanted to free myself of my girlish infatuation with my stepfather.

I suppose I have succeeded. What next? My education, too, has been completed.

50

Eliza

Chère Maman,

This letter will be the final one I write to you from Paris, for tomorrow I sail for home.

I know you expected me to stay through spring, but circumstances make that impossible and—I believe you would agree—no longer desirable. Besides, I am eager to be there when you bear my sister or brother, which Papa says will be soon.

Caroline left with all her trunks and her maids Hélène and Ernestine yesterday. (I sent Ernestine off with my blessing. She would hate Virginia!) Caroline is to marry General Murat early in the new year, to everyone's satisfaction but especially hers.

Hortense has also been called to Malmaison. Her situation is not so happy, but I have become very close to her

*in these past few days especially, and she is resigned to it. It
is very likely she will marry Caroline's brother Louis, who is
not handsome and does not make up for that fact with
charm and wit.*

*Eugène de Beauharnais has gone off to Italy to be some
sort of official there. Although the incidents at our school
were hushed up, I'm certain none of us—and especially
Eugène—will ever forget them. After everything that
happened he couldn't bear to remain in Paris.*

I regret, a little, making such a fool of myself with
Eugène. I realize now, of course, that it was a silly fantasy.
We are so different, worlds apart.

And besides . . . I open the box of mementos I have col-
lected in my time here and take a note from the top of the
pile of theater tickets, advertisements, and little trinkets. I
received it the day after the performance, from Armand. The
creases in the paper are starting to become tears, so often
have I opened and reread his words.

Chère Eliza,

*I hope you will eventually forgive me for everything. As
to what "everything" is, that is what I wish to tell you in this
letter.*

*At first, I meant to remain your enemy. I meant to play
you for a fool, with the help of circumstance and my own*

selfish need to find a way to leave the life my family—such
as they are—has laid out for me.

But I could not remain insensible to your sweetness and
beauty. Yes, although you are still very young, I can see
that you will become a beauty to rival Hortense herself.

I read those lines over and over again. Me? A beauty? Had he written nothing more, I would have been happy. But his letter continues to explain that Hortense persuaded him to write to Madame Campan, informing her about Madeleine. As to why he agreed? He admits that he thought by ingratiating himself to Hortense, he might put himself in a position to be given lucrative commissions for portraits once he left school. And now that his family has declined to support him any longer, that day is imminent.

He also assures me that, contrary to what I believed, nothing was my fault. None of what happened can be laid at my feet. Madeleine's tragic end could never have been prevented by me, once it all had been set in motion by her and Eugène.

You were the perfect innocent, his letter says.

I shall, I know, be much less trusting in the future.

A gentle knock interrupts my writing. *"Venez!"* I call. To think that soon I shall leave my French behind and become once more a girl from Virginia. Then everyone here—including Armand—will be nothing but a dream.

I turn as my door opens. "I wanted to come and see you, to give you a gift before you leave."

"Hortense!" I run to her. We embrace with genuine affection. "And I wanted a chance to tell you again that I wish I had not tormented you the way I did with Caroline. I didn't know she intended to tease you so. It was wicked of her, and I'm sure she's sorry, too."

She smiles. Now there is always sadness in her smile. I know what she's thinking.

"Michel was not worthy of you," I say, taking her hand and making her sit with me in front of the fire.

She looks surprised. "You knew?"

I nod. "I overheard you in the ballroom. I stopped Madame Campan from entering."

She smiles, but it is not a happy smile.

"You will find someone else soon," I say, feeling more like an older sister than a younger school friend.

"I fear that it is not for me to choose. Now that Bonaparte is first consul, my mother's expectations are even more pressing."

I know she speaks of Louis, Napoléon's ugly, uninteresting brother. Madame Campan couldn't wait to announce to the school that not one, but two matches were certain to be concluded within the month. "How can she ask it of you?" I say. "You will be married to her brother-in-law! Your stepuncle, if there is such a thing."

This makes Hortense smile her cheerless smile again.

"In time you will understand. A match of convenience is not so very terrible. One expects so little; one is bound to be pleasantly surprised."

"I wish I could stay for Caroline's wedding. I'm certain it will be magnificent." I sigh.

"Actually, I have heard that it is to be a private affair. Napoléon doesn't want tongues wagging about extravagance at a time when he is trying to get the finances of a country in order."

Too bad for Caroline, I think. "Well, I'm sure she'll be glad to be married, even if it isn't a grand event."

We both stare at the flickering firelight for a moment. I shall miss Hortense especially. It has been a short time, but we have shared so many experiences. "Do you hear anything from Eugène?" I cannot help asking. The last time I saw him was in his bloody uniform, carrying Madeleine to the wagon. Although I have given up all desire of being anything to him, I will never forget his kiss.

"He is working very hard. I had a letter. He said to remember him to you."

I don't really believe her. I'm sure Eugène has other things on his mind. An awkward silence falls between us.

"I also had a letter from Armand," she says.

I try not to act too interested. "Oh? Has he left school now?"

"Next week," she says. "He's thinking about emigrating. There is no future for him here, poor fellow."

"To Africa?" I ask, my mind leaping first to the places where France has a foothold.

"He mentions America, actually." She doesn't look at me when she says it, pretending not to expect me to be very interested.

And I do my best not to act interested. America is a large country. And perhaps he will decide on Boston or New York instead of somewhere near Virginia. There are more opportunities for artists in the cities. Still . . . "You said you had a present for me!" I say, then realize perhaps I shouldn't sound so excited about it, especially as I haven't yet told her that I have a parting gift for her.

"You'll probably hate it. But I couldn't think of anyone else who should have it." She stands and goes to the door.

I'm confused. "Is it somewhere else?"

"Follow me. It's downstairs with your trunks, waiting for the final bit of packing."

I take a candle and walk with Hortense down the wide curve of dark stairs to the vestibule. I think of that first time, when Caroline and I stole out in the night. It was only a few short weeks ago, but I feel as if I am a completely different person now. It was the beginning of everything. The beginning of my life.

I see the pile of trunks. I had to buy two new ones to fit all the gowns I have bought here, some while my mother was here, a few new ones just in the last few days so I can take them with me and lead the fashions back home. To the side is a partially wrapped panel leaning against the wall. Hortense walks over to it and pulls the cloth away that covers its front.

I bring my candle close, letting the light softly and gradually reveal what is there. "It's exquisite." My eyes fill with tears as I see Hortense looking out at me from a beautifully painted canvas. "I shall treasure it always."

"It was painted last summer, by someone you know. My mother wanted to give it to Louis, but I persuaded her not to."

The portrait captures Hortense's sweetness and beauty so perfectly. "Is it . . . ? Did he really do this?" I ask. I had no idea Armand was so gifted. "I shall think you are in the room with me whenever I look at it." *And I shall remember the feeling of Armand's hand in mine, too,* I think. This gift is too generous, and too perfect. "I have only a bauble to give you, I'm afraid," I say. "It's in my room."

We climb the stairs, arm in arm now, and slowly, as if we both know this will be our last time together.

I give Hortense the sapphire pendant my mother bought for me to wear to my first Parisian ball.

"Oh, no, it's too fine!" she exclaims.

"No, I insist. It's poor in comparison to your portrait." And, I think, perhaps if she is ever in difficulty she could sell it and come to America. I don't tell her that, though.

"When do you leave?" she asks.

"Very early tomorrow. Please don't feel you must see me off," I say. "I don't think I could bear it."

"It's late. I must let you sleep, and I see I have interrupted you writing a letter." She nods to the desk, where I left my quill in the inkpot and the sheet of paper in view.

There is no point in prolonging our good-byes. We embrace.

"I'll never forget you," I say.

And I may never see you again, I think, fearing that it's true.

EPILOGUE

Eliza

The carriage ride to Honfleur was uneventful. An elderly lady, Mrs. Higginbotham, is acting as my companion on the voyage home. She will give me no trouble. She sleeps most of the time. I expect to be left to myself. Thanks to Madame Campan's instruction, I know how to blend into French society tolerably well, and will enjoy it if there are tea parties or dances on board with the officers.

The journey will be long, and I am looking forward to being home, although I don't regret a minute of my time in Paris and Saint-Germain. My trunks are already on board the ship I shall take to New York, where I will shed Mrs. Higginbotham and be met by one of our slaves.

Our slaves. I wonder if Papa would consider freeing them? Surely we could afford to pay them some small wages, or let them work for room and board. I would do it in honor of

Madeleine, and everything I learned from her about the price of real freedom. It didn't matter that she was half African. She deserved love and the liberty to live her life just as much as Caroline and Hortense did. Just as much as I do.

Perhaps that is the most important thing I have learned here. *Liberté, Égalité, Fraternité.* It's what the French fought their revolution for. Madeleine wasn't just my equal, she was superior to me in so many ways—in her passion, her talent, and her willingness to do whatever it took for the sake of love. I will try when I am home to be open to seeing such things in people who are different from me, either because their skin is not white, or because they don't have the advantages that I have been fortunate to come by.

We sail on the tide in a few hours. It is cold, but the day is clear. I do not wish to sit inside a café with my chaperone and sip tea until it is time to leave. I don't know when—or if—I'll ever set foot in France again. I'd rather walk by the quay and watch the laborers loading crates onto the ships. I wonder where they are all going?

The breeze is brisk, and I pull my cloak around me.

"Mademoiselle Eliza Monroe?"

I jump. I don't know anyone here, and I left Mrs. Higginbotham dozing in front of a fire in a quayside café. When I turn toward the voice, I am dumbfounded to see Armand de Valmont.

"Armand!" I want to throw my arms around him, I'm so happy to have this last chance to see him, but I restrain myself. It would not do to make a spectacle when I have assured Mrs. Higginbotham that I was only going for a brief stroll.

He smiles and removes his hat. He is wearing clothing like a common laborer and carries a portfolio. "I go to America to seek my fortune," he says, gesturing toward the ships in the harbor.

"On the *Serendipity*?" I ask, suddenly excited that perhaps we will have more time to become acquainted.

"No. I'm on a merchantman. I have no money for a proper passage. I'm working my way across, sketching for the shipping company."

My heart sinks as quickly as it flew into the clouds. "Where will you land?"

"Boston. There is an established society there, where members may want their portraits painted by the latest sensation from Paris." His eyes sparkle with mischief.

"New York has wealthy residents as well. And Philadelphia, and—"

He steps closer to me. "I'll look for you, Eliza." His eyes are kind and sad at the same time. I wonder why I didn't really notice them when we first met.

"Hortense gave me the portrait," I say, suddenly feeling awkward.

"I told her to." He touches my cheek with his cold fingers. "You have a wonderful future ahead of you. I am very glad to have met you when you were but a sweet girl."

He speaks as if this is a final parting, and my throat squeezes shut. He nods and strides away.

"Armand!" I call.

He turns, but does not come back. Instead, he makes me a low, courtly bow, sweeping his hat across so that it skims the dirt beneath our feet.

I smile. I should feel sad, I know. But instead, I am elated. Now I know that nothing can stop me. And I know I have not seen the last of Armand.

Author's Note

I almost couldn't believe it was possible when I discovered that Eliza Monroe, Hortense de Beauharnais, and Caroline Bonaparte all went to the same boarding school in Saint-Germain-en-Laye. That this was the school run by Jeanne Louise Henriette Campan, who survived the revolution and the *Terreur* despite having been mistress of the bedchamber to Marie Antoinette, made it all the more wonderful. Yet discovering the details of their relationships, or much more beyond that they were all students of the school at one time or other, proved rather difficult.

Eliza was first enrolled at the age of eight, when her parents came to Paris in the midst of the *Terreur*. She was a student for the three years the family remained in Paris, until they left for home in 1797. She had met Hortense de

Beauharnais and formed a friendship with her, but Caroline Bonaparte was not yet a student during that time.

When the Monroes returned to Paris in 1803 for James Monroe to broker the Louisiana Purchase, Eliza spent another year in the school. By this time, Caroline was already married to Murat, and Hortense had been wed to Louis Bonaparte. Nonetheless, Eliza and Hortense continued to be friends as the Monroes went back and forth between London and Paris. The fact that the family attended Napoléon's coronation as emperor of France in 1804 is an interesting footnote.

I have taken several liberties with the sketchy details of life in Madame Campan's school and the timeline of events in Eliza's life. There was no trip to Paris in 1799; Elizabeth Monroe had just given birth to her first son in May of that year and would not have traveled abroad. But it would have been in keeping with her character to chance a hazardous ocean crossing with her child—which she did on both occasions that her husband was sent to France to represent the U.S. government. This was notable because she suffered from what the family called rheumatism—probably rheumatoid arthritis—and must have gone through a great deal of pain for the sake of keeping her family together. Plus, Elizabeth was a true Francophile, speaking quite good French and celebrated as *la belle Américaine* by the French media. During their first stay in Paris, the Monroes actually purchased a small château, which they turned into a center of society and diplomacy, a sort of haven during a period when so much of the city was virtually destroyed.

But at that time, Eliza was too young and Caroline Bonaparte was not yet even in Paris, let alone at Madame Campan's school. To make the connection of all three girls plausible, I chose 1799 as the year in which they could be together. Both Hortense and Caroline were, in fact, at the Académie at that time, sent to be out of the way during the events surrounding 18 Brumaire. I had only to manufacture Eliza's presence and add two years to her age. This timeline also allowed me to have all three of them interact with a dramatic turning point in French history.

Concerning the relationships among the Bonaparte and Beauharnais clans: the enmity between Napoléon's family and Joséphine was a fact, and it extended to the children, who were seen as usurpers of Napoléon's affection and support. Caroline was the youngest of three daughters, and had four older brothers as well. By the time she came along, Madame Bonaparte paid little attention to her education. She was virtually illiterate when she came to Madam Campan's school as a teenager.

Hortense tried to be friendly with Caroline, but their relationship was never a warm one. However, Hortense was devoted to her brother, Eugène.

The relationship of Napoléon and Hortense has been the subject of much speculation and rumor in the past. One nineteenth-century account suggests rather salaciously that they were lovers. That Napoléon was very fond of both of Joséphine's children is indisputable, however. When he threatened to divorce Joséphine over Captain Charles, it was Hortense who pleaded with him on her mother's behalf. I have chosen to treat the complex relationship between stepfather and stepdaughter by giving Hortense a kind of hero-worship crush on Napoléon. This was a way for me to explain why she would eventually agree to an arranged marriage with Louis Bonaparte in 1802, who was unattractive, unambitious, and not a particularly nice person.

Caroline's passion for Murat is well documented, as is the fact that Joséphine intervened to overcome Napoléon's objections to the match. She saw it as a possible means of softening the family's dislike. Her tactics did not entirely succeed, as Napoléon eventually divorced her so he could marry someone else and produce an heir.

Although Joséphine lived out her life quietly, the rest of Napoléon's relatives populated the royal courts of Europe. Caroline and Murat were given many honors. Her titles stacked up to include *Princesse française*, Grand Duchess Consort of Berg and Cleves, Queen Consort of Naples and Sicily, Princess Consort Murat, *Comtesse de Lipona*. This power and influence was not well used by Caroline, who remained headstrong and unpopular for her entire life.

Napoléon favored Hortense and Louis by making them

king and queen of Holland. They had three sons, the youngest of whom later became Napoléon III of France.

Eliza eventually played an important role as hostess in her father's White House, often taking the place of her ailing mother at state occasions. She married a prominent attorney and named her daughter Hortense, after her dear friend. A portrait of Hortense Bonaparte remained in her possession throughout her life. Although Eliza was generally seen as a haughty, rather snobbish person, she selflessly cared for victims of a fever that broke out in Washington during her father's term. After the death of her mother and her husband, Eliza returned to Paris, converted to Catholicism, and lived out her life in a convent.

Aside from a glimpse of post-revolutionary life in France, this novel gave me an opportunity to explore eighteenth-century issues of race and slavery. The French First Republic officially abolished slavery in 1794. Yet Monroe had slaves, and while serving as governor of Virginia in 1800 called in the militia to suppress the slave uprising known as Gabriel's Rebellion. His actions were swift and unmerciful, with twenty-five slaves hanged in the most brutal way to serve as a deterrent to future rebellions. In his biography of Monroe, Harlow Giles Unger notes that "Monroe nonetheless confessed his doubts about the long-term consequences of his handling of Gabriel's Rebellion..." (*The Last Founding Father,* p. 142).

The difference of attitude between the French and the Americans with regard to slavery, as well as the growing abolitionist sentiments in different parts of the world, must have had some impact on an impressionable young American at the time. By making one of my main characters part black, I found a way to force Eliza to confront the injustice of a system that America depended upon for economic prosperity. Whether she actually had these shaded feelings remains unknown.

As for Madeleine and her mother—they are fabrications of my own imagination. There is no evidence that Eugène de Beauharnais ever had a liaison with an actress, or that there was a Creole actress at the Comédie Française. This is a work of fiction, after all, and Madeleine inserted herself onto the page and simply would not let go of events.

ACKNOWLEDGMENTS

A novel is not the product of one person's hard work and dedication. It is the result of work by a whole team of people whose only wish is to bring the best possible book to the public. Therefore, I would like to thank my agent, Adam Chromy, for his tireless support and work on my behalf, as well as all he and his team have taught me about writing novels. Equally as important is my editor, Melanie Cecka, whose painstaking critiques and notes really helped me pull this novel with its different points of view together into a coherent whole. I would also like to thank Stephanie Cowell and Susan O'Doherty for reading and commenting on early versions of the manuscript. It takes time and effort and is an invaluable service. Also to thank is the copy-editor, Nicholas LoVecchio, who keeps me honest and helps me avoid embarrassing gaffes.

In addition to the people who have directly touched this book, I must mention my community of authors. We all know how difficult it is to write a book: the uncertainty, the self-doubt, the triumphs and disappointments. I know I can turn to my writer friends for help and comfort when the going gets tough. I have had moral support and sound advice from many fellow authors at Novelists, Inc. In addition, I would like especially to thank Michelle Cameron, Christy English, Christopher Gortner, Sandra Gulland, Mitchell James Kaplan, Caroline Leavitt, Mary Sharratt, Anne Easter Smith, Libby Sternberg, and Sandra Worth for their enduring friendship and camaraderie.

Finally, thanks to my wonderful family, who are my strongest supporters: Charles, Cassie, Chloe, Kurt, Sofia, Ella (okay, well, Sofia and Ella are a little young to understand yet), Laura, Christopher, Joy, Avery (he'll understand someday, too), Keith, Jenny, Vivica, Duff, Barbara, Will, Rowan, and Maria. And my dad, Ed Dunlap, who reads everything I write even though he prefers science fiction.